COLOR OF
love

Color of Love – Citrus Pines Book 2

Copyright 2021 © Lila Dawes

The author asserts the moral right to be identified as the owner of this work.

No part of this book may be reproduced or transmitted in any form or by any means, including but not limited to: graphic, electronic, or mechanical, including photocopying, recording, taping, or by any informational storage retrieval system without advanced prior permission in writing from the publisher.

This is a work of fiction, and is not based on a true story or on real characters.

Dedication

To all the men and women who have fought for our freedom and given their lives, energy, time and mental health to keep us safe. From the bottom of my heart, thank you.

For anyone struggling, please know you are not alone.

This book is a work of fiction and contains themes which could be triggering: Anxiety, depression, panic attacks, PTSD, war flashbacks, suicide mention and violence.

Contents

Dedication	iii
Contents	iv
Chapter 1	6
Chapter 2	22
Chapter 3	33
Chapter 4	47
Chapter 5	63
Chapter 6	79
Chapter 7	92
Chapter 8	111
Chapter 9	128
Chapter 10	138
Chapter 11	149
Chapter 12	162
Chapter 13	177
Chapter 14	191
Chapter 15	201
Chapter 16	214
Chapter 17	230
Chapter 18	240
Chapter 19	254

Chapter 20	267
Chapter 21	282
Chapter 22	294
Chapter 23	306
Acknowledgements	320
About the Author	322

Lila Dawes

Chapter 1

Any second now I'm in danger of being able to talk about myself... Justine Valentina Rodríguez-Hamilton thought, fighting an eye roll. The man sitting opposite her was so engrossed in talking about himself that he hadn't even noticed her boredom. She ran her eyes over his rust-colored hair, then took in his ruddy complexion and pale blue eyes. He was very attractive, smartly dressed and had nice manners, but his conversation skills were definitely lacking. She tried to remain attentive but if she had to listen to him talk about tractors one more time, she was gonna lose it.

She was *sick* of dating. There were slim pickings in her small town so any new bachelors she heard about through the gossip grapevine she pounced on immediately, investigating them for any potential to become Mr.

Justine Valentina Rodríguez-Hamilton. She tried not to come across like she woke up every morning and spritzed herself head to toe with *Desperation* by Calvin Klein, but she felt like Charlotte in that episode of *Sex and the City* where she was ranting that she was exhausted from dating.

Her current date Tommy was from the next town. He had recently bought a farm and he was looking for a ~~farmhand~~ wife to help him run it. Although Justine was looking to settle down, a farm was not where she wanted or needed to be. No, thank you. Not that there was anything wrong with farming, it just wasn't her thing. For starters, she wouldn't be able to do her actual job, which she loved.

She was a psychologist, she loved her work, relished delving into the complexities of people's thoughts and feelings, learning the way their brains worked. She loved that her job combined academics and patient care, and that every day was different. Her drive to help people was what kept her motivated to continually grow and develop her skills. In her spare time, she liked to flex her creative muscles by writing music and performing occasionally here at The Rusty Bucket Inn. Her life was well-rounded, it was as full as it could be, but there was something missing. Something that couldn't be filled by working on a farm, darn it.

She didn't exactly have lofty ambitions for life. It's not like she wanted to be a millionaire married to Chris Evans...*drool*...or even become a world-famous musician. She just wanted a normal life, a strong career and marriage to a wonderful man followed by the typical two point four children. It wasn't very forward-thinking of her, but she was traditional at heart, raised in a traditional household. She could almost feel Susan B. Anthony turning in her grave.

Justine had done the other stuff. She had a successful career, owned her own home and had been fully independent since she was eighteen years old. She had ticked off all the items on her 'Checklist of Life' except the man and the kids. *So, thanks for everything Susan, truly, but I'll take it from here.* She sighed deeply, she just needed to keep going and to believe that these things were coming, but damn she was tired.

"Do you have much experience with udders?" Tommy asked her, interrupting her deep thoughts.

She offered him a smile, "I'm afraid not, I'd be udder-ly useless."

"Not a problem, you can always learn," he replied, her lame joke going straight over his head, banging the final nail in the potential romance coffin. *Dios mio.* She sighed inwardly and reached for her glass of rosé, downing it. Tommy was good-looking but far too serious for her. She definitely had a type: the men she went for tended to be preppy businessman types, smart, mature, funny, emotionally available family men. A bit like her father actually. *Ooh don't open that door.*

Her parents had met when they were in their senior year of high school. Justine's grandparents had just immigrated from Mexico. Her mother, Valentina, didn't speak very much English at the time. One afternoon after school, some of the local boys were trying to take advantage of her naivety when Justine's father, James, swooped in and saved the day. He was besotted with the Mexican beauty, and they had been together ever since, true high school sweethearts.

It was a fairy-tale, and Justine wanted the fairy-tale too and wouldn't settle for anything less. She wanted that perfect, easy, all-consuming love that you only read about.

The kind of love her parents shared, that her brothers had with their wives, and that her friends Christy and Dean had recently found. When she was around them, she could see it, feel it, in everything they did, it lifted them up. She sometimes found it hard to be around them, on days when she struggled to keep up the happy-go-lucky *'I'm not gonna die alone!'* façade. So, when would it be *her* turn?

Justine's lungs constricted in mild panic; her parents had been nearly twenty years younger than she was when they met. When would she catch a break? She'd begun to panic that she would be alone forever. She was thirty-four and time was running out if she wanted to find her true love and start a family.

"Oh, look, I need another drink," Justine said, leaping to her feet, then her manners kicked in. "Would you like another beer?" she asked. Her date nodded, and she tottered over to the bar, her heels clicking on the wooden floor. She placed her empty glass on top of the bar, sighing again.

"Hey babe! What are you doing here tonight?" Taylor, one of her best friends and part owner of The Rusty Bucket Inn, cooed at her, coming out of her office. Justine hiked her thumb over her shoulder towards her date.

"Ooh he's cute, what do you think?" Taylor asked, but Justine shook her head sadly. "Aw I'm sorry hon, another rosé?"

"Yes please, a large one, and a beer too."

Taylor turned away to get the drinks. "You're looking mighty fine tonight, FYI. You're even giving me feels!" she called over her shoulder. Taylor always complimented everyone; she was such a sweetheart under all her sass. Justine ran her hands over her orange satin dress.

"Thanks, Tay. You know exactly what to say to cheer me up," she laughed.

She felt her mood lifting, not only was she feeling down about the whole single thing, but she was stressing about work. Well, about a new client in particular. Blake Miller, the town's new deputy sheriff. She had successfully managed to avoid him so far, not wanting to meet him before their first session tomorrow. She didn't like having personal relationships with her clients, she felt that they came to their sessions with preconceived notions of her and behaved differently, and how else could she help them if they weren't authentic with her?

She would start from scratch with Blake so he would come to his session open-minded, fresh and raw. She wanted to delve into his psyche, immerse herself in his thoughts and feelings until she understood what made him tick. He was intriguing, something about him drew her. Maybe it was because he had a list of problems as long as her arm.

He was a widower, ex-military, suffering from PTSD, insomnia, anxiety, depression *and* he was hard-faced and emotionally stunted...*come to mama!* He presented her with a true professional challenge. She'd never had a client like him before and she was eager to get inside his head, even if she was a little scared she might be out of her depth.

Her mind scoffed at the thought of him, how this gorgeous man had been sent to her town, as though the universe were mocking her. He was definitely the most attractive man in Citrus Pines, and the most serious. Although she preferred men who didn't act like the world would end if they smiled, watching Blake Miller frown around town these last few weeks had made her seriously reconsider her type. *Goodbye comedians, hello Mr. Broody.*

But it didn't matter, she couldn't have him. As his new

psychologist she was bound by her ethics, to treat him and not develop any personal attachments to him. Which was fine because Blake wasn't her type, he was too *messy*, and Justine didn't do messy. She was a perfectionist. When she met her one true love, he wouldn't have any emotional baggage, he wouldn't have been married before, he wouldn't be emotionally stunted and unable to connect to others. She would be his only love; they would be soulmates and live happily ever after.

Justine was pulled out of her thoughts by a loud, high-pitched giggle. She turned to see her friend, Beau, entering the bar with a cheeky-looking blond woman on his arm. He gestured to a booth in the corner, the blond giggled again and went to take a seat. Beau headed towards the bar, smiling when he saw Justine.

"Evening Justine, don't you look beautiful. Who's the lucky guy?" he asked, friendly charm coating his words. She nodded in the direction of her date and Beau peered over her shoulder.

"Not bad!" he exclaimed as Taylor put Justine's glass of rosé on the bar.

"Then why don't you date him?" Taylor drawled sarcastically. Justine rolled her eyes, *Lord, here we go.* She hated getting caught in the middle of their spats. Christy wasn't the only one of their original friendship group who had recently moved back to town. Beau had returned to Citrus Pines after living in L.A. for the last fourteen years. They had all been friends as kids, he and Taylor at one point had been best friends. Then they had a falling out and shortly after, he had moved away. She was so glad he and Christy were home, their group was back together, and everything felt right again. Well, despite Beau and Taylor's obvious hatred for each other, but you can't have everything.

"Hello Taylor, I see your sunny disposition is brightening up the bar this evening as usual," he drawled. Taylor shot him a withering look and moved away to fetch Tommy's beer.

"You're not usually one for dating on a school night," Beau teased Justine.

"Desperate times and all that," she shrugged. He was right, normally she wouldn't be on a date during the week but with tomorrow being her first session with Blake, she needed something to take her mind off her nerves.

"Well, let me know if you need rescuing at all," Beau said, and Justine gestured towards his date, who currently had her hand in her bra trying to get her cleavage to really *pop*.

"You too."

Beau glanced at his date and chuckled, "I think I'll be fine, she's a little handsy but I like that," he replied loudly, his gaze flickering to Taylor's back before moving away again and Justine thought she heard Taylor snort.

"Two beers Taylor, hold the arsenic. Bring them over to us whenever you're ready," he said, then winked at Justine and sauntered away.

"Thank you!" Taylor called after him sarcastically.

"You're welcome!" He threw back over his shoulder and Justine watched as rage reddened Taylor's cheeks.

"You brought that on yourself, *chica*," she said, and Taylor turned her glare on Justine.

"Card or cash?" Taylor seethed through clenched teeth. Justine laughed and handed over her credit card. As Taylor walked off to grab the card reader, Justine felt heat envelope her, followed by the heady scent of spice and sin. She recognized the scent, it was already ingrained in her. She turned and found herself face to face with a pair of silver eyes that had haunted her dreams for months.

Her new client had entered the bar.

*

Deputy Sheriff Blake Miller parked his squad car in the lot of The Rusty Bucket Inn and switched off the engine. He sat there for a moment, contemplating going inside. He wasn't a big fan of crowds, they tended to be a trigger for him. Despite being honorably discharged from the military four years earlier, Blake still suffered from PTSD. He had been relieved to find out he was being transferred from the large, bustling Anderson County to the sleepy, rural town of Citrus Pines in a much smaller county. There had been conditions attached to the transfer: he was also doing it to save his career.

Blake had had a tough few years. His wife Katie had committed suicide while he was on tour with his military unit. He'd been devastated and guilt-ridden by the loss, and incapable of continuing with his unit, psychologically unable to perform his duties effectively. He was a great soldier, an asset to the unit and had never had any issues before, which is why he was discharged before his issues risked any of his fellow soldiers' lives.

He came home to grieve but he soon found himself struggling to manage with nothing to do to occupy his thoughts. So, he joined the Anderson County Sheriff's Department, and began training to be a deputy sheriff. He worked hard, proving himself over and over again, pushing himself to the limit and eventually he was ready to start campaigning to become sheriff.

He loved his job but after everything that happened, the trauma and stress started to build up and he fell into a downward spiral culminating in displaying poor judgment over a call that came in one day. There was a report of a suicide attempt, on top of one of the buildings in the town center. He was the closest responder and despite not being trained to handle this specific situation, he decided to attend to try and contain the incident before help arrived.

His lack of experience ended in disaster. The woman jumped. She screamed all the way down and then…silence. He still heard it in his dreams, sometimes even when he was awake. A shudder tore through him, and he shook his head. *Don't spiral into your thoughts tonight.* His sheriff had called him into the office a few days after the incident and given him an ultimatum: *'Sort yourself out or you've lost our support for sheriff.'*

So here he was. Citrus Pines was currently without a sheriff. Blake was sent in as a second deputy with the ambition that he would soon become the new sheriff if he worked on his mental health. Yes, he was glad to be out of the big county and into a small town for the sake of his mental health. But he also knew that small town life was close-knit: everyone knew everybody's business. Blake just wanted to be left alone, he didn't want anyone discovering what a mess he was.

His move had come with conditions. He had to visit a psychologist once a week and work through his issues. The psychologist had to report weekly on his progress and if no progress had been made, he was gone. He'd seen therapists, psychiatrists, and psychologists in the past, but no one had helped. Granted, he didn't try very hard, he wasn't exactly the poster boy for good mental health. But he hadn't connected with any of them, they hadn't known the right way to reach him, and he'd shut down each time he was passed on to someone new. His guard was so high now he didn't think it would ever come down.

He didn't hold out much hope for the new psychologist that he'd been assigned to, Dr. Rodríguez-

Hamilton. A small-town psychologist was likely to be more of a quack than the big city boys had been. Blake's only hope was that the doctor wasn't ingrained in the community and therefore unlikely to share anything he learned about the new deputy with friends. Blake was dreading their first session tomorrow, which is how he found himself in the parking lot of The Rusty Bucket Inn. He needed a stiff drink to help him relax if he had any hope of sleeping tonight.

He steeled himself, trying to calm the anxiety eating away at him and went inside. Luckily it was a weeknight and not that busy, it tended to get crowded at the weekends which was partly why Blake came tonight. He wanted to learn to cope around crowds again, he wanted to push himself, but not far enough to send him spiralling, he needed to take baby steps. He glanced around the rustic bar; he really liked it here. It was cozy, the epitome of small-town vibes and it had a good, honest feel to it. He knew the owner, Taylor, and liked her too, having helped her out on a couple of occasions.

He took in the surroundings: the rock and roll music playing softly in the background, the glasses clinking, and the low murmur of conversation. He scanned the crowd, taking note of everyone, assessing each of them for any potential threat. He planned his exit strategy in case of emergencies, a habit from his military days that he just couldn't shake. He went over to the bar and leaned against it, waiting for Taylor to serve him.

He noticed the woman standing next to him, hell, had noticed her the second he walked in. The orange satin dress she wore hugged her sinful curves tightly like it had been poured onto her. The color of the dress complimented her mocha skin in a mouth-watering, pants-tightening, palm-sweating way. Her chocolate hair cascaded down her back in soft waves. She tossed her hair, and he was immediately enveloped in a cloud of vanilla and cocoa. *God, she smells good.* The heady scent filling his nostrils so thickly he could practically taste it. She turned to face him, and he felt like he'd been punched in the gut. It was *her*.

He had seen her around a few times when he'd been called here by Taylor. Each time he spotted her, she disappeared after a few minutes, and he didn't see her again. He didn't even know her name, she was a mystery to him. Her eyes, a couple of shades lighter than her hair, reminded him of warm honey; widened when she saw him.

He ran his gaze over her, lingering to truly take her in. Her bowshaped mouth was painted red, and had formed an O of surprise. She had a small mole in the corner of her mouth that was begging to be licked. He tried to steer his thoughts away from going down that path, but his eyes continued their journey. Her breasts were the size of a handful, not large and not small but her hips had a delicious flare to them. Her long legs were hidden by the dress, but her dainty feet were strapped into a pair of sexy black sandals.

There was no denying she was a beautiful woman, her features perfectly put together, her body designed by every teenager's fantasy. She was a temptress, he could tell, luring men with her wiles and showing them exactly what she could do with that mouth and body.

Her brow furrowed at his perusal. He hadn't meant to be so blatant but this was the first time he had gotten a good look at her and he wanted to make the most of it before she disappeared again. She ran her eyes over him in turn, her stare bland and bored before she turned away, immediately dismissing him. Did little Miss Sinful not like what she saw? Didn't think he was good enough for her?

He chuckled to himself and muttered, "Don't worry, honey, I'm not interested in you either."

She stiffened next to him. *Shit,* he hadn't meant for her to hear him. He opened his mouth to apologize for acting like an asshole, but she tossed her hair again, grabbing her drinks and walking away. Blake watched her go back to her date, curvy hips swaying as she went. Damn that was sexy. Although he usually preferred his women more subtle and demure, everything about Miss Sinful screamed the opposite.

Still, that was no excuse for objectifying her the way he had, he'd clearly not been in social situations for a while, his skills were more than a little rusty. Judging by how tight his pants were getting while he looked at her, he also needed to get laid. It had been far too long. Blake shook himself and turned back to Taylor who was watching him, a smirk on her face.

"Hey Blake, how ya doing?"

"Good thanks, how's business? That ex of yours turned up again?"

"Nah, you must have scared him away for good."

"Glad to hear it, any problems you just give me a call."

"Will do, what can I get ya?"

"I'll have a whiskey soda, thanks."

He looked around the bar while she poured his drink, his stomach doing little somersaults at the groups of people clustering together. A few more people had come in after him, and he was starting to feel nervous about the size of the crowd. His eyes landed on Miss Sinful again and he could just about see her face over her date's shoulder. She looked bored. Taylor put his drink down on the bar and her sharp emerald eyes followed to where he was staring, and she smirked at him again.

"Stare any harder and I'm gonna try and set you two up," she joked.

He shook his head. "Nah thanks, she's not my type, just trying to place where I know her from."

"Not your type, huh? Well, she's here a lot, she performs here, you should check it out. She's singing next weekend."

He nodded and Taylor turned away to serve a group of guys who had crowded round the bar. Blake started to feel uncomfortable but pushed himself to stay there. Forcing himself to endure the discomfort, harness it and overcome it. But try as he might, he couldn't. The men got rowdier, the volume in the bar increased. His eyes swept around the room, trying to find something to latch onto to ground him. His gaze clashed with Miss Sinful's, her soft honey eyes seemed to lighten as she stared at him. He looked away, not wanting her to witness his rising panic. He jolted as the group of guys all burst into raucous laughter. His breathing started to speed up, he felt himself growing hot, his palms sweating.

A loud *crack* from behind him had him spinning around, ready to strike out, but it was just a ball rolling off the pool table, landing on the wooden floor. Taylor shouted at the guys to be careful, and Blake turned back to the bar, trying to get himself under control. He squeezed his eyes shut, trying to calm himself down. He gripped the cool bronze railing on the bar, attempting to use the sensation to ground him. His breathing remained labored, he could feel his panic attack rising, he tried to fight it down as his surroundings started to blur together.

"Hey man," a deep voice said from behind him before a heavy hand clamped down on his shoulder. Startled, Blake switched into combat mode, grabbing the hand, and flipping his attacker over his shoulder. The body crashed into the barstools and landed hard on the floor. Blake stared down at the man, his fists raised, teeth bared, ready to use lethal force if necessary. But as he stared into his enemy's face, his surroundings came back into focus, and he realized he'd attacked Beau.

Beau stared up at him from the ground, a mixture of anger and confusion on his face. Blake's breath sawed out of him as he realized what he'd done.

"Shit, sorry man," he muttered, his voice like gravel through his tightening throat. He needed to get out of there, needed to be away from the crowd. There was silence as everyone watched him. He needed to get away from these prying eyes before they figured out just how fucked up he was.

He stormed out of the bar and into the warm night, the thick air and citrus scent suffocating him. His chest began to tighten as he got into his squad car, his hands shaking as they jabbed the key into the ignition and he slammed his foot down on the gas, tearing out of the lot. He finally slowed down a few blocks later and pulled over on the dark, quiet street. He couldn't control his breathing, his panic attack in full swing, his vision blurred, his hands gripped his knees tightly as he struggled to regain control of his body. He was fighting a losing battle, knowing it would consume him. He surrendered, his weakness overwhelming him and then passed out.

When he awoke a few minutes later, his breathing had returned to normal, but his body ached, tired from the strain, tired from stress, just *tired*. He waited a few minutes before starting the engine and driving home. When he got into his house, he went straight to bed, praying his exhaustion would override his insomnia and he would finally get some rest.

*

The next morning, he got up, dressed in his uniform of black t-shirt and jeans, clipped his badge to his belt and his gun to his hip. He headed over to Dr. Rodríguez-Hamilton's office, trying not to think about what had happened at the bar last night. He was due at the doctor's office first thing and then after his hour-long session he could head to the station and start his working day.

It was another bright, sunny day in Citrus Pines. The gentle tang of lemons drifting by on the breeze, pine needles littering the pavements; it was peaceful and quiet. So far, he wasn't missing Anderson County. He didn't have any family there, they were back in California, still pretending he didn't exist. His only friends had been his co-workers and they had all abandoned him when it was clear he wasn't okay.

He watched as the small businesses began to open up, a few owners waving at him. He reluctantly returned the gesture. He pulled up outside the practice, parked the squad car and, with a sense of trepidation, he went in. He was greeted by an older woman who sat behind a desk, dressed in a smart pantsuit. She offered him a bright smile.

"Hello Deputy Miller, you're right on time," she said gently.

"Good morning," he read her nameplate, "Hilda."

"You can go right in, Dr. Rodríguez-Hamilton is ready for you."

Blake looked toward the door, the pit in his stomach growing. He thanked Hilda and went over, knocking sharply on the door. He took a deep breath and entered. The office was brightly lit by natural light shining in through the large windows. It was decorated in soothing cream and brown tones with large leafy green plants dotted around the room. There was a long brown leather sofa and a matching armchair facing it, separated by a glass coffee table.

Bookcases filled with books on psychology, psychiatry and human behavior stood along one wall. His eyes landed on the cream desk at the other end of the room and the black leather high-backed chair, which was facing the wall, hiding his new psychologist.

"Dr. Rodríguez-Hamilton?" he called, shutting the door. The chair swiveled and at the same time he was hit with the scent that tantalized him in the bar last night. *Oh shit*, his stomach bottomed out as he came face to face with his new psychologist. Miss Sinful herself sat there, a professional smile frozen on her bowshaped mouth. She stood up and gestured to the sofa.

"Nice to meet you Blake. No need to be so formal. Please, call me Justine."

Shit.

Chapter 2

Justine stared at Blake. His silver eyes held nothing except darkness and despair, and she wondered how they looked when he was happy. Immediately she disregarded the thought, *he's a client,* she reminded herself. She kept her smile fixed on her face, hoping if she acted casually enough, he wouldn't notice her cheeks heating or hear the pounding of her heart.

They stared at one another in silence before he tore his eyes away and let them roam around the office, his hand still gripping the door handle so tightly his knuckles blanched. *He's showing signs of anxiety, he's planning his exit route, looking for weaknesses in the building's structure.* Oh yes, he was exhibiting symptoms just standing there.

A bubble of anticipation fizzled inside her: this was what she'd been waiting for. He wouldn't be easy, he definitely would be a challenge, everything about him screamed hard, ahem, metaphorically speaking. After witnessing his outburst last night, she knew there were some deep-rooted issues and she couldn't wait to get her hands on him, again, metaphorically of course.

"*You're* Dr. Rodríguez-Hamilton?" he asked, his eyes flicking back to her. She nodded and stood up, gesturing to the couch again.

"I sure am, but just call me Justine, I'm not a *doctor* doctor, I can't prescribe you anything, not that you might need anything. I can see from your file you've been on medication before and didn't want to try again, unless you've changed your mind, that is, but I do have a PhD." She clamped her mouth shut to stop her babbling, and sighed internally. She was meant to be the one in control.

He slowly walked towards the leather couch and by the time he was sitting down his expression had completely shuttered. She was afraid that would happen. She seated herself opposite him, smoothing her purple knit dress over her knees, feeling nervous and trying not to come across like she was out of her depth.

"So, welcome to your first session. How are you feeling?" she asked enthusiastically, wanting to create a sense of excitement and joy that he'd taken this step, even if it wasn't his choice. He rolled his eyes, not even trying to hide his reaction and she was surprised at the blatant rudeness.

"Did you not like that question?" She narrowed her eyes, assessing him. He pursed his lips at her inspection.

"It's just the epitome of cliché," he muttered, his deep voice gravelly as though the words had been dragged from his throat. She tried not to shiver at the sound. *He's. A. Client!* she scolded.

"You might find it clichéd, but I find it polite to

inquire after my client's wellbeing," she retorted. He pursed his lips again and he folded his arms across his wide chest. She bit her cheek, annoyed at herself for her snappy tone, *he's already adopted a defensive posture and closed himself off.*

Despite his reaction she wasn't concerned, she'd known he would be a tough nut to crack, something she would relish breaking down. Also, unlike some of her other clients, he was required to be here by the terms of his employment, she had plenty of time to break down his barriers. She didn't need to play her trump card yet and he was sorely mistaken if he thought she wouldn't get under his skin.

"Feel free to make yourself at home, you can remove your jacket, and your shoes if you wish," she said, kicking off her heels and crossing her legs. He didn't move, just stared at her, his expression unreadable. She didn't speak again, just continued to let him watch her. She knew he was assessing her, trying to figure her out and see what her weaknesses were but she had none. *That's not true,* her brain piped up, but she shoved the thought away quickly. After another five minutes of silence, she tried again.

"How have you found the move from Anderson?" She already knew that she wouldn't get a response, she just wanted to show him that she wouldn't be fazed by his actions. A muscle twitched in his jaw, he clearly had something he wanted to say but didn't want to break his silent treatment. She nearly laughed at such childish behavior coming from a thirty-eight-year-old man. If he wanted to play this game, then she was all in.

She settled herself more comfortably in the chair, tucking her feet up under her, rolling her shoulders, massaging her neck, this would be a *loooong* hour. She couldn't deny she wasn't enjoying being the full focus of his attention, she reveled in having this beautiful man studying her, and she wondered what he saw. It meant she was also able to openly stare at him, something she hadn't been able to do all the other times she'd seen him, when she'd been too busy avoiding him.

She took in his features: long, black lashes surrounding those startling silver eyes, his dark eyebrows were thick slashes across his forehead. His brow was tightly pinched, he was definitely one of those men who looked good all moody and broody. He had a cute nose perched above that flat, mulish mouth. She would love to see him smile, she bet it would be beautiful. *Stop fantasizing!*

His square jaw was set firmly in displeasure, his beard was in definite need of a trim and his biceps bulged angrily from where he folded his arms across his chest. *Did he work out?* She wasn't normally a fan of muscles but seeing his made her feel all funny inside. She tried not to drool. *Maybe preppy businessmen aren't my type after all.* She couldn't see anymore of him without looking away from his gaze and she refused to let him win their staring contest.

They sat like that for an hour. Occasionally he quickly glanced out the window whenever there was a loud noise and she felt a flare of triumph each time, but he always swiftly met her gaze again. Luckily, there was a clock behind him on the wall.

"Well, we're done for today." She stood and headed around to her desk. "Looks like we're in for the same time next week too so, I'll see you then."

She lifted her head, but he had already left the office, the front door banging shut behind him and she sat down with a sigh to make her notes. While she wrote she assured herself that her disappointment was stemming from a professional point of view rather than a personal one. When she finished, she went out to see Hilda.

"Did the first session go well?" Hilda asked, smiling up at Justine with affection. She and Hilda had become very close while working together. Hilda was like her work mom, although they spent time together away from the office too. Hilda had developed an interest in cooking the last few years and when she'd asked Justine to teach her how to make some traditional Mexican dishes, Justine had been thrilled. She had spent her childhood in the kitchen with her mom, learning culinary secrets, life lessons and the odd curse word in Spanish.

Justine sighed. "He spoke one sentence in the whole hour."

Hilda tsked, handing her a list of her messages. "It's the quiet ones that always have the most to say," she said wisely.

"I don't think he's quiet, he's just stubborn, but I hope you're right," Justine replied. She thanked Hilda for her messages and went back into her office.

Blake was complicated, that was for sure. His outburst at The Rusty Bucket last night had surprised her. She hadn't realized his symptoms simmered so close to the surface. She couldn't work out whether it was the crowds, the noise or being touched without his awareness or consent that had set him off. There was no mention of his triggers in the file that she had received so she would need to keep her eyes open to try and figure out what they were.

She put Blake out of her mind, focusing on her next client, a woman named Jodie who went bankrupt spending all her money on original 1800s fashion. Jodie liked to dress up and host luncheons with her stuffed animals. *And yet she's still got more experience with men than you,* her brain taunted. It was true, Jodie also dressed her husband in the same clothes as her, and he liked it.

Justine tried to be present for the session, but she was a little checked out, she couldn't stop thinking about Blake and what she could really do for him, the change she could make to his life, if she could handle it. Jodie didn't want to change what she did, she just wanted to complain about why society couldn't accept her. Blake *needed* to change, for the sake of his career, his sanity, even his life.

*

Blake was fuming. God, she'd pissed him off something awful. He'd assumed Dr. Rodríguez-Hamilton would be a man. Foolish and old-fashioned on his part, but he had not assumed that Dr. Rodríguez-Hamilton would be some wily temptress who had more than beauty and brains. With her as his new psychologist she had the ability to *own* his thoughts, to break him apart from the inside out, leaving him a shattered, broken shell. And *fuck* that scared him.

He had stormed out of her office as soon as their time was up, not wanting to be around her for another second, fearful of what her probing gaze would uncover about him. He jumped into his cruiser and sped off down the street to the station.

Obviously, she had taken 'Therapy101' at college he scoffed, thinking about how she asked him how he'd *felt*. But he hadn't expected her to call him on his rudeness; she had a backbone and wasn't a shy little wallflower. He would have told her to shove her niceties if he wasn't required by the terms of his contract to be there. She had him by the balls on that one and he didn't enjoy it one bit.

But just because he was required to attend their weekly sessions didn't mean he was required to talk to her. The way she'd sat there, her honey eyes beseeching him to open up and surrender his innermost thoughts and feelings had him all riled up. It had been hard to maintain eye contact with her the whole time, she was clearly unaware of her effect on men. It annoyed him even more that he was fighting arousal the entire time.

He definitely needed to get laid, and soon, making a mental note to go to the bar one night to find a woman who was interested in something with no strings attached. He didn't get into relationships, he didn't get close to people, he didn't get attached. The only person he had ever come close to loving had been his wife Katie, but even then, it was with the rose-tinted infatuation of a teenage boy.

He pulled into his designated parking space outside the station, a perk of small-town life, and went inside the building. The old wooden structure should've been knocked down and rebuilt years ago but instead it just got patched up every now and then. And necessities added in, like electricity, air-conditioning and indoor plumbing. It was a small, quaint building and as much as he joked about how rundown it was, he felt comfortable here, like it was a second home. He went inside and the cool air from the AC hit his face.

"Morning, sir," called Jim, his receptionist. He was an elderly gentleman who struggled with bouts of absent-mindedness but he'd been around for decades so Blake couldn't get rid of him. Also, he kinda liked him, not that he would admit it to anyone.

It was a small office, just made up of him, the other deputy, Austin, Jim and the five patrolmen. Their desks sat facing each other in the middle of the station with Blake and Austin's offices running along the back wall next to the break room. The rickety stairs in the corner led down to the restroom and the two holding cells, one of which was full of police equipment and filing cabinets. Things were pretty slow in Citrus Pines.

"Morning Jim, busy day today?" Blake asked, pushing aside his still burning anger from his morning session. Jim knocked a stack of files on the floor and Blake tried not to roll his eyes.

"Oh yes, sir, busy day indeed," Jim replied, ducking down to pick up the papers.

"You don't need to call me sir, Jim," Blake reminded him, picking up his messages from the notepad next to the main phone.

"I know, sir, but it's hard to break old habits," Jim said, smiling up at Blake and his bad mood melted away further. Blake nodded and headed into his office passing the patrolmen and waving in greeting. He dropped the messages on his desk and started moving around the stack of files which were...sticky? He lifted his fingers to his nose and delicately sniffed. Strawberry. Understanding dawned and he closed his eyes, threw back his head and yelled.

"AUSTIN! GET IN HERE!" He heard movement in the office next to him and then Austin blundered in.

"Yes, Deputy Miller?" he asked, worry lining his features. Blake took him in, floppy blond hair, too-young face, and a smear of something red and sticky down his white shirt.

"Did you have a donut this morning?"

"Why, yes, I did! How did you guess?" Austin replied, his expression one of awe.

"Because these files you left on my desk are covered in strawberry jelly," Blake growled, and Austin had the decency to look embarrassed.

"Ah, sorry about that, won't happen again."

"Good. Now, what are these?" Blake asked, sifting

through them, avoiding the sticky patches. Austin slowly came further into the room, approaching Blake like he would an angry bear.

"These are the leftover cases from Sheriff Black that you requested?" Austin replied. Blake nodded.

"Yes, great. Thank you, you can go now." His tone still surly, Austin bobbed at him and then hurried out. Just as Blake was looking into the first file, Jim wandered in with another note for him.

"The Neighborhood Watch Society is meeting on Monday night. I didn't know whether this was something you wanted to attend or if it was more Austin's speed?" Jim said. Blake kicked back in his chair, swung his long legs up on the desk and thought for a moment.

"How often do they meet?" he asked.

"It's every Monday at seven for an hour or so."

Blake thought about it. He needed to gain the trust of the town so that when he was ready, they would get behind him as he ran his campaign for sheriff. This would be a good way to support the town, without getting personally involved. He could remain professional and keep them at a distance while also becoming engaged with the community.

"No, it's fine, I'll handle it," Blake said, taking the note from Jim.

"Yes, it'll be good to give Austin a break for a bit, he's been running himself into the ground trying to manage things before you turned up, have you seen how tired he is?"

"Would you say he's done a good job?" Blake asked. Jim eyed him and opened his mouth, then closed it again. "You can be honest; I would prefer it." Blake added firmly. If he was to become sheriff, he needed to have confidence in his deputy.

Jim sighed and closed the door to the office for privacy. "He did a good job alright, but not with that young woman Rebelle when she turned up one day wanting to file a complaint."

Blake scrubbed a hand over his jaw, tugging on the strands of his unkempt beard. "Rebelle? I've heard that name before?" he asked.

Jim nodded and sank down into one of the chairs opposite Blake's desk. "Yes sir, Rebelle Black was married to the previous sheriff." Jim looked about him furtively then when he spoke again, he dropped his voice to a whisper. "Some folks say it was her that shot him a few months ago. But the autopsy was inconclusive, could've been suicide, could've been accidental or it could have been *murder*."

"Why would she kill him?" Blake asked, leaning forward, getting drawn into the intrigue. Jim looked around again.

"Well, some say he wasn't a very nice man, nothing concrete obviously but I wouldn't have been surprised if she did it in self-defense."

"Interesting. And you say she came here for help? Was this before or after he died?" Blake queried.

"A few weeks after. I couldn't hear much but I think she was getting harassed. Austin just told her he would look into it and shoved her out the door, none too gently if you ask me." Jim harrumphed, disapproving of the aggressive display towards the woman.

"Has she been back since?"

"No, and I don't blame her either."

"I'll have a look into it a bit more, I think. We can't have a resident thinking they can't turn to us if they need help."

"My thoughts exactly!" Jim agreed, leaning back in the

chair, getting comfortable.

Blake tried not to smile. "Thanks for your help, Jim, you can head back out now."

Jim leapt up. "Oh yes, sir, very good. I'll mark the NWS meeting on your calendar and you just need to head to the address on the note there."

Blake chuckled as the old man hurried out, then his thoughts turned more serious. Call it jumping to conclusions, but he didn't feel right about what he'd just heard. Maybe there was nothing in it, but he made a note to look into the old sheriff in a bit more detail and maybe follow up with Rebelle and see if everything was okay.

He started leafing through the files that had been placed on his desk, making calls, updating case notes, and generally doing everything he could to keep his mind off how soon his next session with Dr. Rodríguez-Hamilton would come round. And fighting the urge to abuse his power and run a background check on her, so he could find out more about her to put them on an even playing field next time they met. He didn't like this feeling of vulnerability he had, she knew plenty about him, and he knew nothing about her.

Chapter 3

Justine went to the bar after work to meet Taylor and Christy for dinner. When she entered, Taylor was just finishing up her shift and handing over to Kayleigh, her newish barmaid, so Justine went and settled herself in a booth.

She glanced around the bar to see who else was here and spotted her date from the previous night with another woman. *Well, that was quick,* her pride prickled. Not that she could be mad, she'd given him no sign that she was interested in another date. Justine's mom had messaged her last night to say the neighbor's son was recently divorced and looking to get back out there. Valentina had kindly passed along Justine's contact details which under most circumstances would be fine, but he was twenty years older than Justine, and gay.

Taylor appeared beside her, distracting her by flopping into the booth, lacking any kind of grace.

"Sorry, babe," she said, tossing her red mane over her shoulder, the light reflecting off the golden highlights scattered throughout the long tresses.

"Don't worry, I've only just got here," Justine assured her.

"We've been hella busy today," Taylor sighed deeply, but beneath the tired exterior Justine could feel Taylor's energy buzzing away, and knew she loved it.

"That's great. The bar is doing so well, all because of you!" Justine gushed, so proud of her friend. Taylor had bought a fifty percent share of the bar when the owner, Bob Ingles, was looking to sell up. She could only afford fifty percent at the time, with help from her ex-stepbrother, Dean, but promised Bob that she would turn the place around and within a few years she hoped to make enough money to buy the other half.

"Well now I'm all yours, and Christy's too. Where is she?" Taylor asked, looking around.

Justine shrugged. "Maybe she got held up writing, you know what she's like now, so full of thoughts and ideas."

"She's probably just sucking face with my brother. Gross," Taylor muttered, sticking her finger down her throat but again, Justine knew she loved it.

"Can you believe how happy they are?" Justine asked, smiling.

"Sickening, isn't it?" Taylor replied, and they both laughed. Justine, Taylor, and Christy had been friends since kindergarten but when they were eighteen and about to graduate from high school, Christy ran away. After her mother died when she was fifteen, Christy had had an abusive relationship with her father, and finally she couldn't take it anymore. A few months ago, her father passed away and she was forced back to town for the first time since she left.

She had arranged the funeral and sold the house with every intention of heading straight back to New York when it was all finalized. What she hadn't counted on was bumping into Dean, once a long-time crush of hers, now the town's most eligible bachelor. They'd gotten off to a rocky start but with spending so much time together, soon they could no longer deny their feelings.

Their chemistry had been electric, palpable, a living, breathing force to be reckoned with. After weeks they finally surrendered to their feelings and Christy had moved home permanently. Now they were living together, engaged and Justine and Taylor had never been more thrilled that their friends had finally found true happiness.

"You love it, they've both never been happier, and every time you see them it chips a little bit of ice off that block where your heart should be," Justine joked.

"Dang it, it really does. Anyway, on that theme, I have an idea of my own that I wanna run past you both, whenever she turns up," Taylor said. She looked around again and then waved. Christy appeared and plonked herself down into the booth next to Justine, her blond curls bouncing as she did.

"Sorry I'm late, I had car trouble," she said, not meeting their eyes. Justine looked to Taylor who was smirking.

"Car trouble with your brand-new car?" Taylor asked, raising a skeptical eyebrow at her. A brand-new car Dean had made her buy since he was worried sick whenever she took her old one out.

"Uh huh," Christy nodded, her cheeks flushing.

"And I bet you just had to take it to your closest

mechanic?" Justine teased.

"Maybe…" Christy hedged.

"Christy, your shirt's on inside out," Taylor said, and Justine snorted with laughter.

"Okay fine, so we fooled around at the garage, that's why I'm late. Damn, that man gets me revved up," she sighed. Justine nudged Christy as she slipped into a daydream. Christy shook herself then headed towards the restrooms to fix her shirt. When she came back, shirt on the right way, she turned to Justine.

"So, how's your dating life going?" she asked.

"Miserably. There are no decent guys left in this town," Justine pouted.

"There's Beau?" Christy suggested, but Justine shook her head.

"Nah, I couldn't do that to Tayl-him," she replied, checking herself last minute to stop from saying something stupid.

"I've seen someone we could set you up with…" Taylor said cryptically. Justine rolled her eyes.

"Let me stop you there-"

Taylor interrupted. "It's Blake!"

Mierda! She knew they would push him on her sooner or later, but she couldn't explain to them why she couldn't go out with him, she didn't want to reveal that he was her new client.

"He's really not my type," she replied.

"Sexy? That's not your type?" Taylor countered.

"Like Beau you mean?" Justine shot back, her arrow hit its mark and Taylor glared at her.

"Whatever. Look, that's what I wanted to speak to you both about. I've had an idea I wanted to run by you," she started as Kayleigh came over with their drinks. She put them on the table gently, not spilling a drop and then bobbed at Taylor before leaving. Taylor pinched the bridge of her nose.

"I swear to Jesus if she curtsies at me again…"

"Your amazing idea?" Christy interrupted, distracting Taylor from her Kayleigh rage.

"Yes! What do you think about me hosting a Ladies' Night here at the bar? But, like, a classy one, no strippers, more like speed dating and cocktails? There's only a couple of bars in the area, and they don't do this so mine would be the only bar around for miles that does. It's a big point of difference."

"That's a great idea!" Christy enthused. Justine agreed.

"Yes, as long as you can guarantee plenty of sexy men then I'm definitely here for it!" Justine replied, matching Christy's excitement. This was good news. Being able to ~~trap~~ gather all the sexy men in one room for her to work her way through to find Mr. Right? *Perfecta!*

"Amazing, well I need to get permission from Bob as he's still a partowner, but I think he'll be fine with it. To Ladies' Night!" Taylor crowed and lifted her glass. They clinked and cheered.

They talked as they ate, listening to how wedding plans were going with Christy and Dean. When they finished their food, the crowds started drawing in, but Taylor stayed calm and let Kayleigh control the bar.

As Taylor and Christy bickered between themselves, Justine sipped her drink, her thoughts slipping back to the singles night. This would be perfect, maybe she would meet the man of her dreams there. She was getting more and more worried that she would end up alone. Also, she was sick of being a thirty-four-year-old virgin. *Damn traditional values!* Justine was an old romantic and had been saving herself for her future husband, but her loneliness was beginning to consume her.

She wanted to be touched, was desperate to experience the feelings and sensations that others felt when they were intimate with someone. She'd never even had a proper make-out session before. She was missing out on so much by trying to save it all for someone who hadn't had the decency to present himself to her in a timely manner. She didn't want to miss out any longer, listening to the way Christy talked about Dean and vice versa, seeing the way they looked at each other like no one else existed, it was killing her not to experience that.

Later that evening, Beau and Dean both came into the bar, having some bro time, which Justine thought was super cute. Dean smiled at Christy and Justine could practically feel the heat flaring between them.

That's it! Her mind made up, she decided she was just going for it. She would still be looking for Mr. Right but now she was also looking for someone to become intimate with, Mr. Right Now. Excitement sizzled through her at the thought that soon she would meet the man she was going to give herself to. Only problem was, the first person who came to mind was someone she had no right thinking about so intimately.

*

The rest of the week flew by and before Justine knew it, she was at The Rusty Bucket with her friends on Sunday night. Taylor was pouring drinks and chatting to them in between serving customers. Christy and Dean were dancing on the small, makeshift dancefloor, and she and Beau were trading dating horror stories. Beau threw back his head and laughed, long and loud at her joke and as she stared at him, she wished she found him attractive.

He was stunning, there was no denying it: dark hair, high cheekbones, hard square jawline, and eyes that were so pretty and warm they could melt even the coldest of hearts. He checked off the majority of her key requirements: he was a businessman, smart, mature, emotionally available and definitely wanted a family. She and Beau could make beautiful babies, but he didn't make her heart sing. They had even kissed recently; well, she had attacked him in another desperate attempt to avoid Blake noticing her. He had been a nice kisser, but she felt zero spark and alas it wasn't meant to be. Beau laughed at another joke, and she spotted Taylor glaring over at him. Taylor was the other reason it wouldn't work with Beau…

When Beau went to get some more drinks, she opened her purse, pulled out a mirror and began reapplying her lipstick. Over her compact she saw Blake enter the bar. He looked around, his eyes wide, pupils dilated, and with his brows pinched tightly, he was looking anxious.

When he spotted her, their eyes clashing, a frisson of heat stole through her. She hadn't seen him or heard from him since their session. He continued to stare at her, and after a moment she looked away, not willing to play this game in public. She didn't want to draw attention to their relationship, she didn't want people knowing that she was treating him. It was private. If he wanted people to know then he could tell them, but she wouldn't.

Her treacherous eyes returned to him as he approached the bar and sidled up next to Beau and she watched the two of them talking. The bar was too noisy to hear what they were saying but she held her breath, remembering how he'd attacked Beau only a few days ago. They talked for a few minutes; she tried to read their lips but to no avail. She could just wander over there, nonchalant as hell, and—eavesdrop? *No, you don't care what they're saying!*

They seemed to be having a pleasant conversation and

then Blake stuck his hand out, Justine held her breath. After a pause, Beau clasped his outstretched hand, and they shook. Justine let out her breath in a whoosh as she relaxed, pleased they had cleared the air. She was proud of Blake for being the bigger man, it must have taken a lot for him to admit being in the wrong, which showed a level of maturity that was definitely *not* attractive to her, no, not at all. *No, don't go ticking qualities off the list, he's not ever going to be considered as a candidate, he's your client.*

Beau clapped him on the back, spoke to him for a moment longer and then came back to Justine with their drinks. "He is one interesting guy, I would love to get to know him more," he said.

"Oh, yeah?" she asked, curious about what was said between them, but trying to pretend she wasn't.

"Come on, I know you wanna dance," Beau said, changing the subject and taking her hand. She swallowed her disappointment when he didn't say any more about Blake and pulled her onto the dancefloor next to Christy and Dean and a few other couples. The music changed into a slow, romantic song, but Beau just pulled her against him and they started to sway.

It was comfortable, she enjoyed the closeness and friendly affection. She relaxed and placed her head on his shoulder, knowing nothing was expected between them. As they swayed, moving in slow circles, she soon had a view of the bar, her eyes immediately seeking out Blake, but only so she could make sure he was okay and not feeling anxious.

When she found him, she was surprised to find he was already watching her. His eyes shining brightly, reflecting the neon lights from around the bar. He watched her intently as he sipped his drink, his tongue sliding along the rim of the glass. She fought a shiver and felt herself heating under his stare, vibrations traveling through her body and heat pooling low in her belly. Soon she was facing the other way and her attention turned back to Beau who continued chatting merrily about the renovations he was doing to the house he'd just bought from Christy.

As they continued moving in their slow circles, she got another view of the bar, and yelped as she spotted Blake watching her again. Beau looked down at her, concerned. She just pretended she had hiccupped. *Dios, what is wrong with you, chica? It's like you've never seen a man before!* She tried to look over Beau's shoulder at Blake, but he was so damn tall, and she was only wearing pumps.

She waited, holding her breath, her heart pounding as they slowly turned again. But just as the bar came into view, Beau spun them the other way and she nearly cried out in frustration. *What's wrong with you? Stop looking for him and stop thinking about him!* She tried to put him out of her mind but as the bar came into view for the fourth time, she realized Blake wasn't there and her disappointment was intense.

"You okay?" Beau asked over the music, looking down at her with furrowed brows. She pasted a smile across her face and nodded. She tried to distract herself by telling Beau about the Ladies' Night Taylor was organizing now she had been given the green light by Bob.

"Oh yeah? That sounds awesome, so single men are welcome?" he asked, a spark of mischief gleaming in his eyes, she just laughed and nodded. When the song finished an upbeat number started and they all danced together, tune after tune blasting out. Justine danced until her feet were raw and that night as she slept, her dreams were full of stolen glances with a mysterious deputy sheriff who had the most captivating eyes she had ever seen.

*

On Monday night Blake found himself outside the small community hall, watching as residents from Citrus Pines entered the building, chatting to each other. All day he had gone back and forth in his mind over whether he should've asked Austin to attend instead. Blake wanted to serve his community but also keep them at arm's length. It was better he didn't get close to anyone at the moment, he was constantly so on edge that it was only a matter of time before he lashed out again, potentially hurting someone.

He stood in the dark, torn. Did he go in? Did he leave? He recognized Dean entering the building, and was surprised that he was going to the meeting. Blake assumed that these programs were usually run by old ladies only wanting to get in everyone's business. Dean was a pretty nice guy, he'd spoken to him a few times, and he was someone Blake would be happy having a beer with if he ever felt like trying to make friends, which he didn't.

If Blake didn't go in, then what else was he going to do? Go home and stare at the four walls of his house and wait for another panic attack? Sit there all night watching TV and willing his body to finally sleep? The prospect of a bleak evening pushed him to come out of the shadows and walk into the building.

Once inside, he looked around. A square table took up the centre of the room with chairs surrounding it. The refreshments table on one side held an assortment of pastries and drinks, and most people were congregated around that table. Blake stood in the doorway feeling awkward, he actually felt nervous, what the fuck was that about? *This is where having a friend would come in handy*, his brain mocked. He didn't know who to approach, who to speak to, or even how to act and he started panicking, his anxiety rising. Then Dean spotted him and broke away from everyone, coming over. He held his hand out to Blake.

"Hey, man! Nice to see you," Dean enthused, and Blake grasped his outstretched palm.

"Thanks, nice to see you too," he replied, and was surprised to find that he meant it. Okay so maybe, *maybe* he missed male company. God, why was he being so lame about this? He didn't know what to say to Dean next and started freaking out internally at his lack of social skills. Luckily for him, Dean took over.

"Is this your first meeting?" Dean asked.

"Yep, not really sure what happens at a Neighborhood Watch Society meeting," Blake tried to smile but lately that didn't come naturally.

"No problem. I can introduce you around if you like, so you can get a feel for who everyone is?" Dean offered. Blake felt some of the tension ease from him.

"Great, thanks."

Dean took him over to the people gathered around the pastries and started introducing him. He met the school principal, a couple of small business owners, some healthcare workers, local council members and stay-at-home parents. Everyone he was introduced to was friendly and each wanted to speak to him about their various ideas and thoughts for the town. When he finally broke away, Dean came up next to him, chuckling.

"Sorry, I should've warned you they would pounce on you."

"You're not kidding, I'll need to bring a notepad next time just to keep up with the demands," Blake replied, and Dean just slapped him on the back.

"Come on, buddy, it's about to start, you can sit with me." Dean said, leading him over to the table. Blake tried not to get excited like a damn teenager over sitting together. The meeting was called to order by Janet Hayes, the leader of the local council. She ran through the minutes of the previous meeting and Blake could feel himself getting lost in his thoughts until a loud bang startled him. His heart began pounding, what was that? Where did it come from? He looked around, alert, hunting out the threat, concerned for the safety of everyone in the building.

"Sorry I'm late!" called a smoky voice that could only belong to one person. He looked up and saw Justine hurrying in to take a seat in the empty chair opposite him. As she sat down, she met his eyes and froze for a moment before that cold professional smile slid into place.

"Hey Justine, you know Blake, don't you?" Dean said by way of introduction.

"Pleased to meet you, Blake," she replied smoothly, and he inclined his head. She turned to Janet.

"Sorry, Janet."

"That's quite all right, dear." Janet replied before continuing on with reading the minutes. Blake felt even more on edge than he had been before, knowing she was here. That she was so close. Why couldn't he seem to get away from her at the moment? He had seen her more times this last week than in all his time so far in Citrus Pines. He discreetly watched her, concentration furrowing her brow, pinching her lips in the cutest way as she listened to Janet.

He turned away, mad at himself for getting distracted and staring like a creep. Had he not gotten his fill during their first session? Apparently, that hadn't been enough though, just like last night at the bar when he couldn't take his eyes off her while she danced with Beau. He had ended up leaving, annoyed with himself because instead of looking for a hook-up, he wanted to storm over to her and Beau and rip them apart. *Why were you even bothered?* He couldn't answer.

She cleared her throat, drawing his attention to her again. She swallowed and his eyes tracked her throat as it bobbed delicately with the action. Her tongue swiped across her plump bottom lip, and he felt a sharp lance of arousal hammer through him, his cock twitching in his jeans. *Goddammit.* He tore his eyes away and focused on Janet again. But Justine's scent soon made its way over to him, cocoa and vanilla, a sinful combination. It drove him wild, his thoughts going crazy until he was sitting in a meeting full of people with a hard-on. He bit his cheek in frustration at getting aroused so easily like a damn teenager.

The rest of the meeting passed by fairly quickly, Janet spent the time filling him in on what they usually did. They talked about local issues and ran through development requests for their own properties or for the town. Residents reported any suspicious activity they'd noticed and on a few occasions ran civilian stakeouts to catch suspected criminals in the act. They were even working on how to branch out into monitoring cybercrime to protect some of the kids at school from internet trolls.

He was really impressed with everything they'd done. They had caught criminals themselves and the town was safer because of the work they did. By the time the meeting was over he had invitations to visit the school and the council offices to look at the work they were doing there.

He chatted to Dean briefly as everyone started filing out of the hall and when he looked up, he was ~~disappointed~~ pleased to see Justine had already left. He made his way home and worked out for a couple of hours before heading to bed. He lay there, staring up at the ceiling, willing sleep to come but as usual it eluded him. His mind filled itself with thoughts of his new psychologist and how her thick hair would feel wrapped in his fist as he drove into her, her cries of pleasure ringing in his ears.

He was still thinking about her when the sun rose the next morning which riled him up even more. He definitely needed to get laid; that was the only reason he'd been thinking about her so much. He'd overheard Taylor talking at the bar the other night about the singles event that she was organizing. Maybe he would swing by and see if he could meet someone who would be up for a quick, no-strings-attached fling. That should solve everything.

Chapter 4

The next few days passed quickly and before Justine knew it, it was Wednesday morning, and she was waiting for Blake to turn up for his second appointment. She couldn't deny that she was looking forward to this session. Part of her wondered if he would actually turn up, because even though the sessions were mandatory, he seemed determined not to work with her. She couldn't deny the way her heart raced as the handle to the office door turned and he entered.

"Morning Blake, how are you?" she asked cheerfully, gesturing to him to take a seat on the couch. He didn't respond, just watched her as he came around to sit, his eyes piercing her. He was wearing his standard uniform of black t-shirt and jeans, plain clothes but on him they looked-*stop!*

She fixed a smile on her face as she sat down opposite him. He didn't attempt conversation, she sighed inwardly as it became apparent they would have a repeat of last week. That was fine by her, she'd keep asking all the things she wanted to ask. Again, she had all the time in the world and at some point, if he wanted to keep his job, he would have to open up to her.

"How are you settling into the town?" she asked. He rested one ankle over the opposite knee and folded his arms but didn't reply.

"It was nice to see you at the NWS meeting the other night. Are you going to be coming every week?" she asked. That didn't have anything to do with helping him, she just needed to know where she could expect to bump into him outside of work so she could prepare herself.

She had been overwhelmed when she'd rushed into the meeting late and met his cool eyes across the table. She'd felt his stare on her for most of the meeting and fought every instinct she possessed, refusing to meet his hard gaze and leaving as soon as the meeting was over. She couldn't explain the way he made her feel. Even now she had so many emotions roaring through her and she didn't know what any of them meant.

He didn't answer her question, just continued to trap her with his stare. She switched tactics, deciding to bring up something she was curious about.

"Do you want to talk about the incident at the bar last week?" she asked. A muscle ticked under his left eye but other than that he gave no reaction to her question.

"Why did you attack Beau?" Another facial tick. For some reason seeing him fight his impulses really…intrigued her. She felt heat stirring low in her belly and something unknown passed between them. She arched an eyebrow at him and continued.

"Was that a reaction to being surprised or do you just not like men prettier than you?" A bold question, she hoped to get a reaction out of him, wanted to make him sweat. But other than a fierce clenching of his jaw, there was nothing.

After the continued silence she wondered if keeping up her professional front was triggering his standoffish behavior; maybe if she relaxed a little then he would too. She removed her suit jacket and her shoes, took her hair out of its high ponytail and softened her features when she looked at him. He narrowed his eyes at her as if to say, *I know what you're doing*. But still nothing.

Half an hour later she grabbed a notepad and pen and just watched him as he watched her. She loved being able to openly stare at him, taking in the contours of his face. Every now and then she sighed and wrote something on her notepad then continued watching him. He frowned at her each time she did it, his glare spurring her on to push his buttons and she couldn't deny that she got a thrill out of it. It was obviously bothering him, and she knew he wanted to ask what she'd written but he wouldn't dare. That would show he cared, and judging from his behavior he didn't care about anything.

"How many panic attacks do you have in a week?"

Jaw clench. Eye tick. No response.

Just as time was about to run out, she fixed him with a contemplative stare, and came to sit next to him. Her hair fell forward, as she brushed it to the side, she spotted his hand grip his knee tighter.

"Tell me about your wife, Katie." A statement, not a question and one he didn't take well. His nostrils flared, his jaw cracked, and his fists clenched. She was pushing him, but he wouldn't react. He didn't even turn to face her, just stared straight ahead at where she'd been sitting before. A moment later their time was up and, as though he had a timer set, he got up and left her office without a backward glance.

She frowned after him. How the hell was she going to reach him?

*

Blake sat in the parking lot of The Rusty Bucket again, working himself up to go in. It was Saturday night, the busiest night of the week. He had done well Sunday when he came in and tested himself though he hadn't stayed long, he wanted to quit while he was ahead. *That's not why you left,* his brain reminded him helpfully and he replayed Justine dancing with Beau. Blake couldn't figure out what the deal was between the two of them. He also couldn't figure out why he cared so much that it consumed his thoughts. He kind of liked Beau and didn't want to keep turning into a raging, testosterone-fueled manbeast whenever the guy so much as looked in Justine's direction.

Blake knew that Dean and Beau were best friends and he guessed he could admit it would be kind of cool to hang out with them. They were pretty much the only guys in town that were a similar age to him and with similar interests. And though Blake hated to admit it, he was beginning to feel kind of lonely. He still got nervous thinking about spending time with anyone. He could have an anxiety attack and then they would realize how messed up he was. Maybe it was just easier to keep people at arm's length.

Before he could decide, he needed to make sure he could keep himself in check when socializing with others. Tonight would be a big test. It would be packed inside the bar, hot and loud, and people might accidentally bump into him. There were a lot of scenarios that could trigger him, but he needed to do this to see if he had made any progress at all. Maybe if he had made progress, he could stop seeing Justine. Just the thought of that relieved him. He took a deep breath and then went inside.

The place was packed. He kept his head down, trying to stay calm and made a beeline for the bar. He ran his eyes around the room as usual, memorizing his escape route in case of emergencies, counting how many people were in the bar, who might be considered a threat. He spotted Beau, Dean and Christy huddled together, but not Justine. Not that he had expected her to be here but if they were here, she usually wasn't far behind.

"Hey Blake, you came!" Taylor called when she saw him.

He frowned. "Were you expecting me?"

"It's Justine's gig tonight, didn't you come to hear her sing?" she asked, raising her voice over the music currently playing.

He tried to keep his expression neutral; he hadn't realized that was tonight. But now he was glad he'd come, he wanted to see her perform. Although he didn't want to admit it, she intrigued him. He also needed to discover more about her, to find her weaknesses. Then if he knew hers, he might not feel so vulnerable around her all the time.

"Happy coincidence," he replied with a slight smile so she wouldn't think he was a stalker.

"You're gonna love her! Whiskey soda, right?" she shouted over her shoulder as she walked away.

"You *are* a good bartender."

"I know, right?" she gushed, and he fought a chuckle. He looked around again. A group of older men in a booth were having a heated debate, the raised voices drawing his attention. His palms started sweating but he tried to stay relaxed. He turned away, distracting himself and saw Beau waving to him, he waved back but didn't make a move to join them. Tonight would be too risky, he was already on edge.

Taylor brought him his drink and as he raised his glass to take a sip, he spotted Justine joining her friends. His drink stalled halfway to his mouth when he saw her, she looked…he didn't have words. Her silky chocolate locks were pulled into a bun on top of her head, two tendrils loose, framing her face. Her eyes were smoky and sensual, and her lips wide and plump, covered in a rich purple lipstick.

Her orange satin dress was strapless, leaving her delicate shoulders bare, her flawless skin on display. The dress pulled tight across her breasts, enhancing her cleavage. His throat dried, he was baffled by his response. He preferred sweet angelic-looking women, not blatant sex goddesses.

Or do you just not like men prettier than you?

Her words from their session this week had haunted him, he'd read far too much into them. Was she just being nice, or did she really think he was pretty? Did he want her to think he was pretty? He couldn't stop the words from playing around and around in his head until it was all he was thinking about.

As though she heard his thoughts, her eyes flicked to his and widened. They stared at each other, tension passing between them before he gave in, and nodded his head at her in greeting. She stared at him a moment longer before turning back to speak to Christy. He threw back his drink in one gulp and gestured to Taylor to pour another.

Why hadn't Justine acknowledged him? That was the second time she had done that now. Was she just trying to remain professional? He rolled his eyes, why did he care? It was getting harder and harder to keep quiet during their sessions. He had to bite his tongue to keep from answering her questions, from spilling information that no one else knew about him. Could he trust her, could she genuinely help him?

He couldn't believe she seemed content to just let them sit there in silence, openly assessing him with that hot stare of hers. He liked listening to her talk, that voice of hers was so sexy, he didn't want to admit it, but he spent most of their sessions being turned on, imagining what her moans sounded like. She was getting under his skin, and he *hated* it.

Taylor brought him another drink and a big smile before the music in the bar turned down and the crowd fell silent.

"Good evening everyone and welcome to another amazing Saturday night performance by Justine! Y'all know the rules, no bar service during the performance and I swear to Dolly Parton if anyone talks, I'll drag your ass outside myself. Oh, and only me and Christy get to dirty dance."

Blake's eyes moved to Christy who looked around, embarrassed. "Take it away, Justine!" Taylor finished then whooped loudly and started clapping, glaring at everyone in the bar until they did the same. She put the mic down, dimmed the lights and he watched as Justine took her seat on stage and strummed her guitar.

He watched as a sense of calm appeared to wash over her, confidence cloaking her as she lost herself in her music. She opened her mouth, and the most magnificent sound came out. Her singing was beautiful, soulful, and heart-breaking. Her smoky voice changing with the music, husky where it was warranted and sweet when required.

He was captivated by her, during a particularly slow, sultry song she began vocalizing and moaned softly on the final note, the sound exactly what he'd been imagining during their sessions, and he hardened painfully. To hear her moan like that while he stroked inside her, he pictured her splayed out underneath him, her nails clawing his back, her head thrashing as he worked her. His mouth ran dry, he gripped his thigh tight and then all of a sudden, he was startled out of his daydream by the volume around the bar increasing.

What the hell? He'd been so out of it he hadn't noticed she'd stopped singing, that people were crowding around him trying to get to the bar, shoving past him. A bark of laughter right in his ear made him jolt in his seat. How could he have stopped paying attention, what sort of soldier was he?

The bar faded around him, replaced by desert as he was transported back to the worst memory he had of his last tour of duty. He and one of his buddies from his unit, Walker, had been out on a routine patrol. He and Walker had been laughing one moment and the next Walker was lying on the ground, blood pouring from his thigh and shoulder. He'd been shot by waiting rebels and in an instant Blake turned lethal. He spun, rifle raised, alert and immediately located the enemy. He shot twice, one bullet to the head and one to the chest.

Blake stayed calm, keeping his panic inside, as he lifted Walker into his arms. Walker's face was already ashen from the blood loss. Blake ran, fear pushing him to run faster than if his own life depended on it. He ran back to base, praying the whole time that Walker would make it, he nearly dropped him a couple of times, his hands so slick with blood. He'd made it back and lasted through a tense wait for the chopper to arrive and evacuate Walker. His friend had nearly died on his watch because he'd been too busy joking with him to do his job and keep an eye on his surroundings. Blake had failed him.

His chest tightened, his breathing grew shallow, and his vision began to cloud, the desert fading in and out, merging with the bar. A panic attack was moments away, he could feel it. He reached out blindly, not knowing what or who he was grabbing on to. He stumbled off his stool, his stomach roiling and he looked down at his trembling hands, covered in blood. He needed to get out of here and fast but there were so many people, what was his exit strategy? He couldn't remember, what the fuck was wrong with him? This is what he trained for!

Blake stumbled his way to the door and jerked it open, the cool evening air enveloping him. He took in huge lungfuls, trying to calm his breathing but it continued to quicken. Blake fumbled in his pocket for the keys to his car and managed to make his way over to his vehicle. He couldn't drive though, not like this. He would just have to sit and wait for it to pass, where the *fuck* were his keys? His panic reached breaking point and he felt a hand on his shoulder, he spun around, ready to attack.

"Hey, come on, find your way back," her husky voice washed over him, soothing.

"Get away from me!" he shouted, he turned to shove her away. Didn't she realize she was in danger? She grabbed his arm and pressed him against the car, the metal cool on his back.

"Blake, listen to me. Take a moment, pull yourself back from this. You can do it," she soothed, her voice remaining calm and steady. His eyes adjusted in the darkness; the bright orange of her dress became his focus point. She flattened her palm on his chest, over his pounding heart. She grabbed his hand and placed his damp palm on her chest, over her heart.

"Focus on the rhythm, focus on my breathing and the steady beat of our hearts," she intoned. He tried but he couldn't, he needed to get away. He wanted to break apart in private, no one could help him, least of all this seductive siren.

"I can't..." he choked out, gasping for air and she shushed him gently.

"You can do this, you can, Blake. Find a focus point, start thinking of something. Your favorite sports teams, list them. Favorite songs, name them, pick a color and associate objects to that color, distract yourself, give yourself something to focus on as a way to pull yourself back."

His mind raced. Any second now he would pass out, that was what usually happened, he couldn't bear the thought of doing that in front of her.

"You need to work with me or I'm gonna lose you. Blake, I need you to trust me."

He ran through what she'd said, he played basketball years ago but didn't really follow it anymore. *Color, pick a color.* The moonlight shone down bouncing off her orange dress, snagging his attention and he stared at it. *Yes, orange, okay, oranges...basketballs...*his mind blanked.

"You can do it, just focus, keep thinking," she encouraged him. *Oranges, pumpkins.... foxes.... Carrots. Justine's dress...*he slowly gained control of his breathing, his nausea began to fade, and his vision started to clear the more he stared at her in that dress.

"Good, that's so good, Blake! Keep going, I'm so proud of you!" she cried, and he met her stare, looking at her properly for the first time. Her warm eyes, shining up at him in the moonlight, her wide mouth parted in the most beautiful smile.

His breathing deepened and he felt the heat of her palm on his chest, seeping through his thin t-shirt. He realized his palm, the one held to her chest, was no longer covered in blood. The skin beneath his hand was delicate, soft, as silky as her dress. Her cleavage rising under his palm with each inhalation and his eyes couldn't move away from her, drinking her in.

The air thickened between them; heat radiated from them both creating a heady sensation. Neither of them said anything, just kept their hands on each other, both of their breathing ragged as they moved in sync. His mouth was dry, his body exhausted, his mind empty and yet he felt more alert than he had in years.

The evening breeze blew a tendril of hair across her face, and it settled over her bottom lip, the scent of vanilla wafting to him. He had to fight the urge to reach up and brush the strand away.

Or do you just not like men prettier than you?

Her words hammered across his mind. Did she like the way he looked? Did he care?

"You did it," she whispered, and his eyes moved back to hers. She was looking up at him, her expression so open and genuine that his chest ached. He snatched his hand away from her abruptly. He had, he'd done it, he hadn't passed out, he'd pulled himself back. She had helped pull him back. He looked at her, bewildered and unable to explain what just happened.

"Thank you," he said around the lump in his throat, his voice rough.

"Whatever you did, that's your technique for helping with your anxiety and panic attacks. I can show you more Blake, just let me in." Her expression was so earnest, it twisted him up inside. He couldn't let anyone in, didn't want anyone to see how truly fucked up he was. He couldn't. He pulled away from her, dug his keys out of his pocket and unlocked his car.

"Sorry I ruined your performance," he muttered, and opened the door, refusing to meet her eyes.

"You didn't," she replied softly, stepping back so he could get in. He needed to leave, needed to be away from her, too vulnerable after what they had just experienced together. He shut the door and started the engine and drove away.

He made it around the lot and was nearly out of sight before he gave into the urge to look in his rear-view mirror. He raised his eyes and found her, still stood in the parking lot, bathed gloriously in the moonlight, orange dress floating around her in the breeze, watching him go. He sped off before he turned around and did something stupid.

*

Justine came into the office earlier than normal, excitement waking her up before dawn, like a kid at Christmas. Today was her first session with Blake after the incident at the bar on Saturday night and she had high hopes for what they would get out of today.

She replayed that night in her mind. As soon as her set had finished, she looked out into the crowd and her eyes immediately found him, like they always did. His expression had been glazed, but as people swarmed around him, trying to get to the bar in the short interval, he had come back to himself.

She'd noticed his breathing change, his eyes darting around and the way he stumbled off his stool. She knew he'd been triggered and was on the verge of a panic attack. When he'd tripped out of the bar she had immediately gone after him, needing to make sure he was okay. Which he wasn't, not that he would admit it, *stubborn ass*. His eyes were panicked, ferocious and lethal, as they'd swung to her, even in that moment though, he had been in control. He hadn't hurt her the way he'd attacked Beau. She knew she could reach him if only he'd let her, she just needed a connection.

She shivered as she remembered how her hand felt, pressed against the hard, muscled wall of his chest. The way his big palm had fit to her chest, and she'd prayed her heartbeat didn't run into overdrive. His hard callused palm partly covered her dress and partly covered her sensitive skin, abrading it wonderfully. She'd stared up at him, watched him wage a war against his own instincts and conquer them. His mind was powerful, he controlled himself did he even know how difficult that was?

Her stomach clenched as she pictured the moonlight shining down on him, creating a halo around this tortured beautiful devil. She needed to stop thinking about him like that, he was her client, nothing more. *Then why did you put on a nice dress and spend ages on your make-up*, her brain piped up. She told it to shut the hell up.

She heard Hilda come in and went out to greet her.

"Morning Hon, you're in early," Hilda said, and began bustling about the office.

"Yeah, busy day with clients and I needed to make some notes, I've got a bit behind," she lied, hoping Hilda wouldn't see through her charade.

"You're so dedicated." Hilda gushed, and Justine felt a pang of guilt. They chatted for a little while before Justine went back into her office and made some notes on other clients. She glanced at the clock and saw it was nearly time for Blake's appointment. Her heart started to speed up in her chest and she took a deep breath to calm herself. She was just excited because they'd made progress, not for any other reason, purely professional.

By 9.15am she wasn't excited, she was angry. *Where the hell was he?* Five minutes later she heard the door open and a deep rumbling voice echoed through the building. She stood up, peering towards the door hopefully like a teenager with a crush, and she mentally checked herself. He came in, his eyes raking over her from head to toe then he cleared his throat.

"Sorry I'm late, I was dealing with a police matter," he said, and shut the door. She smiled at him brightly, sure he was late, but he'd actually *spoken* to her.

"Thanks for coming, it'll be a shorter session if that's okay as I'm back-to-back all day," she replied. He nodded and sat down on the couch, folding his arms over his chest. His expression was wary and guarded. When he said nothing more, her heart sank with disappointment. Really, were they back to this?

"How has your week been?" she asked, knowing he wouldn't answer. She had hoped after Saturday night that they were past this but obviously not. She tried not to let the disappointment show. Instead, she stood up and grabbed her small recorder from her desk, wondering if he had looked at her ass when she bent over. *Oh my God, cálmate, pinche calenturienta!* She gritted her teeth against her devilish thoughts and set the device to record, placing it on the coffee table. She was through playing nice with him.

"Are you okay if I record our session?" she asked.

"No, I'm not." he replied curtly.

"Okay then." She offered him a professional smile but made no move to turn the device off. He stared at her, his eyes flicking to the recorder, and back to her. That muscle ticked under his eye again. He opened his mouth and then clamped his lips shut.

"Anything to say?" she taunted him.

He fixed her with a hard stare, his eyes hot with anger and something else she didn't recognize. "Why did you ask, if you're not going to do what I said?" he gritted out.

She smiled at him again in that way that she could tell pissed him off.

"I wanted to see how you reacted to not getting your way," she replied simply. His lips thinned to a mulish line. She took a deep breath and sighed when he didn't respond.

"What triggered you on Saturday night?" she asked, again not expecting an answer. She saw guilt flash in his eyes briefly. What did he feel guilty about? Something to do with his flashback? Or because he said he'd ruined her performance? Did he care about her?

"Did you behave like this with your other psychologists?" she pressed. She wanted to give him a hard time, she wanted a reaction and was through playing their silent game. Was he like this with everyone or just her? She noticed he didn't seem to have many friends, not much of a social life. Did he have a girlfriend? Had he had one since his wife died? She had a mischievous idea…

"When was your last sexual relationship?" she asked. His nostrils flared, she loved when they did that—ah—because she knew she was getting to him. He fixed her with a calculated stare, something wicked gleaming in the depths of those slate eyes then he reached over and flicked off the voice recorder.

"When was yours?" he asked coolly. Her heart thud in her chest at his words. His eyes captured hers, the silver depths swirling hypnotically, pulling her under and in that moment, she wanted to drown in them. She felt hot all over, her face flushed, and her body ached. For what, she didn't know. She opened her mouth and closed it again, he'd stumped her. Realizing he had done this on purpose to shut her up, she fixed him with a facetious smile.

"We're not here to talk about me. How many times a day or week do you have panic attacks, Blake?" she asked, getting up and taking the recorder back to her desk. She put it down, straightened a pen that was askew and picked up a business card. She went back over to him and stared down at him. He matched her look but didn't answer. She slid her card across the coffee table to him and caught his eyes staring down the front of her dress. Goosebumps spread out over her skin at his blatant perusal. Another trick to throw her off. *Damn, it nearly worked as well.*

"My number is on there. I'm available to speak to any day, at any time, if you need me," she said, sitting back in her chair. They continued their stare-off again until the end of the session, shorter today because he was late.

She stood up. "Well, I hope you found this to be another thought-provoking session?" She walked back to her desk and by the time she turned around he was leaving the room. She noted with triumph that her business card was no longer on the table.

Chapter 5

Saturday night was girl's night. Justine, Taylor and Christy used to do sleepovers when they were teenagers but when Christy left town, that had stopped. Now that Christy was back, they picked up the tradition again and did it once a month. They all turned up at Taylor's, in their pjs, ate snacks, drank cocktails, and watched scary movies before falling asleep in a pile on the floor. It was the highlight of Justine's week every time; so what if they were in their thirties now?

Normally she wore her cozy flannel pajamas, but the temperature had risen towards the end of the week, so she changed into a cotton shorts and tank top set. She grabbed the fresh batch of fudge brownies she'd made and got into her car to head for Taylor's. As she drove down the dark country roads to get to The Rusty Bucket

Inn, singing along to the radio at the top of her lungs, her thoughts veered towards Blake, where they seemed to go far too often lately.

He was an enigma. Brooding, serious, mysterious and the way he held himself screamed *alpha male*. She'd never met a man like him. Annoyingly, she couldn't get him out of her head, mainly because he was wreaking havoc in her professional life, refusing to drop his guard and let her help him. She'd never had a client this stubborn before and she began to wonder what it would take to break him. Had his other psychologists given up on him because he couldn't be helped or because he didn't *want* to be helped? Whatever it was, she wasn't a quitter; he would have to quit her first.

What was he doing now? It was late, was he in bed? Was he in bed, *alone*? She bit her lip, she didn't care what he did, she only cared from a professional viewpoint. Frankly if it helped him, he could bang his way through the town, and she wouldn't bat an eyelid. She huffed. Okay maybe she would care a little.

He was attractive, there was no denying it, and intense in a way that made her want to bask in his attention, roll over and submit to him like a little kitty cat, just wanting to please him. She felt heat pooling in her core at the thought of pleasing him. Ugh, she needed to hurry up and start exploring intimate relationships.

The first Ladies' Night was taking place next weekend at the bar, and she couldn't wait. She was so busy thinking about how many men would turn up, that she didn't notice the streak of orange that dashed in front of the car until it was too late. She screamed and slammed on her brakes, but she felt the distinctive thud as she hit the fox. She slowed her car, pulling off to the side of the road, her tires crunching over dried leaves and twigs at the edge of the forest.

She sat there for a moment, trying to get her breathing under control. She squeezed her eyes shut, knowing she was going to have to go and look for the fox. She loved animals and couldn't bear the thought of it suffering. Her only thought was that hopefully it had been hit hard enough that it was already dead and not lying in agony.

It was pitch black outside, not a soul around. The bright lights of her car illuminated the road ahead. She rooted around in her glovebox and found the flashlight she kept in there for emergencies, took a deep breath and got out. The balmy evening air warmed her, the silence of the night so intense it was deafening. She flicked the flashlight on, shining it over the road as she began walking back. Her footwear consisted of fluffy black sliders which were rapidly filling up with twigs and leaves, not the best footwear but she hadn't expected to be traipsing around in the dark.

She continued walking until she spotted tire marks on the road, most likely hers. She looked around. She couldn't see anything, then she heard a faint whine. Her heart pounded in her chest, her brain screaming at her to get back in her car and drive off. But she couldn't, she couldn't leave the animal out here to suffer. She steeled herself, mentally put on her big girl panties and turned her flashlight towards the row of trees edging the forest. Calling herself all kinds of idiot, she stepped off the road and into the trees.

*

Blake lay in bed, tossing and turning, willing himself to sleep. He thought that if he went to bed earlier, it might take him a while to drift off, but it would still be earlier than normal. Apparently not. He finally gave up just after eleven and got up, his insomnia not willing to give him a much-needed break. He was on edge, antsy in a way he hadn't been for a while. He had worked himself hard today, working out for hours, punishing his body, willing it to collapse with exhaustion but that had the opposite effect. His body ached but his brain was wired.

He looked out of his bedroom window, the breeze ruffling the trees, the moon high and bright in the clear sky. It was the perfect night for a ride. He smiled to himself, the first genuine smile he'd had in weeks as he changed into jeans and t-shirt. He pounded down the stairs, grabbed his helmet and leather jacket from the hall closet, stuffed his feet into his black Doc Martens, pocketing his keys and phone.

The evening air smelled fresh, a hint of citrus teasing his nostrils, the scent that surrounded the town. He went around the side of the house. The police cruiser that he used most of the time was parked on the driveway but inside the garage sat his precious baby, his Triumph motorcycle. He hadn't ridden much recently and couldn't wait until he was flying down the open, deserted roads of the rural town.

Opening the garage, he paused. There she was, her sexy black paint and metal shining at him in the moonlight. He felt his smile widen. He put his helmet on and swung his leg over, seating himself on his Triumph, adjusting his weight. He turned the ignition, the engine roared to life, loud and purring. The vibrations calming him, the sound soothing his nerves and centering him. He revved the engine and the sound reverberated off the brick walls of the garage then he sped out onto the street, feeling invincible.

As he drove out towards the back roads where he could really push the bike to the limits, he felt amazing. Why couldn't he feel like this all the time, so carefree and relaxed? He took several deep breaths, the breeze rushing through his helmet and sinking inside his lungs.

He rode into the night, everything else falling away, until on a long stretch of road, he saw a car up ahead. He slowed the bike slightly when he spotted the driver door was wide open and the headlights were on. *What the hell?*

His adrenaline kicked in as he surveyed the situation. A late night, empty road, no one around for miles, what danger lay ahead? All his positive, calm energy disappeared when he pulled up alongside the empty car. He killed the engine and got off the bike, resting it on the kickstand. Pulling his phone out of his pocket, he called the station.

"This is Deputy Miller, has anyone reported a car abandoned at the side of a road? Any reports come in at all tonight?" he asked when one of the young officers answered. There was a pause as the officer checked the system and Blake looked around, scrutinizing the area.

"Not that I can see, sir," the officer replied.

"Can you run a check on some plates for me?" Blake read out the plates and as he stood waiting for the info, he heard a noise in the brush next to him and spun, eyes trying to focus on the pitch black of the forest.

"Who's there?" he called, injecting a layer of menace and authority into his tone. The hair on the back of his neck stood on end as he waited. Nothing. He heard another twig snap, closer this time. His breathing deepened, there was nothing worse than knowing an enemy could see you, but you couldn't see them.

He closed his eyes, sharpening his instincts, homing in on his years of military training to guide him. When he heard another twig snap his eyes shot open, there, just to the left of him. He ducked down behind the car and crawled around the side, ready to attack whoever was roaming in the woods so late at night.

As they came closer, he stilled himself, he didn't have his gun with him for protection, he would need to rely on his fists. He smiled to himself in the dark, *no problem there, I've been itching for a fight.* When the assailant came closer, he pounced, grabbing them, and shoving them against the trunk of the car. A high-pitched squeal rang out and he jolted back, looking down into the wide, startled honey eyes that had tormented him for weeks.

"Justine?" he rasped, his mouth going dry as he took in her disheveled appearance. He ran his eyes over her, checking her for injury. What he wasn't prepared for was the most adorable orange and green pajama set that he'd ever seen. The material was dotted with cartoon carrots in ninja outfits and read, *'I'm skilled in carrate'*. His lips twitched at the pun. His humor faded when he took in her long, toned legs stretching on for miles, long enough to wrap around his waist and hold on for the wild ride. He shook his head, dislodging the thought. Her feet were shoved into fluffy...were they slippers?

"What the hell are you doing out here?" he shouted, backing away from her, his nerves getting the better of him when he realized he could've seriously hurt her.

"Me? What the hell are *you* doing out here?!" she yelled back, her eyes narrowing at him. He frowned at her, surprised she wasn't afraid of him.

"I'm out here because I was checking what the hell this car was doing here!" he shouted again, annoyed that even though he was the one in charge, he was explaining his actions to *her*. He still held his phone in his hand, he lifted it back to his ear and said goodbye to the officer on the other end. He ran his eyes over her again, lingering, he noticed her nipples hardened under his stare. It didn't look like she was wearing a bra.

"Are you alright? What are you doing out here in your pajamas?" he asked, glancing around, to make sure no one else was going to jump out at them.

"I'm heading to a…sleepover," she began, her voice dipping on that last word and her cheeks flushed. He became inexplicably angry, fury flooding his veins at the thought of her heading over to some guy's house so late. He knew there was only one reason for a 'sleepover' at this time of night: a booty call.

"I hit a fox with my car and was looking for it, I wanted to check it wasn't injured. I found it, it's still alive. I've got a blanket in my car to wrap it in. I'm going to try and find somewhere to take it for help." She shivered, and it took all his strength not to wrap her in his arms and warm her up. He needed to get away from her, he could feel the nervous edge starting to creep back into his veins, but he couldn't make his legs walk away.

"I know somewhere we can take it," he replied gruffly. He was calling himself all kinds of stupid for helping her when his mind screamed to stay away whilst he felt so vulnerable, but it was his duty to help his citizens.

She pushed past him, and tendrils of her hair coasted across his cheek in a silky caress, the scent of her washing over him, heating his blood. She opened the trunk of her car and bent forward. He tried not to stare at the round globes of her ass peeking out from the bottoms of her cotton shorts but failed miserably. She grabbed a blanket and slammed her trunk shut, switching on her flashlight again.

"It's this way," she said, and marched on, taking the lead, like she wasn't wearing skimpy pajamas in the middle of nowhere, at midnight. Dammit *he* was the deputy, he should be in front, protecting her from any danger lurking in the woodland.

He tried to overtake her, but she shoved him out of the way, snapping that he needed to stop trying to lead when he didn't know where he was going. It sounded like she called him something unpleasant in Spanish: he would need to Google that later. She shushed him when his boots clunked along the forest floor, snapping all the twigs, and crunching through the dried leaves.

"Every animal around for miles will hear you coming!" she hissed at him. *That's the point,* he thought, he wanted to scare away anything that could hurt her. He kept close to her, letting her lead but keeping an eye out for any movement around them. After a few minutes she stopped dead and for all his training, he didn't notice and slammed straight into her. Her soft body coming up against his, his arms banding around her to stop her from falling. His face buried in her hair, that familiar scent ratcheting up his desire. Because of course he was traipsing through the forest in the middle of the night with the one woman he couldn't stop fantasizing over. *Hello erection, nice to see you again, how long's it been, a few hours?*

"You need to be very still, and quiet," she whispered, and she shone the flashlight into the brush and sure enough there was the small fox. Laying against the base of a tree, breathing shallowly, its eyes darting around wildly. It opened its mouth and let out a soft, high-pitched bark.

"I know honey, I'm sorry I hit you, but I'm gonna help you now, you'll feel better soon, I promise," she cooed at it and Blake stared at her. Was it charming that she was cooing at this wild animal? Yes. Did it chip a small chunk out of his defenses? Damn right it did.

He took the flashlight from her and kept it illuminated on the fox as she slowly crept over to it and wrapped it in the blanket she had. As she lifted it into her arms, it let out another pained bark, the sound echoing around the forest and hitting him hard in the chest. They quickly tramped back out to the road and then she stood there, looking down at the bundle in her arms, shivering. He sighed internally as he stripped off his jacket, thinking he was an ass for not doing it sooner.

"Here, give me the fox," he said, and held his jacket out to her. She eyed him suspiciously but handed the fox over. When he took the bundle, she wrapped herself in his jacket and he instantly got irritated. Irritated that she'd covered up all that gorgeous skin of hers that was begging to be licked. Irritated that she looked adorable as fuck as his leather jacket swamped her. And irritated that he noticed all these things.

"Come on, this way," he growled, angry at his runaway thoughts. He carried the fox past her car and towards his bike.

"Where are you going?" she called after him, her smoky voice had him fighting a shiver. She stood at the driver's side of her car.

"Do you know where this place is?" he asked her pointedly. She shifted on the spot under his harsh scrutiny.

"No," she muttered.

"Exactly, we'll take my bike, it'll get us there faster and give us a better chance of helping this little guy," he said, and turned back to his bike. He held out his helmet to her, he only had one and would rather she wear it to protect that pretty little head of hers. He swung his leg over the bike, careful not to jostle the tiny injured bundle in his arms. She stood next to him, the helmet gripped tightly in her hands, eyeing the bike warily.

"Do you trust me, Justine?" he asked, holding his breath, not understanding why he needed to know her answer more than he needed air to breathe. She nodded, relief flooded him, and he held out a hand to her. She hesitated before sliding her palm into his, a jolt of electricity rocketing up his arm at her warm, soft touch. She placed her other hand on his shoulder as she got onto the bike and settled herself.

"Here." He brought her arms around his waist and settled them around the fox so that she had her arms wrapped around him and the fox together.

"Hold on tight," he commanded through gritted teeth as her heat came up against him, her soft breasts pressing against his back. He started the engine and pulled away, not too fast, to give her a chance to get used to the feel of the bike. Her knees gripped the side of his hips, tightening as they turned into the corners. She leaned in slightly, surprising him, she was a natural. He wondered if she'd been on the back of a motorcycle before and vowed to hunt down whichever man she'd done it with and hurt him.

He tried to distract his raging thoughts by focusing on where he was going. He'd done a little investigating since he heard about the incident with Rebelle at the station. He was trying so hard not to become drawn in and deeply ingrained in the town, but with the NWS meetings, Justine, and his curiosity over the incident with Rebelle, he was failing miserably. It turned out she owned a little farm on some land which she had inherited when her husband, the previous sheriff, had passed away.

Blake had driven past it during the week while on patrol, curious to see what she'd done with it. She had turned it into an animal shelter, the *Take A Chance* rescue shelter. Hopefully she would be able to help them tonight. He didn't know why but it would trouble him if the fox died, not just because he didn't want an innocent animal to die but because he didn't know how he would react if he saw Justine upset.

They rode out of town quickly, the bike tearing through the streets faster than her tiny car could have and before long they arrived at the farm. The sound of the bike must have alerted Rebelle to their presence because she was coming out the front as he and Justine were getting off the bike. He took in Rebelle - she was a tiny slip of a woman, delicate, petite, too thin and too gaunt-looking for someone so young. Her brown hair floating about her cheeks in a delicate pixie cut, her doe eyes wide with alarm at the sight of these two strangers on her property in the middle of the night.

"Rebelle Black? I'm the new deputy sheriff, Blake Miller, pleased to meet you. Sorry to disturb you so late but we have a bit of an emergency you might be able to help with," he said, helping Justine off the bike while protecting the wounded bundle she carried.

"Hi Rebelle, it's been a long time, it's great to see you," Justine said quietly. Rebelle just eyed them both carefully. "I accidentally hit this fox and he needs urgent care. Is that something you can provide?" Justine continued. Rebelle stared at the bleeding animal in Justine's arms, who chose that moment to let out another pained bark. She nodded, stepping forward and taking it gently from her.

"I know an emergency veterinarian who can take a look at him." Rebelle's voice was soft, her demeanor gentle, submissive even, and in that moment, Blake made up his mind. No matter what the town gossip was, there was no way Rebelle murdered her husband.

"Do you want me to take you?" Blake asked, coming to stand next to Justine.

"No, I'll take my truck and go now. I'll let you know

what happens," she said to Blake, and he nodded. She turned and headed towards where her truck was parked without a backwards glance.

"Thank you!" Justine called after her in the dark. Rebelle waved over her shoulder and got into the beaten-up old truck, gunned the engine, and drove off. Next to Blake, Justine shivered, her adrenaline probably wearing off.

"Come on, let's get you back," he said, and started walking back to the bike but realized she wasn't following him. She was staring after Rebelle, looking worried. The level of concern she had for the injured animal surprised him. She was compassionate and genuinely worried and that melted his heart a little bit more.

"I'll let you know what happens when Rebelle updates me," he said, and she turned to meet his eyes in the moonlight. She nodded and then came after him. He got back on his bike and waited until she was sat behind him, helmet back in place and she tentatively wrapped her arms around his waist, her palms lifting up and flattening against his chest. He couldn't help but notice how perfect she felt pressed against him and he fought his urge to pull her onto his lap, starting the engine more aggressively than he should have.

The drive was short and silent. In no time at all they were back at her car. She got off the bike and removed his helmet, shaking her long hair out and running a hand through it. She handed it back to him and then shrugged out of his jacket.

"You can keep it if you like, until you get to your…sleepover." He nearly choked on the word, knowing soon she would be wrapped in the arms of someone else, moaning in ecstasy.

"I'll be fine now, it's not far," she said, and turned

away. He pulled the jacket on, trying to ignore the warmth it still held from her body or the lingering cocoa and vanilla scent that enveloped him. He watched her go back to her car, before she turned back, the moonlight bouncing off her hair and showing him those silly cotton pajamas one last time.

"Thank you, Blake," she said softly, the words reaching him on the breeze. He swallowed the lump that formed in his throat as he watched her, the image of her standing there looking so stunning now tattooed into his brain. He nodded and tugged his helmet on, revved the engine and shot off before he pulled her against him and crushed her mouth to his.

He didn't sleep that night. He tossed and turned again, this time from picturing Justine, naked and spread wide for him in his bed, begging him, pleading with him to make her come. He got up and had a cold shower, already worked up before the day had even truly started.

*

Justine turned up to the NWS meeting on Monday night absolutely exhausted. Stifling a yawn, she waved hello to a couple of the older women she knew and made her way to the refreshments table, scanning for coffee. She'd hardly gotten any sleep and was suffering for it now. To be fair though, she hadn't meant to be up quite as late on Saturday, getting to Taylor's place late thanks to the fox incident. Then she'd spent all of Sunday until late researching PTSD triggers and treatments.

She had also spent most of the weekend trying not to think about her client in an inappropriate way, but it hadn't gone well. What was wrong with her? Why couldn't she get him out of her mind? The way he had looked at her the other night, the moonlight sparkling in his silver eyes, lightening them, bewitching her. His pale skin becoming pearlescent in the moonlight, his features harsh, dark slashes in contrast. He'd looked tragically beautiful, his scowl etched deeply across his face, her reluctant hero. She would bet her life that he only ever considered himself the villain when he was anything but.

He was a complex mix of standoffish but helpful, uncaring but compassionate and he was throwing her through loops. The level of care he had shown for an animal *she'd* injured had shown her his softer side, and goddamn it was endearing. She'd realized that he wasn't lost at all, he just needed to be brought back to himself.

She watched as he walked into the village hall for the NWS meeting, a gaggle of ladies rushing him in their eagerness to vie for his attention. She watched him over her mug of steaming coffee as he tried to answer all their questions while his arms were filled with the multiple casseroles they had made him. This helpless, gorgeous, *starving* new man in town that they needed to look after. Did he even realize what a big hit he was with everyone?

She smiled to herself as she watched him, slipping back into the daydream that had plagued her since Saturday night. The new one where when he'd slammed her up against her car, it was with passion. How good he felt when she'd wrapped her arms around him, holding on as they rode through the night, the muscular wall of his chest hard and unyielding in her grip. Her body was instinctively drawn to him, molding with his as they leaned into the turns of the road together. And the way he'd stared at her before he left her, like he was seconds away from ravaging her sex-starved body, had her fighting shivers but she knew she was just fantasizing again.

Her core throbbed sharply, bringing her back to the present from her daydream. She didn't understand her attraction to him, he wasn't what she normally liked, and she needed to nip this in the bud. He was a client, nothing more. She could never cross that line, her ethics wouldn't allow it, no matter how much her body begged for it. Besides, rebellious leather-wearing bad boys were a phase she grew out of when she was eighteen. She was looking for something different now, something lasting. She wanted a love that set the world on fire.

Blake lifted his head, met her eyes and started disentangling himself from his fan club and headed towards her. *Was he walking in slow motion?* He was wearing his leather jacket again. God, he looked good in that. She had been wrapped in it the other night, the leather warm from his skin, his scent lingering like spice and hot nights, it was like she was wrapped in *him*. She shook her head as she fought another shiver. *Roll on Ladies' Night where I can try and find a man to pour all this frustration into.*

"Evening Blake," she said, trying to keep her tone even, once he was in front of her.

"I just thought I'd let you know that I heard from Rebelle about the fox. She's going to be fine. Just a broken leg and a pretty deep cut in her side that the vet stitched back up," he replied, not returning her greeting. Straight to the point as usual, that was fine by her, but she still felt a twinge of disappointment at his lack of personal engagement. *Maybe that's another symptom, is he trying to shut himself off from everyone?*

She smiled. "That's great, I'm so relieved, thank you. Which vet was it? I'll swing by and pay for the treatment."

He plowed a hand through his hair, fingers snagging on the curls that had started forming. She would love to run her fingers through it, tugging the strands tightly as his lips worked his way down her neck and…

"Don't worry about it, it's been taken care of," he

replied gruffly, distracting her from the thoughts that she wasn't meant to be having anymore.

"What do you mean, it's been taken care of? Did Rebelle pay for it?" she asked, concerned she'd caused Rebelle undue expense. His mouth flattened into its usual unhappy line.

"No, I covered it," he said, not meeting her stare. He paid for it? *How...sweet.* The action really surprised her, it was such a nice thing to do, so at odds with his frankly frequently off-putting personality. She wondered if, try as he might, he cared a lot more about the town and the people in it than he let on.

"Blake, you didn't need to do that," she said softly. He shrugged, looking around the room. "It's nothing."

"Let me give you some money for it, it was my fault in the first place and you helped more than enough in the moment. I'm so grateful you turned up when you did," she said, sincerity coating her words, desperate to try and connect with him. His eyes swung to hers, their color swirling to a dark silver, enthralling her.

"I said it's nothing." His tone was standoffish and left no room for argument. With that, he spun on his heel and went over to talk to Dean who had just come in. She stood there, not entirely surprised that when she'd been nice to him, his walls had shot straight back up.

The meeting was called to start a few minutes later and she drifted off into her thoughts. When it was just her and Blake together in the forest, he'd spoken to her, shown a different, caring side of himself. Like being away from the town, alone with her, had opened him up. She needed to break down those barriers once and for all, and now she had an idea of how to reach him. Shooting him a knowing smile across the table, she knew just what to do to crack this man.

Chapter 6

When Blake pulled up outside Justine's office for his next session, he saw her waiting outside leaning against her car, and he just knew she had something planned. Something he wasn't going to like. He tried to ignore the punch of lust that hit him low in the gut as he took her in. Dark hair swinging from a ponytail, a lacy white sundress with large orange flowers played at the tops of her knees, the contrast against her delicious skin had his palms sweating. She had large, round white-rimmed sunglasses perched on top of her head and her dainty feet were encased in tennis shoes. Wherever they were going, it was outdoors. He sighed and got out of his car.

"Morning, Blake," she called with a little wave. God, he loved the way she said his name, like she was sighing and his blood heated. He came over to her and nodded in greeting.

"Don't you want to know why I'm meeting you out here?" she asked.

He still refused to play her game. He didn't feel like he could open up and tell a stranger all his darkest innermost thoughts, no matter how beautiful she was. He had to admit though, it was getting harder to stay quiet. The problem was, he didn't want to talk about all his issues, he wanted to talk about her.

"School field trip?" he replied with a sardonic smile. He noticed her eyes dropped to his mouth and a smile lit her face. He had to look away from its dazzling brilliance, an ache forming in his chest.

"Exactly, get in!" She gestured to her little three door Toyota. Could he even fit in there? He reluctantly went around to the passenger side and got in. Her usual scent of cocoa and vanilla immediately consumed him, this time honey was added to the mix. Images plagued him of his face buried in her hair, inhaling the intoxicating scent while his hands roved her body. Did she taste like honey? He shook his head, dislodging the thought before he got another hard-on—that was definitely bound to make things awkward. When he was buckled in, his knees practically to his chest, he turned to face her. She shot him another brilliant smile and put her sunglasses on.

"Road trip!" she sang as she peeled away from the curb and he fought the laugh trying to work its way free. She didn't speak to him again for the whole journey, which annoyed him although he couldn't explain why. They drove away from town, past the turning for the bar and kept going. A short while later she pulled over at the side of the road.

There was nothing around for miles, just trees as far as he could see. He watched as Justine got out of the car and took a deep breath. He got out, taking in his surroundings. They were at the edge of the forest they'd been at a few nights ago. He felt a pit growing in his stomach, he didn't like being in large open areas, he wasn't sure how to get his bearings, or how to protect her if something happened.

"Take a deep breath," she instructed.

He fought an eye roll but did as she said. Inhaling deeply, he detected the scent of pine, fresh earth and the typical tang of citrus. It was wonderful, not that he would admit that to her. She smiled at him, pleased with his compliance.

"This way." She pointed and then marched off into the trees. Reluctantly he followed her, tearing his eyes away from where the hem of her dress flirted with the backs of her smooth thighs. He gritted his teeth and kept his gaze on the forest floor, this would be his toughest session yet. The sound of leaves crunching under his feet, the softness of the pine needles coating the floor, the breeze blowing through the trees, rustling their leaves and branches. It was so peaceful, so quiet, he actually began to relax.

They walked for ten minutes before he heard the trickle of water. He glanced up and saw that they'd come to a small clearing by a river. Justine skipped ahead and perched on a rock and patted the one beside her for him to take a seat. He remained standing, staring out at the flat water with the trees along the bank reflected in its calm surface. When she didn't speak for a little while he looked over at her. She was studying him, a frown on her face.

"I know you won't open up to me," she sighed, and he was surprised to feel a flare of guilt at disappointing her. "Not without knowing some personal details about me. I'm asking you to share your deepest thoughts with a stranger without offering anything as collateral in return."

He didn't say anything, didn't move, just held his breath to see what she would say next. He didn't understand his fascination with her, she wasn't the type of woman he was usually interested in. She was too dominant, too independent, too sexy, and too…experienced. She wouldn't *need* him. He liked to protect, liked to take the lead and he just knew she wouldn't stand for that.

"So, I'm going to tell you some things about me, some things no one knows, or not many people anyway. I'll trust you with this information, in the hope that you'll trust me in turn and let me help you." She looked out to the water and clasped her hands together, not meeting his stare. They sat in silence for a moment. His heart was pounding in his ears, he was on edge waiting for her to speak and reveal details about her life. She took a deep breath.

"My family went on vacation to Disneyland when I was seven. My parents had saved up for years to take us all. Just before we went inside the park, my parents went ahead to sort out our tickets and a man came over and offered to give me a Goofy balloon. Goofy was my favorite and I was so excited. He said it was in his van, so I went off with him to get it. We were nearly there before anyone realized and caught up to us. Sometimes, I have nightmares about what could've happened to me, and what happens to the children who don't get away." She went quiet and he was shocked at what she told him. He was about to say something when she began speaking again.

"When I was getting my PhD, one of my professors made a pass at me, offered to give me better grades if I got on my knees for him. I refused and he hit me, ironically calling me a slut and a whore."

Blake stiffened and cold rage flooded through him.

"I reported him and he got fired. I studied harder and got better grades than he'd been offering, so in my mind I beat him, I *won*. But I still think about the fear I felt in that moment, after being propositioned then hit like that. It's stayed with me all these years and I wonder if I really did win after all," she added.

The sounds of the forest stilled. Blake held his breath, waiting for her to go on. She looked up at him and held his stare, her honey eyes wide pools of emotion and he gobbled up the sight of her vulnerability, devouring it, drowning in it.

Then she said, "My deepest fear is that I'll end up alone. It's pathetic I know but I've never even had a proper boyfriend."

His jaw clenched. Wasn't she with Beau? His second thought barreled into him after his first, wait, she'd *never* had a proper boyfriend? She had to be nearly the same age as him. Did that mean…?

"I believe in true love, the sickening fairy-tale kind, but it doesn't seem to believe in me. Everyone around me is so loved up and I feel lonelier than ever. I've got the house, the job, the family and friends, but not the man. Sorry, that probably sounds ridiculous to you," she murmured.

He opened his mouth, but his reply was cut off by something in the distance. *Wait, was that…?* Her voice faded into the background as the sound grew nearer, soaring above the trees. His breathing deepened and he knew what was going to happen next. His stomach turned, his hands trembled as he raised them to run through his hair, tugging the strands, using the pain to try and keep himself in the present. He couldn't let the memories overrule him. The helicopter soared closer, the blades chopping through the air, the rhythmic sound mesmerizing him, thundering through him. He looked at the forest floor and as the pine needles morphed into sand, Walker was laying at his feet, bleeding out.

"No!" Blake bellowed, pushing his fists into his eyes, trying to erase the image.

"Blake?" Justine called, her voice sounded too distant, too far away. He needed to get away from her, what if he hurt her? He couldn't guarantee what would happen if she was near.

"Get away from me!" He spun away, the sound of the helicopter nearer and he watched as it split the trees in front of him and lowered, landing in the desert clearing that formed in front of them. He was holding Walker, his grip on him slipping and sliding from all the blood pouring out. He felt a hand on his back.

"What are you seeing, Blake?" her soft voice filtered through, trying to anchor him. He couldn't answer her. He was too focused on gripping Walker tightly, trying not to drop him but his hands were so damn slippery, there was so much blood.

"What are you seeing, Blake?" she asked again, her voice firmer. He shook his head. Walker slid from his arms, thudded to the ground, his cry of pain echoing in Blake's ears.

"Answer me, Blake!" Her raised voice commanded an answer from him. This time she penetrated his fear and he responded.

"It's Walker, he's bleeding. I can't help him, it's all my fault!" he cried. The image changed as Justine stepped into the desert and took his hands. Walker was still lying between them on the ground, writhing in pain.

"Blake, listen to me. We need to break the connection

between the past trauma and whatever just triggered you. We're going to try the 'then and now' technique, I need you to stay with me."

His vision blurred, his stomach turned, and cold sweat was breaking out on his forehead. This wouldn't go away, not until it played out in full. He couldn't break the spell.

"Blake, what do you see *then*?" her voice firm, demanding.

He fought against himself, pain searing through his mind. "Then?"

"Yes, in your trauma, what is it you're seeing?"

"Walker, he's been shot, he's dying," he gritted out, sweat dripping down his temple, his muscles pulled tight with tension and ready for action.

"Good, that's good, what do you see *now*?"

He looked around him, the image of her bleeding into the image of Walker, the two twining together and confusing him.

"Blake! What do you see *now*?" Her voice compelled him. His vision cleared slightly.

"You, I-I see you," he gasped as his muscles tightened, fighting the need to act.

"Good, what else do you see *then*?" she replied, her voice becoming louder, but he couldn't answer. He was standing in a military hospital, thousands of miles away, watching as the doctors tried to save Walker's life.

"Hospital, he's lost too much blood and it's all my fault."

"It's not your fault, Blake. He's lucky you got him out of there," she replied, her voice soothing.

"He's screaming in pain, and I can't help him, I failed."

"No, Blake, you didn't fail. What can you see *now*?" Justine countered. He felt her warm hand grip his jaw.

"Stay with me," she commanded.

"I see...argh!" he cried out in frustration, the hospital fading in and out as trees came into view, "I see trees, the forest floor, not the desert." His surroundings cleared, the heat of her body so close to his, pulling him back from the cold clinical infirmary and into his earthy surroundings. Her forehead was pressed so close to his, her palm cupping his cheek, connecting them. He was panting, his breathing calming.

"What do you see *then?*" she asked. He focused and saw nothing now but the trees. And her in that dress, the orange flowers on the material becoming his sole focus.

"Nothing, I see nothing," he rasped. His stomach settled as he came back to the present, his eyes flicked to hers. The warmth shining from them, encouraging him, pride lighting them. The heat from their closeness, their mouths inches apart, breaths sawing out of them both. He couldn't hear anything except the sound of her panting. She stroked her hand over his jaw, grounding him.

He looked at her mouth, that goddamn smart mouth of hers that drove him insane with her goddamn nosy questions. He wanted her, wanted to taste her, see how quickly he could make her moan. His cock hardened beneath his jeans as her eyes dipped to his mouth and heated.

Or do you just not like men prettier than you?

Her words teasing his mind. He was going to do it, his mind screaming at him not to even as his body leant forward, his heart pounding for an entirely different reason now. Did she want him too?

Her words from minutes earlier played through his mind; she wanted the fairy-tale. She was a princess trapped in her burning castle, waiting for Prince

Charming to rush in and save her. But Blake wasn't anyone's hero, he was the villain holding the match. As though she sensed the change in him, she disengaged and stepped away, that professional smile of hers back in place. He spun away, angry with himself for his weakness. He walked back over to the rock and sat down, trying to conceal his arousal from her. She sat down next to him.

"Why was it your fault, Blake?" she asked gently.

"Why was what my fault?" he replied, his voice thick. He didn't want to talk about this, he felt too vulnerable, his emotions scattered.

"Why was Walker's injury your fault?" she pressed.

It was still too raw, he couldn't talk about this, didn't want to. But he knew he couldn't shut her out after she had shared so many details about herself. He waited a long time before he replied, but he didn't answer her question.

"I didn't love my wife."

Justine didn't say anything, just waited for him to continue.

"She was my high school sweetheart. When I was getting ready to move away for college, she told me she was pregnant, so I didn't leave and we got married. But she'd been lying to me. She just didn't want me to leave her. I had no decent skills or education, so I joined the military. Katie grew more and more depressed from her guilt, and it was hard for me to be around her, to constantly placate her when I had this pit of resentment burning away in me. I didn't know how to help her or myself, so I ignored the situation. As soon as I came back from one tour, I signed up for another. For years we carried out this routine. Then one day I got the call that she'd killed herself."

They sat in silence, the breeze ruffling the trees, birds

singing and the sound of branches knocking together.

"Thank you for sharing that with me," she said.

He wanted to roll his eyes at her words but the sincerity in her voice stopped him. He looked down at her sitting next to him. She didn't say anything else, and he was grateful she didn't push him or ask more questions. He felt like he was at his limit, completely drained.

"Let's head back," she said.

They drove back in silence, him staring out the window, wondering how a trip into the woods had ended this way. She had broken him but had been his savior too.

"What was that, what did you do with me?" he asked, not facing her.

"It's called the 'then and now' technique. It's used to help break PTSD sufferers out of a flashback by getting them to focus on what they can see both past and present to help identify that they're no longer in the past," she explained. They lapsed back into silence.

"Thank you," he said quietly after a moment, and when she didn't respond, again he was grateful for that. When they pulled up outside her office, they got out and stood facing each other on the sidewalk.

"I want you to try to use that technique the next time you're triggered and let me know what happens. Consider it homework from our school field trip." She flashed a smile at him, but he didn't respond. After another beat of silence, she sighed.

"Do you have any friends, Blake?" she asked gently. The way she was looking at him stirred something inside him, it wasn't quite pity, but he still felt embarrassment flaming his cheeks. He didn't have friends and he liked it that way, kind of. If he didn't get close to anyone, he never got hurt.

"I'd like you to work on developing some relationships. I want you to explore getting to know people, putting yourself out there and meeting new people. Some people might like to be alone, but it doesn't help you heal if there's no support network in place for you." She stared at him in that way that made him feel like she was seeing him, *really* seeing him. He needed to get out of here, now.

"See you next week, Justine," he said, and turned and walked away, but not before he caught the soft smile she gave him. Damn, she was tearing him up inside.

*

Justine sat down behind her desk, her mind whirring from her session with Blake. She had gotten him to open up and she couldn't believe it. She was thrilled, from a professional perspective and a personal one. She had only meant to see if getting him out of her office would work, if being somewhere less formal would help him relax. She hadn't counted on finding one of his triggers, let alone tackling it together and helping him. Then he'd gifted her with information about himself, insight into his past and some of his other issues.

She quickly wrote up her notes before she forgot them. She found it interesting that he opted to tell her about his wife rather than his military flashback. From what she could gather he was harboring severe issues with guilt and failure, both with what happened on his last tour and with his wife. And she bet that was linked to the incident with that suicidal woman too.

That would be a big focus for them moving forward. She needed him to take her through each incident so she could establish what had happened and how his feelings of guilt had formed, and how she could retrain his thoughts.

She was excited: it had been four weeks but they had a breakthrough. She typed up her notes and emailed them to his superior back in Anderson County as she was required to do each week. This time she actually had some detail to share with him and he would be able to see there had been developments.

She sat back in her chair, thinking. She had known Blake would kick up a fuss about going somewhere, that was precisely why she'd done it. She needed to break the pattern they had fallen into. She had watched him as he stood in the forest, taking deep breaths, letting himself relax. His features had softened, and he'd appeared younger, almost boyish and carefree. She flushed in embarrassment when she thought of the personal details she'd revealed to him. But she had needed it to be something important, it would do no good sharing basic information with him, it didn't create vulnerability and it didn't create trust.

When he'd gone into his trauma, it pained her, hearing him blame himself for something that hadn't been his fault. She'd managed to reach him and pull him back and as they'd stood close together, hearts pounding, breaths heaving, she'd shocked herself when she had nearly kissed him. Nearly begged him to take her in his strong arms and show her true pleasure for the first time.

When she had felt his arousal press against her, she'd almost groaned and thrown herself at him. That was the last thing he needed when he was so vulnerable and raw. She knew he wasn't actually aroused; it was just a physical reaction to all the adrenaline that had been coursing through him. It had been sweet that he tried to hide it, not wanting to make her feel awkward. She shoved her thoughts away, reminding herself that she was meant to be helping her *client*, not lusting after him.

Lila Dawes

She made it through the rest of the day, mainly thinking about what she would uncover through Blake's next sessions.

Chapter 7

Justine surveyed herself in the full-length mirror against the wall in her bedroom. She looked dressy but also like she'd casually thrown something on and not spent hours planning this laid-back look. She ran her hands over the black leather pants that were practically shrink-wrapped to her body, her loose, white strappy top contrasting nicely. She wore her hair down and poker-straight, where it fell to her hips, tickling the backs of her arms when she walked. She added jewelry and make-up to complete the look and, when she was satisfied, she headed out to The Rusty Bucket Inn for the first official Ladies' Night.

By the time she arrived, her stomach was in knots. She didn't know how many people were going to be there. Would any of the men even be interested in her? What if they weren't? What if it was all men she had dated before? At least Beau would be there, he could be her wingman.

"Breathe," she muttered, calming herself before she pushed open the door and went inside.

Taylor had rearranged the bar interior, creating a row of intimate tables for two, so couples could have privacy on their dates. She'd placed a small candle on each table, the glow from the flames creating a warm and inviting atmosphere. Bouquets of roses adorned the bar, and petals were scattered here and there. She had done such a good job bringing the romantic vibes, it looked gorgeous.

A small crowd of men had already formed at the bar, eager to sign up for the evening. A sudden wave of insecurity gripped Justine and she looked around, nervously nibbling on her thumbnail. Overcome with shyness, she didn't know what to do. She spotted Kayleigh serving drinks to the group of men gathered at the bar and wanted to go over to her, but her timidity kept her feet locked where they were. *You are a strong, confident woman, you don't need to be shy or afraid, you just need to be you!*

Justine surveyed the men, not recognizing any of them from town. They were all talking together and laughing loudly, having a whale of a time. Should she go over there and introduce herself, confident as hell? Did she just take a seat and wait? How did this work? Anxiety had her blood pounding and she wished she had asked Taylor for more information before she turned up tonight. Then she spotted Taylor coming out of her office and relief coursed through her; she began to relax.

"Hey!" she hissed, snagging her attention.

"Hey Justine!" Taylor called loudly, drawing the attention of all the men who turned as one to stare at her. She felt herself flush under their scrutiny. One winked at her, another waved.

"That was subtle, thanks," she hissed sarcastically. Taylor just laughed.

"We're about to start, don't worry though, I'll explain everything. I just need to go and get the others from the bathroom," Taylor said over her shoulder.

"The bathroom?" Justine frowned.

"The other women didn't know what to do so they hid in the ladies'. Props for coming in and just owning it, babe!" Taylor grinned at her.

Justine may have only just arrived but she wished she had thought of hiding in the bathroom too. The group of men were still staring at her, she shot them a shy smile and busied herself by rummaging in her purse for a lip-gloss. The door to the bar opened, Beau came in and Justine nearly threw herself at him in relief.

"Wow, you look great!" he said, giving her a quick once-over. "Spin for me," he added, a wolfish smile on his face.

She laughed and smacked his arm playfully. "Stop it! You look great too, are you excited for this?"

"Not many ladies here for the Ladies' Night, might have to start chatting up some of these guys," Beau said, glancing around, disappointment shining in his eyes.

"Taylor's just fetching them from the bathroom," Justine replied, and he perked up. Then Taylor reappeared with at least six other women, none of whom Justine recognized. They must be from the next town over, like the men.

Taylor clapped her hands to draw everyone's attention.

"Okay everyone, are we ready to begin?" The conversation died down until all that could be heard in the background was Meatloaf's dulcet tones singing he would do anything for love, but he won't do that. Justine resisted singing along, she loved all old-school tunes. Eighties music was her favorite but some of those nineties hits couldn't be denied.

"I would like all the ladies to take a seat on this side of the table." Taylor paused while the women eagerly took their places, chairs scraping against the wooden floor in their hurry. Justine perched on the seat at the end of the row, closest to the door, just in case.

"Perfect, now all the gentlemen can take a seat opposite," again Taylor paused while the men looked around nervously before sitting down. Beau was quick to choose a place and sat down across from a busty blond, barely containing his grin. A young-looking man-child sat down opposite Justine and fixed her with a sweet smile.

"Now, everyone has two-and-a-half minutes to chat. You can talk about anything *except* your previous relationships. Let's keep things positive, people. Then at the end of your time the men will move to the next seat, until everyone has had a chance to talk to each other."

Beau raised his hand. Taylor rolled her eyes. "Yes?" she asked through clenched teeth.

"So, it's essentially speed dating? What makes it a Ladies' Night?" he asked.

"It's a Ladies' Night because that's what I said it is," Taylor snapped back, then smoothed her hands over her hair like she was trying to calm herself. "Anyway, at the end of the night the *ladies* get to hand out their number to as many of the men as they are interested in." Taylor finished with a pointed stare at Beau. She started explaining the rules: no touching unless requested yada yada. When Beau raised his hand again, Taylor looked like she was going to lose her shit. But instead of detonating, Taylor offered him a sickly-sweet smile.

"Yes?"

"What happens if more than one woman gives me her number?" he asked, a shit-eating grin consuming his face.

"In the *unlikely* event that *you* get more than one," she began with another pointed stare at Beau. "Then the world would implode and this whole thing would be moot. But for everyone else, you're free to do what you want, as long as the ladies are happy. They run the show tonight."

While Taylor finished explaining everything, Kayleigh came around and took drinks orders for those who didn't get a chance to go to the bar. As Justine looked around, she noticed there was a spare seat halfway down, one of the women had no one sitting with her. *How awkward, does she just have to wait out one of the rounds until a man comes to sit with her?*

"Is everyone ready to begin?" Taylor asked. But before anyone could answer, the door to the bar opened and everyone turned to stare as Blake walked in. Justine's stomach did a series of unwanted acrobatics when she saw him. He'd trimmed his beard, and with his hair slightly long, his curls were unruly in a sexy 'just got out of bed' way. He was wearing a burgundy button-down shirt which fit snugly against his broad, muscled chest and he wore smart black pants.

Her heart pounded as she took him in. He looked dangerous, roguish, absolutely gorgeous and she knew he was the best-looking man in the room tonight. The other women all began assessing him fiercely. *Hands off, ladies, he's mine!* She blinked in surprise. Where had that come from? He wasn't hers and he never would be. She didn't even want him, he had too much baggage, he was too complex, too serious. It was her body that wanted him, the little hussy. Which was exactly why Justine was here tonight: to find someone to take that next step with, because it wouldn't be, couldn't be, Blake.

He looked around the room, assessing like he usually did. His eyes landed on hers but flicked away again dismissively. *See, he's not interested in you either.* A sharp pain pierced her chest at the thought, she brushed it aside.

"Blake, finally! You like to keep the ladies waiting, don't you?" Taylor joked, he offered her a small smile and then took a seat in the empty chair. The woman seated opposite him looked like all her birthdays had come at once and to Justine she looked like was going to launch herself at him. *Not jealous at all...*

She didn't understand what he was doing here. He could barely speak to her, let alone a new woman every couple of minutes. Okay so Justine had told him to start developing relationships, but she didn't think he'd start straight away. She was concerned from a professional point of view, she didn't want him to jump into anything too soon and get hurt, she was *such* a caring psychologist.

"Right folks, the first round starts...now!" Taylor clapped happily and walked away, leaving them all to it. There was a moment of silence where everyone just stared at each other, unsure what to say. Then slowly a few began to talk to the person opposite them. The man-child sitting opposite Justine cleared his throat, drawing her attention away from Blake, who hadn't even looked her way since he sat down.

"I'm Steven, what's your name?" her date squeaked out. *Dios, how old was he?*

"I'm Justine, nice to meet you." She held out her hand, not knowing what else to do and he smiled at her as they shook.

"That's a lovely name," he replied, and they lapsed into silence again. *Dammit why was this so awkward?* She looked down the row and saw Beau charming the panties off his date and even Blake was chatting to his. A lance of hurt speared through her. She saw him every week for their sessions, and he barely spoke to her but here he was a Chatty Cathy! She frowned and turned back to her date.

"How old are you?" she asked, pasting a smile on her face.

"Just turned twenty-one, ma'am," he replied.

Ma'am? Fuck my life.

Her smile faltered slightly but before she could reply, Kayleigh placed their drinks on the table and Justine lunged for her rosé, downed it in one go and demanded Kayleigh bring her another *larger* glass immediately. She and Steven managed to chat a little before their time was, thankfully, up and he moved on. Another man took his place, this one was clearly a sensible age, shaved head, quite muscular with nice eyes. Not her usual type with all those muscles but maybe she needed to start pushing herself outside her comfort zone.

"I'm Darryl. What's your name, beautiful?" he asked, charm pouring from him, and not in a sleazy way. She flushed at his compliment.

"Justine. Nice to meet you," she held out her hand to shake his, but he grabbed it and pulled it to his lips, kissing it softly.

"Nice to meet you too, angel. I've gotta say, I was looking forward to speaking to you."

She flushed again, *now this is what I'm talking about!* A cackle of laughter from further down drew her attention and she turned to see Blake's date giggling away at something he said. *What the hell? Was he being funny? Since when is he funny?! Ugh, stop worrying about what he's doing and focus on you, you've got a goal here so snap to it.* She turned back to her date.

"Oh yeah? Why's that?" she asked, a coy smile playing

on her lips.

"I have a feeling you like to submit, am I right?"

She shook her head, confused. "I'm sorry?"

"If you're looking for a dirty dom then I'm your man, the things I'm gonna do to you…" he trailed off, his eyes running over her, and she suddenly realized what he meant.

She hadn't even had sex let alone dabbled in BDSM. Not that she had anything against it, she just felt like she needed to build up to kinks, if she even had any. A sheriff kink sprang to mind, and she immediately shoved it away. She was disappointed that this guy had jumped straight to sex. Even though that was what she wanted, she also wanted someone to talk to, someone to flirt a little with, not head straight in with whips and chains.

"I think you'd be sorely disappointed with me, I'm far too independent for that. But we could always schedule a chat to discuss where your need to dominate came from?" she offered, smiling sweetly. His smile faltered, but then one merciful minute later another man was sitting in front of her.

He was nice looking, he had a kind smile, dark hair, thinning slightly but he was cute. They chatted and conversation flowed a little easier for them. She liked him, he was a realtor from the next town over, a similar age to her, he had a nice sense of humor and wanted a family. When their time was up, she decided that she would give him her number. Then Beau was sitting in front of her.

"Hey buddy," he crooned at her, and she snorted but relaxed for the first time since the dates started. She didn't need to worry about impressing Beau. Only then did she realize how many men had come her way. She looked up and saw that Blake was just two seats away from her. *Holy shit! He's going to have to sit with me and talk for two and a half minutes. One hundred fifty seconds.* He was currently charming his date, he actually looked pretty chilled, and Justine's heart started pounding as the time ticked on. Beau was talking about his dates, sounded like they were all a hit with him, and then he asked about hers.

"Hmm, one potential so far. Question though, do you have any thoughts on BDSM?" she asked innocently. Beau nearly spit his beer out and a few others looked over at them.

"Sweetheart, that's like going for your first swimming lesson and diving straight into the deep end without any floaties. Maybe work up to it?" he said. He knew about her lack of experience in the bedroom department. She nodded, he grinned and then looked down the row of men.

"Well, looky here, ignore Mr. BDSM. I wonder how well you and Blake would get on?" he teased. She grinned at him, baring her teeth.

"About as well as you and Taylor do," she replied.

Beau chuckled. "Touché." And then time was up, he got up to move back down the row to the next table, winking at her as he went. She shook her head at him, a smirk playing on her lips. He was shameless.

Justine's new date sat down in front of her. Even though two minutes was such a short amount of time to spend with someone, she was exhausted. She turned to look at Blake, he was on the table next to her. If she listened hard enough, she could probably hear him talking. She tried to tune out her date so she could eavesdrop.

"Everything okay?" her date asked. She snapped her attention to him, annoyed he had interrupted her spying and then instantly felt guilty for ignoring him, so guilty that she promised him she would give him her number.

This was not going well.

The next thing she knew, he was getting up and Blake was sitting down. As her eyes met his, her palms started to sweat, and she felt sick. He slid into the seat and eased back, folding his arms over his chest, his huge biceps stealing her attention. He didn't say anything, she opened her mouth to speak but then thought better of it, why should she? He'd been plenty chatty with the other women tonight and every time they'd spoken previously, she'd initiated it.

He began rolling up his shirtsleeves, slowly, exposing more and more of those tan muscular forearms and she couldn't tear her eyes away. *Okay now you have a forearm kink? One kink at a time, lady!* She raised her eyebrow at him in challenge as she sipped her wine. His nostrils flared but he gave no other reaction. After two minutes—she counted every damn second—she gave up.

"Starting to feel like a day at the office," she muttered. A muscle ticked in his jaw and then he shocked her by speaking.

"I thought you were dating Beau?" he said, his eyes drilling into her, bewitching her until he drew an answer from her.

"I'm not sure why you would think that, don't you remember what I said in the forest?"

"So, you've really never *been* with anyone, have you?" he demanded, and then clamped his mouth shut, his brow pinched in confusion like he hadn't meant to say that. Her pulse quickened and heat coursed through her as she realized what he'd asked her but before she could answer there was another man hovering next to them, waiting to sit down. Their time was up, and she couldn't work out whether she was happy or disappointed.

Blake stared at her for a moment longer, his eyes hot

and demanding as though he wasn't leaving until she answered him. She fought a shiver as tingles shot down her spine. Her breathing deepened and her body heated, tension thickening the air around them. What was happening to her body? What was this? The man standing beside them coughed discreetly and Blake blinked, snapping out of their stare-off. He grabbed his drink and stood up.

"Have a good evening," he said, his tone neutral and then went back down the row to his next date. Justine tried to ignore the heat flaring through her, shoving it away as she fixed a bright smile on her face and greeted the man now sitting down opposite her. He was her final date and seemed pretty nice. He was a few years older than her, looking to settle down and start a family which really interested her. When they were finished, Taylor came over to the group.

"Okay, we're all done! Hopefully, that wasn't too painful for some of you. Ladies, if you want to break off over here to make your decision, gentlemen you can wait right there."

The women all stood and walked off to gather around a table that had little slips of paper and pens on it. Justine followed and moments later Taylor joined them.

"I don't know about y'all but the tall, dark and handsome one was tasty!" the busty blond giggled.

"Which one, there's two of them?" another woman replied. Justine looked over at the group of men. There were only two who could be described that way, Beau and Blake. *Would any of them choose Blake?*

"The trainer. He can give me a workout anytime," the blond purred.

"You know, I heard he gave his last girlfriend herpes," Taylor said in a mock whisper. Justine rolled her eyes, *of course.*

"No, he didn't," Justine told the blond, scowling at an unrepentant Taylor.

"Do you know that for sure?" Taylor replied, grimacing. Justine shook her head and shoved Taylor away.

"I think he's really into you, you should definitely go for it," she replied to the blond. The women deliberated a little longer and scribbled their numbers down, but Justine wasn't really paying attention, she was watching Blake, who seemed to be looking anywhere but at her. Taylor came back to announce it was time for the ladies to give out their numbers to the men they were interested in. To Justine's dismay, the women flocked to Blake, practically throwing bits of paper at him, then they ambushed Beau.

Hot anger coursed through Justine, jealousy nipping at its heels. Of course, these women all wanted him, he'd been charming, funny and chatty to them but when he was seated with her, he had pretty much ignored her. He had a good job, nice hair, he was gorg- wait a minute, why did she even care? She didn't, except from a professional point of view. He was her *client* afterall, and his wellbeing was her business. She didn't want him to feel like he was in over his head. It could have a detrimental effect on him, and she only had his best interests at heart.

As she watched him, she noticed he looked a little flustered at the attention and then he caught her staring. He looked away, dismissing her and that pushed her over the edge. She scribbled her number down on multiple bits of paper, then stomped over and gave her number to all the men except Blake, including Beau and the guy who wanted her to be his sub, but *fuck it!* She ignored Blake and threw herself into conversation with all the men. She was so busy talking to them that she didn't notice Blake storm out of the bar, or the angry rev of his motorcycle as he rode off into the night.

*

Blake didn't think he could run fast enough or hard enough to clear the thoughts in his head. He had been sociable last night and had chatted to all the women at the Ladies' Night. He'd appeared engaged with all of them and responded to all their questions. But as soon as he'd got home, every number that had been pressed into his hand had been thrown in the trash. None of them had held his interest or attention. Well, except one but he couldn't have her.

You've really never been with anyone, have you? God, that question haunted him. It had tumbled out, he'd never meant to ask it but once he did, he needed the answer more than his next breath. Except she hadn't responded and that just pissed him off even more. She'd turned the tables on their little game of the silent treatment, and she had won, *again*. He'd walked away with his tail between his legs and his mind running on overdrive.

Did she know how she looked last night? Did she know that every man in that bar had stripped her with their eyes? Cataloguing her body like they knew exactly how every dip, curve and hollow looked? How she looked naked, and like they were going to own every inch of her. He snorted to himself as he pounded the pavement. If anyone were going to own her, it would be hi–

"No," he grunted, cutting off the thought before it was formed, forcing himself to increase his pace, punishing his body for the thoughts in his mind. Was she still a virgin? No, she couldn't be, that was ridiculous.

He huffed out a breath, angry that his thoughts had

immediately returned to her. He kept running along the street and only stopped when a basketball rolled out in front of him. He looked up and spotted Dean and Beau waving at him from the court on the street.

He picked up the ball and was about to throw it back and continue on his way when her words replayed in his head. He needed to build relationships. It couldn't hurt to be a little friendly, could it? And if he wanted to become sheriff here, he would need to start embracing the town and getting involved, becoming someone they could come to with their concerns. Instead of throwing the ball back to the men he jogged over, and they met him halfway.

"Hey, man," Beau said with a grin that Blake no longer wanted to smack off his face now that he knew Beau wasn't dating Justine. Not that it was his business anyway. Dean greeted him and Blake nodded at them both.

"You play?" Dean asked, nodding to the ball in Blake's hands.

"Not really," Blake shrugged, and then jumped into the air, tossing the ball. It sailed through the wire basket with a *swish* and Beau started laughing while Dean just stared in shock as the ball bounced away.

"Fancy a game?" Dean asked, a competitive gleam lighting his eyes. Blake let out a rusty chuckle at how excited he and Beau looked. He shook his head but ducked past them both and raced after the ball. They played until they were dripping with sweat, tearing up and down the court, aggression and testosterone pouring from all three of them until no one could remember the score.

Beau collapsed on the grass next to the court, throwing his arm over his eyes, shielding them from the sun. Dean sprawled next to him, and Blake took a seat leaning back on his forearms, letting the sun caress his face. He felt pretty good. That game had worked a lot of his aggression out, now he felt chilled.

"I heard you were at Ladies' Night with Beau here?" Dean asked after a while. Blake nodded.

"Any ladies take your fancy?" Beau asked, peeking at him from under his arm.

"Nah, I got a few numbers, but they didn't really do it for me," Blake replied, looking away, already knowing where this was going, his chilled vibe starting to wane.

"Not even Justine?" Dean asked.

Blake shook his head again. "You seemed to do pretty well," he said to Beau, changing the subject. Beau shot him a devilish grin.

"Yeah, I got a few dates lined up now," Beau replied.

"Makes a change, normally you do a lot of talking and not a lot of dating, *amigo*," Dean joked.

"Hey, we can't all find the woman of our dreams and be pathetically loved-up like you." Beau snorted.

"He's just mad because I stole Christy away from him," Dean explained to Blake.

"Nah, you're just sour because I kissed her first," Beau grinned.

"That's your first warning," Dean said, holding up one finger.

Blake chuckled as he watched their easy back and forth, a pang in his chest as he realized just how much he had missed having friends.

"You gonna take your dates to The Rusty Bucket?" Dean asked, picking a handful of grass, and throwing some at Beau.

"Maybe, why?"

"Taylor will love that," Dean replied drily, rolling his eyes.

"Well, this thing was her idea," Beau shot back. *Interesting, was there something going on between Taylor and Beau?* Maybe Justine was right and nothing had happened with them? Even as his mouth opened and the words started forming, Blake was annoyed with himself. He didn't want to show interest in Justine, it would only fan the flames, but he needed to know more about her.

"You ever date Justine?" Blake asked, trying so hard to sound casual. Beau shook his head.

"Nah man, we're just friends. She's an amazing woman, no doubt about it. But she's looking for her one and only, and that ain't me. I mean we've kissed but there was nothing in it," Beau said, shrugging. Blake saw red at the image of Beau and Justine kissing, rage consuming him.

"Have you ever thought that maybe the problem is you? That's two of our girls you've struck out with now. Maybe you're just a shit kisser?" Dean taunted.

"Oh yeah, why don't you come here and tell me?" Beau said, puckering his lips at Dean, who laughed and punched him in the shoulder.

"Tempting, but you got a little too much dick for my liking, plus, I'm about to settle down now. I got my one and only, and we're gonna be very happy together." A dreamy sigh left Dean. Blake looked over at Beau and raised an eyebrow. Beau just shook his head, smirking.

"If you're interested in Justine though, I could put in a good word for you," Dean offered and Blake sat up, fixing him with a hard stare.

"Nah, man. I'm not interested, she's not my type," he said, and then immediately wished he could take the words back.

"You like redheads?" Dean asked.

"I'm not interested in dating, period," Blake said, his

tone firm, hoping they would drop it.

"That's cool, just checking, wouldn't want an opportunity for you to slip by is all," Dean said.

Beau laughed. "You looking to play fairy godmother now?"

"I would look badass in a tutu with a wand, admit it," Dean said, and leapt on Beau, sprinkling more grass over him like it was fairy dust.

"Bibbidi-bobbidi-back the fuck up, dude!" Beau shouted, dusting grass off his head. Blake started laughing, it came out harsh and rusty, like he wasn't used to it. Jesus, when was the last time he had honest-to-God laughed? These guys were funny though, and since he'd been with them, he hadn't thought about any of his issues. When they settled down, Dean turned to him.

"We're having a barbecue next weekend, you should come," Dean said casually.

"Oh yeah? Who's gonna be there?" Blake asked, even though he already knew.

"Probably just me, Christy, Beau, Taylor and maybe Justine if she can make it," Dean replied. Blake didn't know what to say. He didn't think it was a good idea because if Justine were there, she might let slip something about his sessions, or he could have an episode. He really didn't want an episode in front of everyone, especially Justine, even though she was his psychologist he'd had too many in front of her now, it was just embarrassing. There was also the possibility that he could do something stupid, like touch her.

"Yeah maybe," he said, noncommittal was probably the best way to go.

Dean shrugged. "The invitation's there if you want it, no pressure." He smiled at Blake. Feeling reluctant to leave but like he should probably quit while he was ahead,

Blake stood up.

"Good game guys. I better get back, got some work to do this afternoon."

Beau and Dean stood up and Dean held out his fist. Blake looked at it before bumping it with his and then did the same with Beau.

"Cool, well I'll see you on Monday for the NWS meeting," Dean said.

"Yeah, and I'll see you next weekend at the barbecue," Beau said, his tone firm like Blake had better show up. Blake smirked, were they forcing him to hang out with them? He couldn't say no to that, could he?

"I'll see you around," he said to both before leaving. He decided to run the rest of the way back but when he got home, he actually felt tired. Instead of heading into the office he sat on the couch and then after a little while, fell asleep. He woke a few hours later from his nap feeling refreshed: the first time he'd had a few hours' sleep in what felt like forever.

He had a shower and grabbed some food. He contemplated heading to the bar for more immersion therapy but panicked. He had been pretty sociable the last couple of days and it had taken a lot out of him. He decided instead to focus on the case file he'd created on the previous sheriff. Blake had spotted a few incidents where there had been complaints made that had been brushed under the rug or potentially covered up. He needed to do some digging but he also needed to be careful: the officers were still loyal to the previous sheriff. Whatever digging he did, he needed to do it discreetly.

His cell rang, distracting him from his work.

"Deputy Miller," he answered.

"Hello Deputy, it's Dr. Michaels from the Citrus Pines veterinary practice, do you have a few minutes to talk

about the fox that was brought in last week?"
Blake's stomach dropped. He already didn't like the sound of this, it could only be bad news. The first thought that rushed through his mind was, how was Justine going to take it?

Chapter 8

Justine's night was not off to a great start. She went to her parents' home for dinner, giving them both a big hug when she arrived. Her brothers and their wives were already there waiting for her, the men instantly taunting her for being late. Then began the traditional brotherly rivalry which ended up with both brothers roughhousing, smashing a vase and then blurting out their wives were pregnant, much to the annoyance of her sisters-in-law. The volume in the room rising by infinite levels as both brothers were scolded by their wives for announcing the news in such a way, before congratulations were passed around.

Justine congratulated both and then escaped to the kitchen under the guise of fetching glasses for a toast. If anyone ever questioned why she liked her space, this was why. She grew up in such a loud, chaotic household, and while she loved her family, she found it hard to be around them for long periods of time. This was why she liked her things to be a particular way: she craved the peace and serenity that was absent growing up.

She paused at the cabinet, collecting herself and digesting their news. It was exciting; and whilst she was obviously happy for them and couldn't wait to be an aunt to a bunch of little nieces and nephews, it hurt too. When would it be *her* turn?

"Are you going to help me cook, *mija?* It's tradition," her mother asked, coming into the kitchen. Her accent was still strong despite living in the country since she was a teenager, marrying an American and raising a family here. Her mother had taught Justine and her brothers all about their Mexican roots and to be proud of their culture. They had grown up speaking Spanish, it was as ingrained in Justine as English, and she couldn't wait to teach her children the language and about their heritage when the time came. *If* the time came…

She turned to face her mother, taking in the gray that now dotted her hair, the lines that bracketed her eyes and mouth. Justine's stomach clenched like it usually did at the idea that her mother was getting older. Her throat tightened with emotions she tried to hide.

"Of course, you still have so much to teach me," she replied. Her mother nodded then gripped her arm tightly and Justine knew what was coming.

"When are you going to marry and give me grandbabies, *mija?*" Her accent thickened with emotion, her concern was overwhelming.

"When I find the right man, *mamá,*" Justine sighed, rolling her eyes.

"Just pick someone already. Look at how much time

you've wasted, you've been so busy building your career, time is running out!" Her mother stared up at her. Her eyes, a shade darker than Justine's, were full of worry. "You need to settle down, you spend so long looking for perfection that you're missing out on what could be a good man who can offer you a good life."

"But I don't just want a *good* life, I want a *great* life! I refuse to settle, *mamá*, end of discussion," Justine huffed, feeling herself getting riled up over justifying her life choices to someone who couldn't understand. She was always so torn. Her parents had traditional values that had been passed onto Justine, who tried to reconcile these within a modern world. Yes, she was independent, but she also wanted a family, and she didn't want to have to justify herself to anyone.

"Okay, *mi amor*, I'll let it go, but time is ticking," her mother sighed sadly, then patted Justine's stomach.

Time is running out.

It took everything in Justine not to open her mouth and scream, *I know! I know all this, it plays through my mind every single second of every minute of every fucking day, I don't need another reminder!* Instead, she pasted a smile on her face, celebrated the baby news and cooked with her mother, making a mental note to try this recipe with Hilda.

Dinner itself was fine although tension poured off Justine, she was ready for one of her brothers to make a comment similar to their mother, but they didn't. Her mother force-fed Justine until she was ready to burst, but her bad mood still hung around. Justine left dinner early, her father walking her to her car.

"Don't let your mother upset you, you know she just wants the best for you," he murmured against her hair, hugging her tightly.

"I know, it just doesn't make me feel any better about

where I'm at in life," Justine grumbled, returning his bear hug.

"Don't compare yourself to anyone, we're all on our own clock, *mi niña*. We're so proud of you for everything you've achieved. Your mother can't help that she's dying to be an *abuelita*," he laughed, his voice deep and gruff, then gestured to her car. "I've topped up your oil, it was looking a little low and replaced one of your wiper blades as it was torn."

She kissed his cheek. "Thank you, *papi,* I'll see you soon." She waved goodbye and got in her car, heading for the NWS meeting. She tried to calm down on the drive over, pushing her mother's voice out of her mind but it wasn't working.

The meeting hadn't started when she arrived, so she went over to the refreshments table, looking for something sweet to drown her sorrows.

"Justine!"

She looked up and saw Dean waving to her. She smiled at him and headed over, her step faltering slightly when she saw Blake standing next to him. When she reached them, Dean dropped his head to kiss her cheek.

"I feel like I've not seen you for ages, Just," Dean said.

"Don't be silly, it's only been a week," she replied, smiling. She loved Dean, had known him since they were kids, he was like a third brother to her, the really annoying, gossipy one.

"Hello Blake," she added, meeting his eyes reluctantly.

"Justine," he nodded at her coolly.

"You think tonight's gonna be as thrilling as always?" Dean teased her; she rolled her eyes.

"I don't think it will ever be as exciting as last summer," she replied, and they laughed at the memory.

"Last summer the ladies were convinced that there was

a gang going round and knocking over everyone's trash cans. They did stakeouts and created the Trashcan Bandits taskforce but never caught anyone. The mystery remains unsolved," Dean explained to Blake.

"What leads did they have?" Blake asked, his tone intense and Justine had to fight another eyeroll, of course *Deputy Sheriff McSerious* would jump on the case.

"None. No one ever saw anything," Justine replied.

Before she could say more, Janet coughed delicately to gain everyone's attention and they began to file over to the table. Justine got caught up behind a group of elderly ladies and the only seat left was next to Blake. Cursing her rotten luck tonight, she sat down. Janet began the meeting by reading the minutes from last week where she just reconfirmed that nothing interesting had happened whatsoever. Justine really didn't enjoy these meetings but as a local business owner and resident, she felt she had to do her bit for the community.

She squirmed in her seat, trying to get comfy and her knee brushed up against Blake's. He jerked at the touch but tried to play it off like it was nothing. *Someone's jumpy tonight.* Maybe he was feeling anxious about being around so many people. She ordered herself to stop being such a grump and moved her seat away slightly so as not to crowd him.

She tried to focus back on Janet but after a moment she noticed Blake sit forward in his chair, the angle putting them closer together, she could feel the heat from his body teasing her, his scent surrounding her, and her eyelids fluttered closed as it now crowded her. *So masculine.*

"I'm afraid to say we have some alarming news to report," Janet started, and Justine focused her attention back on the real reason she was here tonight.

Color of Love

"Some of you may remember our biggest case from last year, still unsolved to this day!" she cried dramatically, and Justine felt her stomach sink.

"That's right, the Trashcan Bandits are back, and wreaking havoc in our town again. They must be stopped! From next week we will use these meetings to conduct stakeouts around the neighborhood in the hopes of catching these rogue individuals. We'll pair off to be on the safe side, you never know these days what people are capable of."

There were disgruntled murmurs around the group and Justine thought she could hear Dean snickering behind her. She turned to make eye contact with him, and he coughed into his hand to cover a laugh. She fought her own laughter, until she met Blake's steady, cold gaze and her giggles died in her throat. *He's too damn serious.*

"Now, I think the best way to pair off is to just go around the table so we'll start from the top, Justine and Blake will be our first pairing, then Dean and Betty…" as Justine tuned Janet out, she felt Blake stiffen beside her.

Shit. Why was this happening to her? Why did the universe keep throwing them together? He was at work, in her personal life and now they were stuck on a stakeout together for God knows how long. Great. Was he going to also be at the next sleepover too? What did he wear to bed? She'd bet he slept naked. He would look amazing naked, all that muscle on display. *Why are you suddenly so obsessed with muscles?*

"Justine?" Blake nudged her and she realized he'd been calling her, and she'd been too busy thinking about him naked to notice.

"Yes, sorry," she replied, feeling herself flush when she turned to face him. He frowned down at her, his dark brows drawn in, making him look all sexy and broody, *damn him!* He swiped his tongue over his bottom lip, the sight had her clenching her fists to stop from reaching for him. *What's wrong with you?*

"So, I'll pick you up at your place at seven next Monday?" he asked. She nodded, resigned to being stuck in a car with him, in the dark, for an hour at least. An hour she would have to fight to keep her thoughts clean and her hands to herself.

"Sounds good," she replied, and he stood up, said goodbye to Dean and started walking off.

"Blake!" she called, a thought dawning on her. He turned to face her, raising an eyebrow. *How did he look so sexy just doing that? Ugh,* please *stop thinking about him.*

"You don't know where I live."

"Justine, I work at the sheriff's office. I know where you live," he replied, his tone cocky. God that fired her up. He smirked at her slightly as if he knew exactly what she was thinking and then he was gone.

*

On Wednesday morning, Blake arrived at Justine's office bright and early, beating Justine herself. Hilda sat him in the waiting room and tried to make small talk with him. He attempted to give her one-word answers to discourage the social interaction, but she kept drawing him in. He was trying so hard to keep the town at arm's length, still not ready to let them into his life yet, his stunning psychologist in particular. But it was *hard*. Literally. He hadn't had this many spontaneous erections since he was a teenager. He needed to get laid, fast. The problem was his body was turned off at the thought of any woman but her. The one woman he couldn't seem to get space from. He scowled as he thought of their pairing for the upcoming stakeout. Stuck in a car all evening, in the dark, her scent and closeness driving him wild. It would be his toughest lesson ever in self-restraint.

"I'm so sorry I'm late!" Justine exclaimed, bounding into the office. Her jacket caught on the door handle, and she yelped as it yanked her back. Her bag slipped from her grip, the contents spilling across the floor. Blake got up to help her and he grabbed the papers that had fallen out, glancing down at them briefly catching the words 'PTSD' and 'treatments'.

"Thank you, please come straight in," she said, when he handed her belongings over. Her eyes were wide and bright, and her cheeks tinged with crimson making her look adorable. *She could be wearing a sack with her head shaved and you'd find her attractive!* His brain mocked.

He took a seat on the couch and watched as she removed her jacket and hung it over the back of her chair. She smoothed her hair down and took a seat opposite him. She looked elegant today in a plain black dress with bright orange earrings and sandals. He tore his gaze away before he started spouting poetry about how luminescent she looked. *Luminescent? Shit, too late…*

"Again, apologies for being late. I was up late last night researching and overslept."

"It's fine, Justine," he replied.

She smiled at him brightly, flashing her straight, white teeth at him. Her smile was so damn sweet he had to fight his every instinct to return it.

"How are you?" she asked gently.

He looked at her for a moment before he sighed internally. He gave up. He wanted to get better and something about her spoke to him in a way his previous therapists hadn't. He believed that she genuinely wanted to help him, and even after he spent weeks pushing her away, she continued to try harder than ever. Blake wanted to be better, he really did. He was exhausted, his issues were *exhausting*. But he was still scared to let her all the way in.

"I'm okay," he replied, nodding his head. She tilted her head to one side, fixing her honey eyes on him.

"Just okay?" she prompted.

"A little tired," he grumbled, only willing to admit his feelings in dribs and drabs.

"Is that from your insomnia?" she asked, and he nodded. "How long have you had that?"

"On and off for a couple of months," he answered, again not looking at her, instead staring out the window.

"Well, you must be exhausted. Did it start after the Anderson suicide incident?" she asked, her voice was gentle, so damn gentle he wanted to curl up in her lap and tell her everything. Her voice soothed him. The husky layer to it stroked over him, liquefying his bones. He had a feeling that if he were in bed, he could fall asleep listening to the sound of her voice. Although if they were in bed together, they wouldn't be talking. He was so busy fantasizing about being in bed with her that he didn't respond and after a moment she sighed.

"Blake, I need you to work with me here. You know I have to report every week on your progress, I'm worried about what will happen to you," she said.

He snorted. "Listen, honey, you really don't need to worry that pretty little head of yours about my career, it's all on me."

Her eyes widened, and he realized what he'd said. He clenched his jaw; he couldn't let her get under his skin any more than she already had. She got up and came to sit next to him, crowding him in with her heat and scent.

"Blake, it's my responsibility to make sure that you have all the help you need. If you want to tank your career by not opening your mouth and admitting you need help, then be my guest. But your mental health is my concern and I don't want the next suicide statistics to include you," she said, her eyes beseeching him to open up.

Her words drove a spike through his chest, he felt like an asshole. Here he was thinking he had a point to prove and in reality, the point he was proving was the complete opposite. He wasn't fine. He knew that. But he was scared to admit it out loud to anyone. She placed her hand on his thigh, the heat from her palm seeping through his jeans, firing him up.

"Did you do the homework I mentioned?" she asked. He cleared his throat and shifted his leg so her hand fell away. He couldn't think straight when she was this close to him, let alone touching him.

"Yes."

"How many panic attacks did you have?" she pressed. He didn't answer, just stared straight ahead. He felt sick. God, why was this so hard? Out of nowhere, he suddenly became emotional.

"Blake, look at me."

But he couldn't, he was scared of what would happen if he faced her. She reached into his lap and took his hand. Her skin was warm, her fingers wrapped around his and squeezed. He felt comforted by her touch, like she grounded him.

"I need you to connect with me. Do you remember what I told you in the forest, those things about me? I was so scared to tell you, but I shared those things because I trust you. I need you to trust me, so I can help you, Blake."

Her voice was strong, her words sincere and they rocked him. He realized he *did* trust her. He just didn't want to be weak in front of her.

He turned to face her, drinking in the sight of her. Man, she was stunning. He couldn't help it, he wanted her. He knew it was wrong, they had a professional relationship, but she was intoxicating. He swallowed around the lump in his throat, he needed to push those thoughts out of his mind. He cleared his throat, and spoke, his voice thick with emotion.

"I had five panic attacks this week," he rasped.

She squeezed his hand in comfort. "Did you try the techniques we talked about?"

"I tried but I couldn't stop them, they didn't work," he admitted, feeling useless that he couldn't control his own body.

"That's okay, sometimes it takes a while to get the hang of them. I wouldn't expect you to get them right away, this is what we need to practice."

A wave of relief crashed through him at her words. He'd been worried that he hadn't been able to control himself, that he wouldn't ever be able to do so.

For the rest of the session, they worked on the techniques and she helped him with his breathing control. They didn't go into more treatments. She wanted to focus on him being able to manage his panic attacks when she wasn't around before they went into more depth. By the end of the session, they were facing each other, both cross-legged on the couch, their knees touching. She'd tried to distance herself, but he kept the connection there, something about her comforted him. When they were finished, she walked him to the door.

"Blake, do you still have my card?" she asked. He nodded. She was pleased about that. She reminded him, "I am here for you any time of day, so ring me if you need me. Or if I'm here, just stop by."

He went to leave, actually feeling lighter than he had in

a while, all because of her. "Thanks for today, I'll see you next week," he said gruffly. She gave him another one of those smiles that made his insides clench and caused all sorts of urges to overwhelm him.

"Looking forward to it," she replied, and waved as he left.

The next couple of days passed by pretty quickly. He had two more panic attacks. He hadn't been able to fight the first one off and had felt so disappointed in himself, but he remembered what Justine had said.

The second one came from an anxiety dream he had where he came home and found Katie hanging from a beam in the garage. He usually woke himself up crying out and then went into a panic attack. This time when he did, he tried to focus on the techniques she had taught him. He tried the 'then and now' technique, but that didn't seem to work as well as it had before.

He tried to list objects like they'd done together in the parking lot of the bar. He decided to stick with the color orange as it seemed to work well enough last time. This time though when he was listing things to associate with the color, all the images that popped into his head were of Justine. Justine's orange dress, Justine's orange earrings, and her orange sandals. It took some work to focus but after a while he felt his breathing returning to normal, his heart rate decreased and his vision cleared. He didn't pass out and that was a huge achievement.

He'd been meaning to swing by Justine's office and let her know the development. He couldn't explain why but he needed to see her and to tell her it worked. She would be so pleased and the thought of how happy she would be put a spring in his step all day.

He had gotten held up at work, some last-minute jobs that needed finishing before the weekend and he finally left the station as it was getting dark. He had to drive by her office to go home and he told himself if she were still there, he would stop by but if she wasn't, he would wait until next week. He tried to convince himself that the anticipation coursing through him was because he had news to share with her on his treatment, and not for any other reason.

He pulled up outside and spotted the light on in her office, the rest of the building was dark, and his stomach dipped at the idea of being alone together. He sighed to himself, he really needed to get his mind out of the gutter. *Nothing is going to happen.* He got out of the cruiser and went over to try the door handle. The office was unlocked so he went in, making a note to scold her for not keeping it locked when she was in there on her own.

*

Ugh, where are they? Justine rummaged down the back of the couch in her office for her earrings. She'd only worn them two days ago, where could they have gone? It was her first date tonight at the bar and she needed these earrings to complete her outfit, they would look great with the white strapless jumpsuit and her orange sandals. She left the couch and rummaged on her desk, trying to see if she'd left them on the surface somewhere. Then she remembered that she'd put them in her drawer, so she wouldn't lose them. *How ironic.*

She rushed around then spotted them ready and waiting for her. She was so nervous about this date, and she needed everything to be just right, including her earring choice. She slid them through her ears, picked up her purse and headed towards the door. She was already running late, and her detour hadn't helped. She looked up and screamed when she saw a tall dark and handsome deputy leaning against the doorframe, arms folded across his chest.

"Jesus Christ, Blake!" she gasped, clutching her chest as her heart went into overdrive.

"I could've broken in here to attack you. You need to lock your door," he said, his deep voice drifting over her. She glared at him, and he gave her that cocky smirk which did things to her insides. She'd barely got him out of her mind the last couple of days, thrilled with the breakthrough that they'd had this week. He was finally starting to let her in, and she could feel their connection growing, deepening.

She turned her attention back to him and rolled her eyes.

"I've only been here two seconds," she told him.

He didn't reply, instead his eyes ran over her body slowly, taking her in. The intensity of them stripping her bare and leaving her breathless, how did he manage to do this to her? Did he do this on purpose or was he like this with all women? His lady-killer good looks suggested the latter. She fought a shiver as he slowly met her gaze again, his harsh eyes melting to pools of liquid silver.

"What are you doing here?" she asked, her voice breathy from the intensity of his stare.

"It's stupid really but, I…uh came to tell you that I've had two panic attacks and during the second one I managed to stop myself from passing out," he muttered, his voice trailing off like he was embarrassed to be telling her. Her joy exploded, and she threw herself at him, wrapping her arms around his neck, pressing her body against his.

"Oh my God, that's amazing! I'm so proud of you!" she gushed. She felt his hands land on her hips, and he set her away from him, his grip remaining tight. She cringed internally, she'd over-stepped, she'd never done that with any other client, but he had finally made some progress and he needed to know how amazing that was. She looked up and his expression was grim, his mouth flattened into a hard line, his brows drawn in.

"Sorry, I got carried away. But you should be so pleased with yourself, that's fantastic progress," she said. He nodded but didn't say anything more. He kept his hands on her hips, his grip flexing, and he held her gaze. He was so beautiful, his thick lashes casting shadows across his cheeks. She had to stop herself from reaching up and brushing a lock of curly, dark hair from his forehead. *Would it feel soft?* He cleared his throat and stepped back into the doorway, the moment over.

"Thanks, I just thought I'd let you know," he said, shrugging it off. *And now we're back to him acting like he doesn't care.* This guy's mood changed faster than she changed her panties.

"Thank you, I appreciate it," she replied, and they just stared at each other, the air around them heavy with tension. His bruising grip on her had left her pulse pounding beneath her skin, she reveled in the sensation, she'd never felt anything like this coursing through her before. Maybe she liked it a little too much? She should leave before she did something stupid, like beg him to kiss her.

"Well, I'm running late, I need to get going," she started, hoping he would get the hint, but he didn't move. The more she was around him the foggier her brain became. She needed to get out of here before she did something unprofessional and not only embarrassed herself but ruined her entire career. *Yay!*

"Where are you going?"

"I...uh, have a date tonight at the bar."

His eyes narrowed. "With one of the guys from the

other night?" he asked, or more like interrogated. She nodded, he pursed his lips and looked away, she could see his jaw clenching. *Am I imagining it or does he seem mad?*

"Do you like him?" he asked, the words coming out like he'd forced them through gritted teeth.

"I don't know," she shrugged, feeling shy.

"You don't know?" he bit back.

"That's right. You know I don't have much experience with this. I'm not sure what it feels like to connect with someone, to know how much you like them or to feel passion for them," her voice increased slightly as she became defensive. *Why was he pushing this?*

He took a step forward. She stepped back to avoid him bumping into her and hit the opposite side of the door frame. He took another step forward, crowding her in, his heat coming up against her. His scent enveloping her, seducing her. He leaned down, his hot, sweet breath drifting over her face.

"Passion is when you can't be around someone without wanting to rip their clothes off. When their every movement speaks to you," he rasped. Her hand came up against the hard wall of his chest, whether to push him back or draw him closer, she really couldn't say. Her eyes fluttered closed as goosebumps spread across her neck and arms at the image his words painted.

"It's longing for someone so much that you can't make it through the day, the hour, without touching them. You would give anything to be close to them, to hear their voice, smell their scent, to taste them. It's yearning. It's aching. It's agony and amazing ecstasy all at the same time. Have you ever felt that before, Justine?"

At his words she sighed, she ran her hand up his chest and around his neck, tangling her fingers in his soft, soft hair. He trailed his breath down her neck, nuzzled her gently, the scrape of his beard against her soft skin had her mouth parting in a soft moan. Heat flared between them, and she felt her core clenching, readying itself.

She needed this man to kiss her more than she needed air to breathe. Her heart pounding in her ears, she tilted her head to meet him, but he pulled back. His arms left her, his delicious heat moved away and when she opened her eyes he wasn't even in the room. She looked out into the main office and saw him heading for the door.

"Blake?" she called, confused.

"Have a wonderful time on your date tonight," he threw over his shoulder, then he was gone, and she wanted to collapse in a puddle on the floor.

Chapter 9

Blake was an idiot. What the hell was he playing at? Why was he taunting himself with her? Did she have any idea of the effect she had on him? The second she mentioned she had a date, his blood had boiled, anger lashing through him, jealousy bringing up the rear. But when she said she didn't know what passion was? His blood had heated, ready to show her. He *needed* to be the one to show her, and he couldn't stop himself from showing her the passion he felt for *her*.

He had gotten carried away. When she'd run her hands through his hair, he'd nearly taken her mouth right there whether she offered it or not. But was she offering it to him? No, of course she wasn't, she was just humoring him. She was his psychologist, they couldn't have that kind of relationship, which was why he was a fucking idiot for showing his hand. He always kept his cards close to his chest and now she knew he wanted her. *Fuck*.

He hit the steering wheel of his car in frustration. As soon as he'd seen her in that outfit, it was game over. The need to be close to her, to touch her, made him stupid. Thank God he'd come to his senses and got out of there before he did something he would regret.

He was sitting in his car, parked on his driveway, his anger coursing through him, along with white hot desire. Desire so strong he'd never felt it like this before. He only felt this way because he wanted her but couldn't have her. If he had her it would go away. Maybe that's what he needed, just have her once, get her out of his system. Or maybe he just needed someone else, to take the edge off. That had been his goal the other night at the bar, but he hadn't been able to get his mind on anyone else but her. He needed to try again, to push himself to forget her.

He went inside his house, he stripped off his clothes and jumped straight in the shower, washing the day away, fighting his urge to reach down and give himself the relief he so desperately needed. He quickly dressed in clean jeans and a sweater, tugged on his black boots and leather jacket, and was soon back in his cruiser, heading for The Rusty Bucket Inn.

Anticipation flooded his veins. He tried to tell himself it was from looking for a woman to spend the night with, but he was lying to himself. He wanted to see Justine and see which man she was on a date with.

He pulled into the busy parking lot, forgetting it was Friday night which meant the place would be packed. He sat in the car for a moment taking deep breaths, his anxiety flaring up when he thought about how many people would be inside. The last few times he visited the bar, he'd managed to keep his cool but because he'd done well for so long it would be typical that he would have a relapse tonight in front of everyone. As long as he stayed calm and worked on the techniques Justine had shown him, then hopefully he would be fine. If he felt an attack coming, he would leave.

He took a deep breath and went inside. When he opened the door, the loud music hit him like a wall of sound. Rock music pounded out as couples danced up a storm and friends laughed and played pool.

He spotted Justine straight away, his eyes always drawn to her. She was sitting in a booth, chatting with her date. When she spotted him, she stopped talking mid-sentence and their eyes clashed together, sparks flying between them. His pulse pounded and he worked his jaw as she dismissed him, turning her attention back to her date. *That's your answer, she's not interested in you, move on.*

He flicked his eyes to the lucky man; it was the bald guy from the date night that he'd overheard asking her to be his sub. He frowned, *what the hell was she doing with that guy?* Considering she had so little experience with men, this guy was not the one she should be using to help her navigate her first sexual experiences. He shook his head and went over to the bar to get a drink, sitting at the opposite end, so he had a clear view of them.

"Hey B!" Taylor called skipping over to him. He wasn't a fan of the nickname, but he let it go, seeing that she was one of the few people in town that he liked. He liked that she was honest and didn't hide her emotions, what you see is what you get with Taylor, no bullshit.

"Evening Taylor, how you doing?"

"Better now I've seen you, sugar. Dean tells me you're coming to the barbecue tomorrow night?" she asked, already pouring him a whiskey soda.

"He invited me. I haven't made up my mind if I'm

coming yet," Blake replied, watching Justine over Taylor's shoulder.

"That invitation has an expiry date, you know," she tsked.

"Oh yeah?"

"Especially since Justine can't make it, you're not gonna bail on us too, are you?"

He turned his attention back to Taylor. *Justine wasn't coming now?* He was equal parts annoyed and relieved. He wanted to spend time with her but also found it hard to be around her without needing to get his hands on her. He did want to spend time with the guys and what else was he gonna do on a Saturday night?

"You know what? Count me in," he said, and Taylor fist-pumped the air and cheered. Justine looked their way, her eyes flicking between him and Taylor and she frowned, her expression turning stormy. *Was she...no, could she be jealous?* She turned her attention back to her date as another, much shorter, man came over to them. Blake watched them curiously. Justine's date introduced them, they chatted for a moment, the shorter one giving Justine a once over before he went back to his table.

"Great, see you tomorrow at eight sharp," Taylor said, putting his drink down on the bar in front of him, then she moved away to serve someone else. Blake turned his attention back to Justine. She kept glancing over at him and frowning. He was so busy watching her that he forgot he was here to look for a date himself.

He quickly surveyed the bar for potential single ladies before realizing he hadn't done it when he came in. He hadn't planned his escape route, hadn't assessed any of the people inside the bar to see who could pose a threat. He was shocked; that wasn't like him at all. He'd been so eager to see Justine, just to make sure she was okay on her date that he hadn't done it. He quickly mapped it all out and then he realized there were no ladies in the bar that he was interested in, save for the one he couldn't have.

Justine's date got up and went to the bathroom. His short friend that came over to them earlier followed closely behind him. Something seemed a little off about it, Blake's instincts cried out, so he decided to do a little detective work. He followed them both into the bathroom, lagging behind slightly to appear less suspicious. Both men were at the urinal when he walked in, so he went into one of the empty stalls and watched them through the crack in the door.

"I'm telling you man, she'd be totally up for it," Baldy said.

"I don't know, I'd rather she agreed to it upfront," Shorty replied.

"You know chicks dig threesomes, and she looks like she's seen some fun before," Baldy laughed.

"I don't know, it doesn't feel right."

"Okay when we leave, meet us in the parking lot and we'll just feel her out, that mouth of hers tells me she's down for whatever."

Blake's muscles tensed, anger pulsing through him and it took all his willpower not to rip the stall door from its hinges and beat them both with it. No way could he let Justine leave with these guys. They washed their hands and left. Blake followed them back out to the bar, and he watched as Baldy went back to Justine and Shorty hovered by the jukebox. Justine grabbed her purse and Baldy put his arm around her waist, leading her outside, winking back at his friend, who downed his beer and left the bar. Blake was right behind them.

He got outside and saw that Justine and Baldy were

talking by her little Toyota and Shorty was making his way over to them. Blake needed a moment to think. He had to interfere, but he needed to not come across like the jealous asshole he was. An idea came to him, a devilish grin crossing his face and he eagerly headed over to them.

"Excuse me, gentlemen, apologies for interrupting but, ma'am, you're gonna have to come with me," Blake said, injecting as much authority into his voice as possible.

"Who the fuck are you?" Baldy spat. Justine's eyes widened in shock when she saw him.

"I'm Deputy Sheriff Miller, that's who the fuck I am and watch your mouth, boy," Blake said, flashing his badge at them. Both their attitudes changed very quickly.

"What's going on?" Justine asked, confused.

"You tell me, ma'am. What were you planning on doing with these gentlemen here tonight?"

She looked at him like he'd gone mad, and he noticed her cheeks flushing in the moonlight.

"I'm gonna need you both to step away from her, she's incredibly dangerous," he lied. When they didn't move, he stormed over to her and grabbed her by the arm, pulling her roughly towards him.

"Hey man, what are you doing?" Baldy shouted, as Blake absconded with the date that he was planning to force a threesome on.

"Blake, what the hell?" she hissed at him. He looked down at her, keeping his face as serious as possible.

"Ma'am, you're under arrest," he said flatly, tugging her towards his cruiser.

"WHAT!" she bellowed, trying to tug her arm free but his grip was too tight.

"What's she under arrest for?" Shorty asked, a tremor of fear in his voice.

"You boys must not be from around here. I've been tracking this little firecracker all over the country. You ever heard of the Manhood Mutilator?" he asked, trying not to smile as Justine spluttered profanities at him, some in English, some in Spanish. The men paled slightly.

"N...no?" Baldy said, his words shaky.

"This little filly right here is the most wanted woman in America. She lures men to her bed with her feminine wiles, acting all innocent and unassuming, lulling them into a false sense of security. Then after she has her way with them, she cuts off their...well the name explains it all."

"Blake! What the fu-" Justine shouted at him, bucking to try and get out of his grip.

"It's Deputy Miller, ma'am. Now turn around and place your hands on top of the vehicle," he commanded. He peered down into her face and winked. She stared up at him quizzically but didn't move.

"Ma'am, I'm not gonna ask you again. Turn around and place your hands on top of the vehicle." He spun her around and she did as he asked. He kicked her legs apart.

"Are you sure about this?" Shorty asked, looking concerned.

"Blake! What the hell is going on?" Justine hissed. He leaned his weight against her, pinning her against the car and she gasped. He bent to her ear, the silky fall of her hair and the delicious vanilla and cocoa scent had him fighting a moan.

"Just play along," he whispered, then turned his attention back to the men. "I've got some crime scene photos in the car if you boys wanna take a look? You've not eaten recently, have you?" Blake asked, wincing for good measure. Justine snorted. He had the satisfaction of watching them pale again and he started patting Justine down like he was looking for weapons.

"No, that's okay," Baldy said, sounding a little shaken up.

"You boys are very lucky I caught you before she managed to get you on your own. God knows what body parts could've been removed." Blake shook his head and concentrated on running his hands over Justine. Her breath hitched in her throat when he brushed across her bare shoulders.

He ran his hands across her back, over the flare of her hips, taking his time, committing her body to memory. He stroked around the sides of her round ass, flaring his fingers over the firm cheeks and sliding his thumb down the crease between them.

Her sharp intake of breath drew his attention to her face. She turned to face him, her tongue darting out and swiping over her lower lip. Her eyelids fluttered closed. *Fuck, was he turning her on?* The thought had his cock hardening in his jeans, desperate to get to her. He should stop touching her, right now, but he couldn't, he wanted to hear more of the delicious sounds she'd begun to make. What started out as an innocent ruse was quickly turning into an erotic body search and Blake became lost in the role of inspector.

"Blake, what are you doing?" she half moaned. He smirked at the sound of his name sighing from her lips, he wanted to hear it when she was splayed under him and he was buried deep inside her. He couldn't deny anymore that he wanted her. It was a visceral, urgent need to have her, claim her body for his until she knew only him.

Behind her he could see the two men watching them. Dammit, he'd forgotten why he was doing this, he bared his teeth at them.

"Dude, let's get the hell outta here!" Shorty hissed, and

they both scurried off to their vehicles, tearing out of the parking lot. Blake chuckled to himself.

"You wanna tell me what that was about?" Justine asked, the moonlight catching her orange earrings. Her voice sounded a little raspier than usual and he realized he was still running his hands over her arms.

Or do you just not like men prettier than you?

Those damn words still haunted him. Did they mean anything?

The door to the bar banged open, startling them both and they leapt apart. He looked over and saw a couple of guys stumbling out, laughing, and waited until they'd wandered off down the road before he turned to face Justine. He needed a minute to get his body under control.

"What the hell was that about, Blake? That was humiliating!" she cried, her expression cold and shut off now.

"I was trying to protect you. You should've heard what that guy was saying about you in the bathroom. You need someone looking out for you if you're going to continue meeting up with strangers. Do you know what they wanted to do to you?" he huffed.

"I wasn't going to be doing anything with them. My date was just walking me to my car! Do you think I'm that easy that it only takes one date and I'll spread my legs?" she spat at him. The thought of her spreading her legs for anyone but him had rage coiling low in his gut.

"Of course *I* don't think that but I wasn't sure if *you* knew what they wanted from you. You said you don't have much experience with guys and I wanted to make sure you were okay," he replied, trying to keep the anger out of his voice.

"I don't need to have *any* experience with guys to be

able to handle myself. You had no right to interfere!" she shouted at him, her chest heaving in the moonlight. He stepped forward, getting in her space.

"Justine, have you ever been with a man?"

"What? Why are you asking me that?" she asked, her anger dialling down in her confusion.

"Because some guys are good guys, and some are bad and that guy you were on your date with was going to try and take advantage of you. You don't have the experience to tell the difference yet and I was just trying to make sure your first experience didn't end up being one you'd never forget, for all the wrong reasons." His anger was getting the better of him. She was fine, she hadn't been hurt but she could have been, and he didn't like the thought one bit.

"Thank you, Deputy Miller, for humiliating me so, what would I do without you?" she muttered sarcastically, she looked away, refusing to meet his gaze.

"Justine, you said this week that you trust me, I need you to trust that I did the right thing for you tonight. I don't want you getting hurt," he said, his tone sincere and after a beat, her eyes softened at him in the moonlight.

"I do trust you, thank you for looking out for me. I mean it, even if you've now made it so no man will ever come near me," she joked, and started walking towards her car. He smiled to himself; he couldn't deny that was a stroke of genius on his part. He didn't want her to be lonely, but he didn't want her with anyone else either.

"You can count on me, Justine. If you need me or don't feel safe, just call me," he called after her. She nodded at him and then left.

That night, he went home alone.

Chapter 10

The next evening, Justine was getting ready for a barbecue at Dean's house. She had expected to be on another date tonight, but word must have gotten out about her being the Manhood Mutilator because the guy canceled on her.

She fought a smile as she thought about Blake's charade last night. She'd been fuming, humiliated, baffled and aroused: a barrage of emotions. She had been so confused by their interaction in her office. Had he just been trying to educate her? Or had he actually been flirting with her? She didn't know, she just knew that she needed him pressed up against her again.

She had been so happy to see him at the bar that she'd barely been able to keep her eyes on her date. Why couldn't her date have intrigued her the way that Blake did? Why did it have to be Blake that she couldn't stop staring at, couldn't stop thinking about? She couldn't have him and even if she could, did she want to? Her body screamed yes but her brain said no, there was so much baggage there. *Damn, I'm in trouble.*

Last night, he had shown her a side of his that she couldn't get out of her head: the protector. He'd stormed across the parking lot to them, in full alpha male mode and shut down the two creeps she'd been with. She already suspected they didn't have pure intentions with her, which was why she'd ended the date so soon. But to have Blake come out and defend her, to tear her away from them and invent such a creative, funny story that still had her laughing even today, was different.

He wasn't as serious as he made out, there was definitely a sense of humor there. Oh, the way he'd pressed her up against his car, running his hands all over her body, controlling what she felt and where, *owning* her body, she shivered now just thinking about it. She needed someone like him to mentor her, like a sex guru. *Is that a thing?* Not that it could ever be Blake, of course. She sighed, putting the thoughts out of her mind, looking forward to spending the evening with her friends, hopefully she could forget all about him.

She grabbed a cab to Dean and Christy's place and when she arrived, she didn't bother knocking, she just walked straight in. Christy had moved in with Dean a couple of months ago and their house was stunning. The place was so warm and inviting, a cozy family home that you just never wanted to leave.

She headed to the kitchen and looked outside where everyone was gathered. Dean and Beau were over at the barbecue, getting it going. Christy and Taylor were sitting around the fire pit, already half a pitcher into the margaritas.

"Hey girl! What are you doing here? How was your date last night?" Taylor asked, waggling her eyebrows. Christy ran inside to fetch another glass and poured Justine a bigass margarita when she came back.

"Oh yeah, weren't you meant to be on another one tonight?" Beau asked.

"Yeah, the guy canceled. I think he had a better offer," she joked, but Christy frowned.

"Asshole," she said indignantly.

Justine laughed. "It's fine, honestly."

"Yeah well, hopefully someone better will come along," Taylor said, eyeing her over her glass, Justine narrowed her eyes at her, suspiciously.

"What do you mean?"

Taylor shrugged her shoulders. "Nothing," she said, innocence dripping from her words, but she wasn't innocent at all. The doorbell rang, distracting them all. Justine looked around. They were all here so who could that be?

"That'll be the guest of honor, let me go and let him in," Dean said, and headed indoors. Taylor was still smirking at her and a sinking feeling settled over Justine.

"What have you done? Who is that?" Justine demanded.

"Shh sweetie, drink your alcohol," Taylor said, tipping Justine's glass towards her mouth and Justine ended up laughing. Her laughter died in her throat when Dean came back with the mystery guest.

"Blake! Nice to see you man," Beau enthused. They did one of those cool guy handshakes that every guy just seemed to get.

"Really glad you came," Dean said sincerely.

"Thanks for having me," Blake replied, and then said

hello to Christy and Taylor and when he turned his stare to Justine, she felt her heart stop as those silver eyes swirled at her invitingly. *Stop lusting after him, immediately!*

"Nice to see you Justine, I thought you couldn't make it?" he asked with a pointed stare at Taylor who avoided eye contact.

"Yeah, I wasn't meant to be. I was supposed to be on a date, but it got canceled at the last minute, something must have spooked the guy," she said, fixing him with a knowing smile. His mouth twitched like he was fighting a grin. She wished he'd just let it out, she was dying to see it.

"Well, I guess it's for the best, you can't be too careful these days," he said, staring down at her. Goosebumps prickled along her skin as she remembered the feel of his hands sliding over her skin and she looked away first, breaking eye contact.

"Take a seat, Blake, I'll go and get you a beer," Taylor said and got up, trying to put him next to Justine but she wasn't fooled.

"I'll help you." She stood up, fixing Taylor with a sharp smile. She grabbed Taylor by the arm and dragged her indoors.

"What the hell?!" she hissed when they were alone. Taylor looked at her, all wide-eyed innocence.

"I just thought you might like to get to know each other before you completely dismiss him as a potential suitor, or at least someone to rid you of your V plates. I don't know how you're still carrying those around," Taylor sighed dramatically as she got a beer from the fridge.

"I told you I wasn't interested in him, and I meant it," Justine huffed, ignoring the crack about her virginity. She knew Taylor didn't mean anything by it and had previously praised her for her restraint.

"And I would *totally* believe you, if your eyes weren't watching him like he's Channing Tatum and 'Pony' just started playing."

Justine flushed. Was she really that transparent?

"I was not! And I already know him well enough from speaking to him at the NWS meetings, so there!" she shot back triumphantly. Taylor looked at her, sympathy lining her features.

"Oh sweetie, I can't wait to watch you fight this to the bitter end, it'll be nearly as entertaining as it was watching Christy and Doofus," she said, jerking her thumb over her shoulder.

"My ears are burning," Dean said, coming into the kitchen with a smile on his face.

"Shush, grown-ups talking," Taylor quipped. Dean wrapped an arm around her shoulders and pulled her into his chest, rubbing his knuckles over her head.

"Asshole!" Taylor hissed as she fought him. Justine decided to use the distraction to escape and headed back outside. Unfortunately, Taylor knew her too well and came charging after her, shoving her out the way. She handed Blake his beer and took the seat next to Christy, so Justine was forced to sit next to Blake. Justine glared daggers at her over the fire pit and Taylor just blew her a kiss.

"So Blake, tell us about yourself?" Christy asked, Blake's beer stalled halfway to his mouth before he took a sip and Justine watched his smooth tan throat working as he swallowed, making her mouth water and she averted her eyes before he noticed her staring. She grabbed her drink and took a big gulp, and as she did so, she caught Taylor's eye and the minx was smirking at her with far too much satisfaction.

"What do you want to know?" he asked.

"Everything," Taylor replied, and he chuckled, the sound warming Justine more than the fire ever could.

"Well, I recently moved from Anderson to-"

"Why did you move?" Christy interrupted him. There was a pause and Justine held her breath, just how much would he tell them about himself?

"I moved for the job and-"

"Interesting, did you leave anyone behind in Anderson? Like, a girlfriend?" Taylor asked, giving him her full, undivided attention.

"No. I'm single if that's what you're asking," Blake replied, and Justine noticed him shifting uncomfortably in his seat.

"How old are you?" Christy's word firing at him.

"I'm thirty-eight."

"Wow a thirty-eight-year-old single man? You're probably ready to settle down and start a family, aren't you?" Taylor took over the questioning and Justine sent her a fierce look telling her to *shut the fuck up!*

"I'm not really the 'settling down with a family' type," he replied smoothly, and Justine's heart thudded in her chest. *Wait, he wasn't?* The idea bothered her more than it should. They weren't together, what did it matter?

"But if the right woman came along…?" Christy jumped on it, leaving the question hanging in the air.

There was a pause and Justine was desperate to hear his answer.

"I think I'm gonna go and chat to the guys. I feel like they're less… interrogate-y…it's been a pleasure ladies," he said, his deep voice caressing over her and he stood up and went over to the guys. When he was out of earshot Taylor turned to them both.

"Well, that went well, better than I thought it would!"

she chimed, and she and Christy clinked their glasses to a job well done.

"You're both unbelievable!" she hissed at them over the fire.

"Thank you," Christy said sincerely, placing her hand on her chest and Justine laughed at the expression on her face. Dammit, she couldn't stay mad at them. To her relief, they didn't question her about Blake and instead they began talking about wedding plans.

She tried to pay attention, but her traitorous eyes kept moving over to where the men were standing, especially when Beau barked out a laugh and she was shocked to see Blake laughing too. His wide smile took over his whole face, the sight of it hit her like a punch to the gut and her breath caught in her throat. It was beautiful: his white, straight teeth briefly flashing, a small dimple popped next to his lip and his eyes crinkled at the edges. He looked so happy.

She was struck dumb at the sight of it, her mouth dropped open and he met her stare. She quickly looked away before he could spot the yearning that was surely on her face. *That's what he said wasn't it, yearning?* His words from the night before in her office consumed her. What was she going to do? He was everywhere, she couldn't get away from him. And now that she could see him bonding with her friends, showing her another new side of him? It just made her want him even more.

The guys brought the food over and Blake offered to go inside and get more beers, the women had plenty of margaritas to keep them going a bit longer. She was starting to feel the warm, alcoholic buzz settling over her.

"That dude is fricking hilarious, and I can't believe he's so good at basketball but never went pro," Beau said when Blake was gone, and Dean nodded along with him.

"Have you got a new man crush?" Taylor teased. For once there was no malice in her words as she spoke to Beau, maybe they'd gotten over whatever their issue was?

"Maybe," Beau grunted. "You seem to like him a lot, that's for sure." There was a hint of accusation in his tone, but Taylor didn't shy away from it.

"We just understand each other, that's all," she replied smoothly, not allowing him to ruffle her feathers.

"Like in the biblical sense?" Beau shot back, and Justine would be lying if she said she hadn't thought about that herself, but she knew that if Taylor was trying to set her and Blake up, there was no way they'd been intimate together.

"Is that any of your business?" Taylor replied calmly, and the air crackled between them. It was too much for Justine, this whole night was too much. She went inside, needing to splash some water on her face. She ran through the kitchen, like a coward, not wanting to see Blake and headed upstairs to the bathroom. She kept running, turned the corner on the landing and smacked into Blake.

"Whoa, slow down," he said, placing his hands on her shoulders to stop her from stumbling. The heat from his large palms setting her aflame. She placed her hands on his chest to balance herself and felt the hard muscles bunching under her touch.

"Sorry," she said, not meeting his eyes as she took a step back.

"Everything okay?" he asked, looking down at her. Concern furrowed his deep brow.

"Yeah, fine," she replied, her tone clipped. He removed his hands and her skin felt bare without his touch.

"I'm sorry about your date tonight," he said gently.

The pity in his gaze was too much for her.

"Are you?" she snapped, and then immediately regretted her display of temper. There was a deep pause between them where she considered whether to apologize or not.

"No, I'm not," he replied, shocking her. The words hung heavy in the air between them, he stepped forward and crowded her against the wall.

"Why are your friends asking about my love life?" he asked. She swallowed thickly, embarrassed to admit what they were doing but he needed to know as she doubted they would stop.

"They're trying to set us up," she replied, reaching up to push him away. Was he trying to intimidate her? "Blake, please," she said, pushing but he didn't move.

"Why would they do that?" he asked. He reached up and brushed an errant lock of hair over her shoulder, allowing his hand to trail over her hot skin. She felt tingles ignite where he touched her, she was so sensitive and receptive to him. She tried not to close her eyes in bliss. Why was he touching her so intimately, did he like her? Could he? The knowledge consumed her, filled her up.

"Because they don't know that nothing can happen between us, because you're my client," she answered, her voice rasping from her, her mouth running dry as those tingles spread through her whole body.

"Is that the only reason nothing could happen?" he asked. Justine's pulse pounded, she needed to get out of here, fast. He pressed his entire weight into her, pinning her to the wall like he'd read her mind. He bent his head and brushed her hair away from her ear before he whispered.

"Do you think I'm pretty, Justine?"

She fought a groan at the sensations tearing through her body, her breathing deepened as she tried to fight her arousal.

"What?" she asked. He nuzzled her ear, the scrape of his beard electrifying her nerves and she fisted her grip on his shirt as her core started pulsing with need. He ground his hips into her, hitting her just right. He was fully aroused, the knowledge flooring her. Had she done that to him?

"I asked you a question. In our second session, you asked if I attacked Beau because he was prettier than me. You said *prettier*. So, I'll ask you again, Justine, and I expect an honest answer. Do you think I'm pretty?" his voice grating out from him. She opened her eyes, and he was all she could see. His gaze turned to molten silver, daring her to defy him. She swiped her tongue over her bottom lip and heat flared in his eyes at the action.

"Yes." The word ripped from her throat before she could stop it and then he was crashing his mouth to hers. His lips were so soft, not at all hard like she'd imagined. He sipped at her, coaxing her, working her until she was moaning, her stomach clenching in need. He tilted his head to deepen the kiss and when she opened her mouth, his tongue found hers. She touched hers tentatively to his and an answering rumble echoed in his chest. Her body exploded with pleasure when he stroked her tongue languidly.

His beard grazed her, the rough feel igniting her desire. *What would it feel like between my legs?* He cupped her jaw, stroking his thumb over the delicate bones of her face, and she sank into him. He worked her mouth expertly, feeding her kiss after kiss until she was arching against his body, trying to pull him closer to her. He wasn't close enough.

His taste was dirty, carnal just as she'd known it would be, and something inexplicably *Blake*. She grabbed onto his strong shoulders and held on as he worked her, showing her his passion, a level of passion she hadn't expected from him. A level of passion she'd hoped was hidden under his rough exterior.

She was feeling everything he'd told her passion would be when he had been in her office and as the thought crossed her mind it was like a bucket of ice had been poured over her. She shoved him away, placing a hand over her mouth. He looked wild and fierce with his desire, every inch the alpha male she knew he was.

"Blake, I can't, you're my client, it's so wrong," she gasped. *What have I done?* Fighting down a sob, she ran into the bathroom and locked herself in. She waited until she heard his footsteps pounding down the stairs before she turned to splash some water on her face.

She was shaking, her body still running on the adrenaline from that kiss. That amazing kiss which was everything romance novels had said it would be when you met the right man. That scared her. He couldn't be the man for her, he was all wrong for her and hello, they couldn't even be together!

She splashed some more water on her face and waited for her shaking to subside. Her body was still humming with arousal, she had to wait until she felt like she could rejoin everyone downstairs. She went back outside, nervous about seeing him but he was chatting with the guys and didn't even look her way when she reappeared.

Chapter 11

Last night's bout of insomnia couldn't be blamed on his PTSD or anxiety, for once. It was all on himself and that explosive kiss with Justine. It had been so hot, he still hadn't cooled down. He just wanted more, he wanted it all, everything she had to give.

It was inevitable, when he'd turned up at Dean's house and seen her, all that mouth-watering skin glowing in the light from the fire, those honey eyes heating when she spotted him, he knew he was going to do something stupid. He just didn't think the opportunity would present itself, and then he'd bumped into her upstairs. Having her pressed up against him got him all kinds of worked up and he needed to know if she felt the same way too.

The short answer was yes, it seemed like she did. But she was fighting it, her damn ethics getting in the way and ruining everything. Not that he blamed her, it was a good thing really, just not when it meant he couldn't have his cake and eat her too.

That kiss. He fought a groan even now. She tasted like sin, just as he knew she would, every movement of their lips dragging him down deeper into the flames of desire. Her soft lips so plump and billowy against his as she gave in, sighing into his mouth with her surrender. The tentative little licks of her tongue had his mind straying to what else she could slide her tongue over. She'd felt so right pressed up against him, turning him into an animal, his need overruling him. Just as he was getting started, she'd shoved him away and locked herself in the bathroom, leaving him standing there, hard and aching for her.

He'd thought if he had a taste of her then that would be enough, his curiosity would be assuaged and he could move on with his life, but he was wrong. He now only had more questions. What would she feel like? Was she as lust crazed as he was? What did she look like when she came apart? What did her moans sound like? Too many questions and not enough answers. He needed more but he couldn't get them. He forced himself out of bed, ignoring his hard-on, it would go down eventually. *Yeah, when you get Justine between the sheets, mindlessly writhing against you,* his mind taunted and he clenched his teeth at the visual that presented.

He had a shower and dressed in a tank top and shorts. He was looking forward to playing another round of basketball with the guys; it was becoming a Sunday tradition. He'd had more fun than he thought he would last night, the fireworks with Justine aside. He felt like he'd been welcomed into the group and he finally belonged somewhere. A sharp ache lanced in his chest which he tried to ignore. He wasn't meant to be fitting in, he was meant to be keeping everyone at arm's length. But Justine was right. He needed a support network if he wanted to get better. He'd been thinking more about what that looked like and who it could be. He needed to get serious about his bid for sheriff too.

Pushing his thoughts aside, he left the house and jogged over to the basketball court to meet Beau and Dean, who were already waiting for him. He dropped his keys and phone in the grass next to their stuff.

"There he is," Beau called over.

"We were beginning to think you weren't gonna show," Dean taunted.

"Yeah, we figured you were too intimidated by us to show your face on this court again," Beau taunted, flexing his biceps. Blake arched an eyebrow at them both as he sauntered over.

"That's big talk considering last time I wiped the floor with you both and sent you home crying to your mama," Blake said, and Beau barked out a laugh.

"Never again," Dean said with mock seriousness and Blake rolled his eyes.

"We gonna stand around all day gossiping like a bunch of old ladies or we gonna shoot some hoops?" Blake asked them, issuing the challenge before slapping the ball out of Dean's hand and dribbling it up the court, his speed surprising them both and leaving them in the wind.

He got in position for a lay-up and jumped, the ball sailing through the net with a satisfying *swish*. Before he could grab it again, Beau snatched it away and ran back down the court with Dean tearing after him. They played individually for a little while and then paired off - Blake and Dean against Beau. Beau managed to duck past them both and took a shot, it bounced off the rim and Blake caught the rebound, heading back up the court with Dean blocking for him. He made an easy shot and he and Dean high fived afterwards. Beau glared at them.

"I don't like this new partnership," he grumbled.

"Don't be jelly, sweetie, you'll get your turn," Blake teased, blowing him a kiss, and Beau flipped him off, laughing. They played hard, dominating the court, aggression and rivalry driving them until hours had passed and they were all exhausted. They collapsed on the grass, the hot sun beating down on them.

Beau turned to him. "Where did you learn to play? At college?"

"Nah, I didn't make it through college. I learned in the military," he started, and noticed the surprise on their faces when he said he'd been in the army. "Sometimes you get a lot of time in-between assignments, but you can't go anywhere, so we set up a little hoop and got a ball. Those were some good times." He sighed, remembering.

"I didn't realize you were in the military," Dean replied softly. "Stupid question, but what was that like?"

Blake was silent for a minute as he thought about how to answer. He didn't want to get too into detail, didn't want to trigger a flashback or anything like that. He'd be humiliated if he had an episode in front of them.

"It was probably one of the best times in my life. It was hard though, obviously. Met some great people and lost some too," he said.

"How come you got out?" Beau asked.

Again, Blake wasn't sure how much detail to go into, he wanted to keep it top line.

"My wife, uh, killed herself," he said simply. Dean cursed under his breath and Beau put a hand on his shoulder.

"I'm sorry to hear that man, we had no idea."

"It's cool, it was a while ago now."

They all sat in silence for a minute and Blake felt like he owed Beau more of an explanation for why he attacked him a few weeks ago.

"Beau, the other week when I-"

Beau interrupted him. "You don't need to explain anything, man."

"I know but I want to." Blake felt sick as he contemplated how much to share, should he even share *anything*? He wanted to get to know these guys and needed to develop relationships, like Justine had said. "I've been going through some PTSD issues, which I'm working through with a psychologist," he added hastily. "But that's why, you know, sometimes I go into old memories and lose where I am. I did that night and I'm sorry about that."

"I appreciate it, man, but you don't need to explain. I think it's amazing that you're coping so well," Beau said, and Dean nodded in agreement.

"It must be really hard to face some of these things, but it just shows how strong you are," Dean said, and Blake could feel the support coming off them both in waves and damn if that didn't give him a lump in his throat. They all sat in silence for a moment, just letting the sun beat down on them, then Beau cleared his throat.

"To be honest, I thought you attacked me to warn me off Justine," he joked, and Dean snorted next to him. Blake punched his arm.

"Is she the psychologist you're seeing?" Dean asked.

Blake nodded, and he noticed them share a look.

"What?"

"Nothing, it's just a shame. You would make a great couple," Dean said.

"I guess she can't really jump into bed with you, probably a violation of rights or some shit right there isn't it?" Beau asked.

Blake just nodded, his mind lost in his thoughts. She probably didn't want to feel like she was taking advantage of him if she slept with him and then treated him. But what if it was more of an arrangement where they both did something for each other? His mind started whirring at the possibilities and he felt himself smiling, suddenly excited about the stakeout they had tomorrow night.

*

Justine was dreading the stakeout, feeling sick at the thought of being stuck in a car with Blake, in the dark for at least an hour. She didn't want to see him, because every time she pictured him, she thought of their kiss. That amazing, soul-searing kiss. She shivered now just thinking about it.

This was why she needed to keep things professional, because how was she going to sit across from him in their next session and delve into his mind when all she could think was, why didn't he palm her breast? Why didn't he storm in the bathroom after her and demand to take her to bed? And why did she want him to? Did he regret it? Did he enjoy it? *Argh!*

She was fighting a war with herself, her head against her heart, and she didn't know which would win, but either way, being with him tonight would ensure that one of them lost. She saw him pull up outside her house, right on time. With a deep sigh she grabbed her purse and feeling like she was heading to her doom, left the house.

"Good evening, Justine," he said when she got into his car, his cheerful voice instantly alerting her. She watched him, something was…different. He looked the same, still brooding, his mouth still flat and unsmiling, but now she knew that it wasn't hard, it was soft, pliant, and delicious. *Shut up brain!*

"Good evening, Blake, how are you?" she returned, buckling herself in.

"I'm just fine, thank you," he purred, his eyes sliding over her, taking in her messy bun, no make-up, hoodie, and denim shorts. The way he ran his eyes over her had her nipples tightening. She gripped her thighs to keep from reaching for him.

"Not exactly dressed for sleuth activity, are you?" he sighed. She looked down at her outfit again.

"I didn't think we'd be doing anything except sitting in the car?" she asked.

"Was there something else you wanted to be doing?" he asked, his voice deepening, and she had to fight a moan at the suggestive tone he used. *You're a professional, you're a professional, you're a goddamn professional!*

"Did Janet tell you where we should start?" she asked brightly, changing the subject. She thought she saw him smile but it must have been a trick of the light.

"She's given me the street name, so we'll just head straight there," he said and then pulled the car away from the curb. The radio was playing softly in the background, a song she recognized. She looked to the console and saw the local eighties radio station tuned in. Her eyes shot to him.

"Eighties music?" she asked tentatively, her heart in her throat. Could they have more in common that she'd thought?

"Guilty pleasure," he shrugged, tension filling the car.

"There's nothing guilty about these solid gold tracks," she replied, and she thought she saw his mouth quirk up. The tension in the car increased and neither of them spoke again. She studied him, reveling in watching him do mundane activities, observing the muscles in his firm forearms flex whenever he turned the wheel. She liked that he drummed his fingers on the steering wheel to the beat of the song playing, that was something she did too.

She began humming along to the song on the radio, thinking about booking another gig with Taylor, she hadn't sung for a couple of weeks now and she needed an outlet for all the emotions she was feeling at the moment.

She felt him staring at her. "What?" she asked, meeting his eyes before he turned his attention back to the road.

"Nothing," he muttered. A short while later, he parked the car on the side of a quiet suburban road with houses lining both sides of the street. "This is where it was reported last week."

"Ooh, the scene of the crime. They must be concerned if they sent the deputy here," she said sarcastically and she saw him roll his eyes.

"You know, you could take this a little more seriously," he murmured, and she watched as he scanned the street. His eyes narrowing every now and then. She would bet he'd memorized every blade of grass swaying in the breeze and infiltrated every shadow that lurked nearby.

"I could but I'm also aware of what this town can be like, having lived here my whole life. It's going to be nothing."

He snorted next to her. "Yes, what a nice sleepy town this is. Like your date the other night, that wouldn't have escalated at all, would it?" he shot back. She crossed her arms over her chest defensively, trying her darndest not to smile at his sarcasm. *Damn him for being amusing!*

"Yeah well, you soon stopped that, didn't you?"

"And I'd do it again in a heartbeat," he said fiercely. She looked out the window, not able to take any more intense eye contact or she would explode. They sat in silence, both surveying the street.

After about an hour something caught her eye, she leaned forward, placing her hand on the console between them, trying to get a better look. Except the console was warmer than she thought it would be. Firmer too. She swallowed as she looked down and saw her palm gripping Blake's hard thigh. She looked up at him, his eyes were sparkling with amusement. She snatched her hand away, flushing. Luckily, the lighting was so dim he wouldn't see her embarrassment. His amusement faded as he realized she spotted something.

"What did you see?" he demanded, back in alpha mode.

"I thought I saw a shadow over there," she pointed, and he turned his attention to the place she indicated.

"I'm gonna check it out," he said, reaching for the door handle and she grabbed his arm.

"Wait!" she cried, suddenly feeling like she should've been taking this stakeout seriously after all. "Be careful."

"Don't worry, I'll be back. We have unfinished business," he rumbled, and then he was gone, his words echoing in her ears. She watched him slink across the road, as stealthy as a ninja. Scratch that, ninjas had nothing on Blake. He blended into the shadows and then she lost him.

She knew she was overreacting, she just told herself that it would be nothing, so why was she worrying? And what did he mean by *unfinished business*? She wanted to chalk what happened between them down to a mistake. Because that's what it had been. A silly, stupid mistake. Okay fine, it was a toe-curling mistake she was dying to repeat but couldn't.

After ten minutes he still hadn't come back, and she

started to panic. What if the Trashcan Bandits were actually a hard-core street gang? Or the Mob? What if it was a serial killer? Her mind ran into overdrive and just as she reached for the door handle to go and search for him, the driver's door opened, and Blake got back in the vehicle.

"I couldn't see anything except a cat," he said. The relief she felt must have been written all over her face. He frowned at her. "Were you worried about me?"

"No," she answered a bit too quickly. He held her stare, a fierce expression consuming his features and she started to burn under the intensity.

"I'm not sorry for kissing you," he growled, surprising her. She didn't think he would bring it up. She didn't respond, she didn't know what to say. She couldn't think about what that meant, she wouldn't let herself. She watched as a calculating look crossed his features.

"I have a proposal for you," he said with a sly smile. She swallowed hard. "I think there's a way we can help each other. We can have a partnership of sorts, an agreement. You'll help me with overcoming my PTSD and anxiety, and I'll open up to you so we can work through it together." He paused, his eyes not leaving her face.

"You'll have to do that anyway," she replied. "If you want to keep your job."

He looked thoughtful for a moment. "True. But I can make it easy on you, or hard."

She glared at him. *Was this sexy bastard trying to blackmail her?*

"Okay, and what is it you think you can help me with?" she asked, sounding bored and as though she was trying to humor him, but her heart was pounding in her chest. His eyes flashed at her.

"I can help you get rid of that pesky virginity you've been carrying around for far too long," he said, a wolfish smile taking over his face.

Her heart stopped, she couldn't breathe, that smile could start wars. She shook herself, replayed his words and the silence surrounding them was deafening.

"What makes you think I want to sleep with you?" she asked when she finally felt she was able to talk. She tried to inject some confidence in her tone, like she was in control even though it was painfully obvious she wasn't. He fixed her with a look that screamed, *bitch, please.*

"Honey, I was there the other night, when you were rubbing yourself against me, moaning…" he trailed off and she gnashed her teeth together. *Damn him!*

"Let me rephrase. I could go and sleep with anyone, why would I choose you?"

"But you haven't, have you?" he asked, his stare probing her, looking for confirmation. She looked away and then back at him and that was all the answer he needed, satisfaction flaring in his eyes.

"You can trust me not to hurt you, that's why. Just like I would be trusting you with my deepest, darkest thoughts. I'd be trusting *you* not to hurt *me*." His tone turned serious and something about his words stuck with her.

"Blake I-"

"It'll be a business deal, nothing more. You can trust me with your body, to help you explore your sexuality and you can help me fix my mind."

"This is ridiculous! You know I can't agree to this. It would be a huge violation of ethics!" she cried, shocked at herself that she was even considering this.

"Not if I'm aware of the terms from the start. You're not taking advantage if I'm willingly giving myself to you.

Body and mind. And it's my own idea," he countered.

"No, Blake. I'm not doing this."

Before she knew it, he wrapped his arms around her and hauled her onto his lap, she straddled his hips. She opened her mouth to protest but he pressed a finger to her lips, and it took every ounce of her willpower not to close her mouth around it. He tucked a loose strand of hair behind her ear, his eyes running over her face, drinking in her features. Her gaze dipped to his mouth, wanting so badly to give in and fit their lips together again.

He stroked over the sensitive skin of her neck, the rough calluses scraping deliciously and she arched to give him better access. He grunted in approval, the air between them turning thick and heavy. Her breasts brushed him every time she took a breath. He palmed her ass, pulling her in line with him. He was hard, thick and her eyes fluttered closed as he rubbed against her, and they found their rhythm.

The sensations flooded her body, driving her wild, making her needy. Her head dropped forward, and he buried his face in her neck, licking across her pounding pulse. She shuddered in his arms as he sucked, hard.

"What are you doing?" she gasped out.

"You wanted me to build relationships, so I'm building relationships," he murmured against her skin.

"Yes, but I didn't mean with me. *God*, don't stop," she sighed as he nibbled her flesh.

"See, Justine? It could be just like this, so good together at night and then the next day you'll be delving into my mind and I'm letting you. Justine, I've never let *anyone* in before," he rasped, and she moaned at his words, rubbing herself against him faster. Was he really offering her something he'd never given another?

"If I'm willing to go ahead with it, if it's my idea, then surely your ethics can't disagree?" he added.

She was so close. Any second now. She could feel her body tensing and his lips ghosted over her throat again, his hand fisted in her hair, and he pulled her against him harder. She was falling and she just hoped he was ready to catch her.

He arched against her and pulled her down at the same time, like he knew it was all she needed. Her climax rocked her, exploding, her breaths coming out in little pants. He continued thrusting, drawing it out and then stilled, shuddering against her. When she came down from the high, she opened her eyes. He was staring at her, an expression she'd never seen on his face and understanding of what they'd just done dawned on her. What had she done? How could she have gotten so carried away?

"You're so beautiful," he said softly, his expression gentle and it twisted something inside her. She couldn't do this, not with him, it was getting too messy, and she didn't do messy.

"I'm sorry, I shouldn't have-" she started, and she shakily climbed off his lap.

"Don't apologize and I started it, not you," he said but he didn't say anything more, like he knew she needed a minute. He started the engine and drove them back to her house. They rode in silence the entire way. When he pulled up outside, she was lost in her whirling thoughts. He cleared his throat, and she was brought back to reality.

"I'll expect an answer on Wednesday," he said firmly, leaving no room for argument. The drill sergeant was back. Dazed and confused, she got out of his car without saying a word and went inside. She had been right, a war had been fought, her heart had won tonight.

Chapter 12

By Wednesday morning, Justine was a mess. She had barely slept, she couldn't eat and now she couldn't even think straight. All she could think about was Blake's proposition, and how alive he had made her feel. Is this what she had been missing out on in life? Because *damn*.

She was at war with herself. One part of her, the horny, slutty part thought it was a great idea, the best idea since panties were invented. The other part of her, the sensible, rational, *ethical* part of her couldn't believe she was even considering it. She was more than a little shocked at herself.

There were pros and cons for each outcome. For example, pro: she would be able to keep treating him. If she could help him control and reduce his panic attacks it would be a huge achievement for her career, and she would have *truly* helped someone. Con: she would be violating her ethics. Pro: she could act out every fantasy that had tormented her since she'd lain eyes on him. Con: it was unprofessional, bad psychologist, bad! Pro: his muscles. *Ugh!* She went back and forth so many times that she broke her brain.

Now, she was sat in her office, nervously waiting for him, and she still didn't have an answer. She heard his deep voice before she saw him. *Probably charming Hilda.* Then he was sauntering into her office, every inch the brooding bad boy and her stomach started fluttering like a swarm of butterflies. He faced her, his mouth unsmiling as usual, but now she knew how soft it was, how it felt and how he tasted, it was branded on her soul.

"Good morning, Dr. Rodríguez-Hamilton," he said slowly. The way he said her name had her mouth running dry and her palms sweating. He closed the door and the distinct *click* echoed around the room. They were alone.

He stalked to the couch, watching her the entire time, like she was his prey, calculating the best moment to strike. Except she wasn't prey. This was *her* office, *her* domain, he'd stepped into *her* lair, and he needed *her*.

The knowledge filled her with confidence. She lifted her chin defiantly and discreetly dried her palms on her pants before standing. She came to a stop in front of him, her heels putting her in line with his shoulder so she still had to stare up at him. But her gaze didn't waver. This alpha male had met his match. In her office, *she* was the alpha. The lead. The female boss. If he didn't like that, he knew where the fucking door was.

"So pleased to see you, Blake. Take a seat," she said, her professional smile frozen on her lips. She watched him sizing her up, contemplating how to handle this. A muscle ticked under his eye, and he slowly lowered himself onto the couch. A frisson of triumph bolstered her as she took her seat opposite him.

"I think today we should focus on talking about Katie. I think how you view your relationship, what happened and the narrative your mind has focused on is behind a lot of the negative emotions and anxiety you're feeling. What do you think?" she asked, pressing her hands over her thighs, oozing confidence.

"I think I'd like to know what your answer is," he replied smoothly. She pursed her lips, *sassy bastard*. She ignored him. *My office, my rules.*

"Tell me how you and Katie met, what was your early relationship like? I believe you mentioned you were childhood sweethearts?"

There was no response, just more of that intense eye contact. She tried again.

"How did it feel when she told you she was pregnant?"

"How did it feel when you rubbed yourself over my hard cock the other night?" he asked casually. She blinked, heat flared through her at his coarse language and the visual his words created. He was trying to mess with her, but it wouldn't work. She wouldn't let it.

"Blake, please try to stay on topic," she chastised. She wouldn't let him get under her skin, no matter how much he affected her. "You said Katie faked her pregnancy to keep you from leaving to go to college. How did you feel when you found out she had lied?"

He didn't reply, just stared at her, assessing. His steel gaze held firm. They had reverted to their first few sessions. Tamping down her growing frustration, she decided to wait him out. The minutes dragged by, at one point she thought she had successfully stifled a yawn, but his damn perceptive gaze missed nothing.

"You look a little tired, has something been keeping you up at night?" he asked genially. She snorted.

"Not exactly your best compliment, are you this good with all women?" she drawled, forgetting herself and where she was, instantly regretting her words. Satisfaction flared in his eyes.

"Take me to bed and I'll show you how good I am." His words were gentle, his tone low but his eyes burned. Her stomach clenched. Take him to bed, like she would be in charge, dominating him. The idea firing her blood. Now she understood her previous date's obsession with dominance. To dominate Blake, to own him, control his wants, actions and pleasure, that would be worth nearly anything. Except her ethics. She whimpered internally, *damned ethics!*

"Agree to my proposition and I'll answer all of your questions. All of them. Otherwise, you won't be getting anything else out of me. Ever." He folded his arms over his chest, his firm biceps bulging, distracting her for a moment and then his words registered.

"This is blackmail! You would really ruin your own career over this? Just to get laid?" she spluttered. He didn't say anything, but a smug smirk had spread over his face when he saw how worked up she was getting. *Gah! Why can't I hide my emotions better?*

"Are you really that hard up, Blake?" she spat, but that stupid smirk stayed fixed on his face.

"You're asking a lot of questions, doctor, but not answering mine. Yes, or no?"

"No!"

Blake pursed his lips again and a flicker of irritation lit his face before quickly disappearing.

"Then I have nothing else to say."

"Then I guess we're done for the day," she retorted,

and stood up expectantly.

"We've got another forty-five minutes left, please take a seat, Dr. Rodríguez-Hamilton." A smug grin crossed his face. He had her over a barrel. *Smug, sexy asshole!* She thought she was going to explode, this man infuriated her. *How dare he come into my office, looking so gorgeous, and manipulate me this way!*

She needed to calm down, she'd been simmering since he came in. It was time to take it down a notch. She didn't want him to see his effect on her or how turned on their verbal sparring had made her. She fixed that smile on her face, the one that seemed to piss him off so much.

"Of course, where are my manners?" she sighed, and at her change of attitude, he narrowed his eyes warily. She went over to her desk and sat down, putting plenty of distance between them. She opened her bottom drawer and pulled out the magazine she kept in there and started flicking through it. She refused to look at him for the rest of the session.

The room was silent, so silent she could hear the rasp of his beard as he ran his hand over his jaw. She waited him out, right until the end. When their session was over, she expected him to leave but he surprised her by getting up and strolling over to her, so slowly, lazily, like he had all the time in the world.

He didn't stop until he was uncomfortably close, but she refused to move back or acknowledge him. He bent down, and out of the corner of her eye she saw he was looking at her magazine. It was only then that she realized she had flicked onto a lingerie page.

He shifted next to her and then he was at her ear, his lips closing around the lobe, running his teeth over it. She gasped in pleasure, unable to hold back and he chuckled, the sound smothering her, drowning her in desire. His big hand flattened on her magazine, his finger tapping the orange bra and panty set displayed.

"That's what I want to see you in when you give yourself to me. Because you will, Justine," he said, his voice hoarse, the sound reverberating through her bones. He nibbled her ear again and then before she could respond he was walking out the door, whistling like he hadn't a care in the world.

*

She needed to get laid, it was as simple as that. It was the only way to forget about Blake and to be able to move on and treat him properly and effectively. The only way to get him out of her damn head. If she got rid of her virginity, then she wouldn't need to make a deal with him so he would have to open up and let her treat him, right?

In their group chat, Taylor mentioned there would be another Ladies' Night on Friday, which Justine couldn't be more grateful for. She was so relieved she could go and find a man to throw herself at, beg him to take her to bed if necessary. She cringed at how desperate that seemed, but she *was* desperate because she needed to get Blake out of her mind, so she would stop aching for him. The man who was all wrong for her yet seemed *sooo* right.

Ever since he came to town, she had struggled with naughty thoughts and dirty urges. Watching him strut around in his leather jacket, with that damn beard, his stupid, big muscles and perma-frown constantly on display, like the rebellious bad boy he was, took its toll on a woman. There was only so much more she could take.

She was so close to giving in. She had avoided him since their session on Wednesday morning, knowing that he only needed to breathe in her direction, and she would scream *"TAKE ME!"* Which was why she found herself pulling up at The Rusty Bucket Inn on Friday night, ready to meet a man. *Come on Mr. Right, hurry up, I'm begging you!*

She reapplied her lipstick, peering in her rear-view mirror, brushing her long hair until it crackled with electricity. She looked down at her outfit, giving herself another once over, her orange crop top and dark blue jeans looked casual but nice. She was ready. She got out of her car and started walking towards the bar. The evening breeze teasing her skin, the scent of pine trees drifting by. She inhaled deeply, the scent calming her. Wait a minute, pine trees and…spices?

"What are you doing here tonight, Justine?" His deep voice, right in her ear. She yelped in surprise and spun around, her hair tangling around her face in the breeze. She came face to face with Blake, his silver eyes glittering down at her in the moonlight, promising her countless wicked nights. She looked around before glaring back at him.

"Are you stalking me?" she demanded.

"Just following up a lead," he shrugged.

"And what lead is that?"

"Police business," he said, his mouth kicked up on one side and drew her attention. His lips looked so soft, surrounded by that dark beard that would abrade her skin so perfectly. She scowled. This was exactly why she was here tonight. The plan was to find a man, have sex, forget about Blake. Three steps, very clear, very simple, very doable. It was a solid plan.

"See you later, Blake." She spun on her heel and marched towards the bar. She felt his heat before his touch. He wrapped his hand around her arm.

"Don't set foot in that bar, Justine."

"Don't tell me what to do, *cabrón*! I'm a single woman and I will do whatever the fuck I want!" she shouted at him.

"Fine, I'm not telling you, I'm…" he gritted his teeth and looked away. "I'm asking you."

She glared up at him.

"Come with me," he said, dragging her around the side of the bar and away from prying eyes. He pushed her against the wall, bringing his arms up and caging her in.

"What are you doing?" she spluttered.

"Stopping you from making a huge mistake," he murmured, peering down at her, every inch the devil in disguise.

"I'm a big girl, I can make my own decisions. I manage it just fine on a daily basis without needing you to step in," she countered.

"This is a decision you would have regretted, trust me."

"Oh yeah, because you know me so well from all our in-depth chats," she replied tartly.

"I know what you want, and I know I'm the only person who can give it to you. I can give you what you need," he taunted her, teased her. Offering her paradise like the snake offered Eve the apple.

"Say yes," he whispered. Her eyes flew to his and for the first time she saw the need banked in them. He was on the edge, could he want this as much as she did? She thought he was just playing a game but now she wasn't so sure.

"I can't, you know I can't and there's nothing you can do to convince me," she gritted out. She immediately knew she said the wrong thing as determination lined his hard features.

"Challenge accepted," he growled before he swooped down. His body pinned her to the wall while his mouth owned hers. He ate at her like a starving man. His kiss wild and dangerous, passion incarnate, full of teeth, tongue and need. White hot need that set her aflame. She moaned and wrapped her arms around his neck and gave in, returning his kiss with abandon.

It was a kiss for the ages, hard, soft and sweet. It was a promise of what was to come and as his tongue stroked against hers, she surrendered. It was like no kiss she had experienced before and he was ruining her for her future husband, because she couldn't imagine anything matching up to this.

She wanted to give in to him, her ethics be damned. It wasn't like she took an oath like other doctors did, it was just—frowned upon. There was a serious chance she could never feel this way again and she owed it to herself to explore it. When she thought about being ninety in a nursing home, looking back over her life, would she prefer the memory of his mouth on hers and the night he could give her, or that one time, out of all the other bloody times, when she did the right thing? As awful as it was, she knew which she would prefer.

She gave in to it, succumbed to her wants and needs and he reveled in it. Little growls left his throat as he devoured her. She tugged at the hem of his shirt, needing to touch his skin. She stroked her fingers across his hard, muscled abdomen before he stilled her hands. He lifted his head, his breath leaving him in ragged pants, his expression fierce.

"Say yes, Justine. I won't ask again."

She couldn't go the rest of her life without knowing what this could feel like, what *he* could feel like, how he looked with his face twisted in pleasure. She damned herself.

"Yes," she whispered brokenly. He grunted in satisfaction and placed a soft kiss to the corner of her mouth, and she fought back a whimper at the sweetness of it.

"I'll come to your place, tomorrow evening," he said, and then he was gone. She was left to make her way home wondering if she'd made a deal with the devil.

*

He knocked on her door, one rap of his knuckles, pause, and then another. As Blake waited for her to answer, he wondered whether she would chicken out. A smirk crossed his face at her surrender yesterday, the relief he felt had been so great, so shocking that he didn't want to look at it too closely. He rearranged his features as he saw her silhouette at the door. She opened it and his heart kicked in his chest.

She was a vision. Her dark, wavy hair cascaded down like a river, begging to have him run his hands through it. He took in her outfit, denim shorts that displayed her long, toned legs that he couldn't wait to have wrapped around him. He lifted his eyes to her baby pink t-shirt that had a cartoon cat wearing a tiara and read, *'Glamorpuss'*. He felt his lips twitch at her adorableness. He liked that she hadn't dressed for seduction and yet he never wanted to bed anyone more.

She looked surprised to see him, he was surprised himself. Not that he was here, that had been inevitable, but that he pursued her so doggedly. He'd never gone to these lengths for a woman before, but she affected him like no other and he needed to have her. If only to give himself peace from the constant thoughts and images bombarding him. And the constant ache in his groin.

She didn't say anything as she looked at him, but something hot passed between them. She swallowed. His eyes caught the motion of her delicate throat working and he couldn't wait to have his lips there, kissing, licking, sucking.

"I've just made some dinner, there's enough for two," she said, stepping to the side to let him in. He came inside, pausing in front of her and at first she looked away. Her eyes darted around the hallway, worry clouding her features, until they hardened. She stood straighter and met his gaze, holding it. *There she is,* he thought and pressed a swift kiss to her lips. He went to pull away, but she softened beneath him, and his resolve crumbled briefly. He swept his tongue inside, she tasted sweet but carnal and he loved it.

When he pulled away, he had the satisfaction of seeing her eyes clouded with desire, and he had to keep walking before he threw her over his shoulder and stomped off to the nearest bedroom, caveman style. That's how she made him feel, aggressive with want and need. He'd never felt that way with Katie.

He put his helmet on the wooden sideboard and she took his leather jacket from him and hung it up on the coat rack in the hall before he went into her living room. His eyes traveled around the room. Light walls and feminine accents gave the space a delicate, comfortable feel. He glanced around, taking in the details of her home, memorizing them, spotting little details like her bookcase, full to the brim, but still organized alphabetically.

He followed her into the kitchen, noting the white cupboards with floral patterned worktops and orange flowered wallpaper that brightened the room. A pink retro-style radio on the side played quietly in the background. It was charming, and so very *her*. She pointed to the dining table in the center of the room and moved to set an extra place for him. He eyed the fragile dining chair suspiciously and slowly lowered himself into it, before trusting it to fully take his weight. She held out a bottle of wine and when he nodded, she poured him a glass, and then she lit the bright orange candle in the middle of the table.

The food smelled amazing. He normally didn't have much of an appetite and had to force himself to eat to keep his strength up when he worked out. It was a side effect of his insomnia and anxiety. But suddenly he felt starved, the smell of spices teasing him.

"I hope you're hungry," she said, placing his plate in front of him and sitting down across from him.

"Ravenous," he replied, his voice deepening with his meaning and she fumbled her cutlery. He tried not to smile, was little Miss Sinful nervous? They ate in silence and as they did, she seemed to get even more tense, her eyes were wide, her movements stiff and forced. She pushed her food around her plate without really eating any. He needed to get her to relax and fast, or she would panic and call an end to their arrangement before it had even begun.

"Do you have any siblings?" he asked.

*

Blake's words pulled Justine from her harried thoughts. She was going crazy, over-analyzing, over-thinking and getting herself worked up. She tried to remind herself that she didn't have to do anything she didn't want to and wasn't ready for. But she *did* want to, more than words would express. She was just nervous.

She was nervous that she might not know what to do and make it awkward. What if she was bad in bed? What if he didn't like her body? She was on edge, and he wasn't helping, turning up looking all sexy and staring at her in that way that made her feel hot and needy. And his all 'discreet' touches and innuendos? Ugh! She was ready to combust. She watched as he swiped his tongue over his bottom lip, she mentally shook herself.

"Yes, I have two older brothers," she replied.

He nodded and shoved another forkful of chorizo quesadilla into his mouth. She noticed he had nearly cleared his plate and she felt a little wave of pride wash over her at how he'd wolfed down what she made. She loved to cook and other than her lessons with Hilda, she didn't get to do it for anyone very often. She glanced down at her own food, barely touched and sighed. She took another bite and chewed but the food was tasteless and settled like lead in her stomach. She was too nervous to eat.

"Do you have any siblings?" she asked, trying to distract herself. There was a pause while he finished his mouthful, she was glad he hadn't talked with food in his mouth, her brothers did that and she hated it.

"Nope, I'm an only child," he replied.

"Are you close with your parents?" she asked, not expecting him to get too chatty. He had a habit of not opening up, although their deal should change that. Her heart thudded in her chest at the reminder.

"Not really, they're hippies so having a son join the military and fight instead of dedicating his life to peace and love sort of ruined any relationship we could've had. I used to write to them when I was on tour but my letters went unanswered. After a few years I just stopped writing."

"I'm sorry to hear that," she replied, she couldn't imagine not being close to her family. Yes, they were loud and nosy and suffocating sometimes, but they were her everything. "You would think they would be so proud of you for being so courageous," she added.

"That's not the way they see it." He shrugged. "It used to bother me, but not so much anymore. I just got used to disappointing people and not getting close to anyone."

His words worried her; did he really think that he was a disappointment?

"Well, for the record, I'm incredibly proud of you. And thank you for your service," she said. There was a pause as her words hung in the air and he stared at her. Something in his expression changed and he smiled warmly at her and nodded, then ducked his head. They continued eating in silence, well, he ate and she watched him discreetly over her wine glass. She couldn't tear her eyes away from this incredible man who fascinated her.

"What about you? Your parents must be so proud of you, a doctor in the family," he said, and she could be mistaken but she thought she saw a hint of mischief in his eyes.

"Yes, they are. Most of the time anyway," she replied, and he shot her a quizzical look. "I'm still single and childless. I don't think *mamá* will be pleased until I'm married and pregnant," she joked.

"Marriage isn't everything," he scoffed, and she bristled.

"But love is and isn't marriage the ultimate dedication of love?" she asked, feeling herself getting defensive. Something dark passed behind his eyes. For a smart person, she could be dumb sometimes, he had effectively been tricked into marriage, so of course he didn't believe in it anymore.

"Would you never want to marry again?" She thought he wouldn't answer but he surprised her.

"I just don't think I could trust someone enough for that, after everything."

"What about starting a family? Do you want kids?"

"You don't need to be married to start a family, Justine." He pinned her with his stare.

She shrugged. "True, I guess I'm just a little old-fashioned that way."

"Miss Independent craves a traditional life?" he gasped, teasing her with his mock outrage.

She laughed. "I know, I'm a walking contradiction. You didn't answer the question."

"Man, you're nosy, aren't you?" he joked, and she laughed again, loving the easy back and forth they had.

"It's kind of my job. Come on, do you want a family, Blake?"

He paused, nibbling his lip in thought before raising his eyes to hers, pain banked in the swirling depths. "I'm too fucked up to be a good father to anyone, so no."

She felt guilty for pushing him but didn't know what to say. He wasn't fucked up at all, it was on the tip of her tongue to say so, but she swallowed the words. He didn't want her platitudes. So, she got up, severing their connection, and took their dishes to the sink. She filled it with water and rinsed them off.

"If you're still hungry I can see what I have for dessert?" she called over her shoulder, switching the faucet off. She felt his heat at her back and then his gravelly voice was right at her ear.

"I already know what I want for dessert."

Chapter 13

She swallowed thickly at his words; her body nearly went up in flames. How did he manage to do this to her? She slowly turned and faced him. His eyes glittered with stark desire, so open and raw. He held out a large hand to her, palm up and she raised her gaze to him, his eyebrow arched in challenge. She steeled herself and slid her palm into his, the hard calluses of his hand abrading her skin in the most magnificent way, tingles branching out from the point of contact. He stepped to the side, letting her take the lead, and with a deep breath, she led him out of the kitchen and upstairs.

Each stomp of his feet on her wooden stairs matched the pounding of her heart. Her palms started sweating, her stomach doing acrobatics like it was going for gold at the Olympics. Why hadn't she put something nicer on?

She honestly hadn't expected him to show up tonight despite what he said. She should have known that he never threatened, only promised.

She led him into her bedroom, cringing internally at the floral patterns that lined the walls and furnishings. It was not a sexy bedroom, it was a flowery, feminine one. As she glanced at the perfectly made bed, her mouth ran dry. She turned to face him, unsure what to do next. He was the first man to ever be in her room, her first lover.

"Relax," he murmured soothingly. He ran his hands up and down her arms. "If at any point you want to stop, we stop, no matter what. You got it?"

She looked up into his eyes. Eyes she once thought so cold and unforgiving now burned, their churning silver color captivating her. She nodded in acceptance.

"Good. Now, is this okay?" he asked, his voice low as he pulled her against him and wrapped his arms around her. Her breasts pressed up against his chest, his large body dwarfing her and she melted against him, feeling safe, protected. She peered up at him through her lashes, her breathing deepening.

"Yes," she whispered. He nodded signaling he heard her. He splayed one hand across her lower back and the other cupped her jaw, his thumb stroking over her cheek.

"Is this okay?" he asked, dipping his head towards her until they were a breath apart. Her eyelids fluttered closed in anticipation, but his kiss never came. She opened her eyes and realized he was waiting for her consent. His sweetness was her undoing.

"Yes," she gasped. He slanted his mouth over hers, kissing her slowly, taking his time to worship her mouth. He kissed her for the longest time, as though he had all the time in the world. She was addicted to his taste and the drugging way his mouth stroked over hers. When he slid his tongue against hers, she moaned and fisted her hands in his shirt. She was desperate to feel his bare chest come up against hers and pressed her body into him in invitation. She felt him tense under her fingertips. *Was he not enjoying this?*

He broke the kiss, nipping her swollen lips gently, teasing her. Pulling back slightly, he ran his hands up her hips, across her stomach and paused just before he reached her breasts, and she nearly stomped her foot in frustration.

"Is this okay?" he rasped, his voice causing goosebumps to break out over her flesh. She watched him, his features pulled tight, lines of strain bracketing his mouth. Was he holding back? That was the last thing she wanted! She threw herself at him, her restraint gone, her nerves defeated, her desire flaring to life. She crashed her mouth to his, banging their teeth together, trying to get closer to him and he growled low in his throat.

"Honey, is this okay?" His hands hovered either side of her, and she realized he was trying not to touch her until she gave him permission.

"Oh, God, yes!" she cried, and he immediately palmed her breasts, swiping his thumbs over her hard nipples, the sensations overwhelming her, directly connected to her core which ached for attention. Her hips rolled against him in reaction. She felt him, thick and hard through his jeans and her eyes rolled back at the contact but it didn't last long because he turned his pelvis away. She pulled back.

"Is everything okay?" she asked, concerned yet pleased to note he was panting.

"Yeah, I just want to take this slowly, for you, but it's harder than I thought," he said, swiping a hand over his jaw.

"I know it is," she purred, and stroked her hand over the hard muscles of his chest and down his stomach to his crotch. He groaned.

"I don't want to overstep or push you to do anything too fast."

"Blake, you have my consent to do whatever you want to do, if you do something I don't like or I want to stop, trust me, I'll tell you."

At her words, he wrapped his arms around her and lifted her up, carrying her to the bed and laying her down gently. He stepped back, his eyes running over her, like he wasn't sure where to start touching her first. She just needed him to touch her, *now*.

"Take off your shirt," she demanded.

*

His cock twitched at her demand, eager to get to her. He smiled at her, enjoying her display of aggression. He did exactly as she said. He reached up and pulled his shirt over his head and tossed it to her. She caught it, smiling, and ran her eyes over his body, drinking in the sight of him.

"Now, your pants."

He tried not to laugh at this new side of her. She was a quick study, he would give her that, but he was in charge here. He looked down at her as he scrubbed a hand over his beard thoughtfully.

"Honey, here I am exposing my chaste, delicate flesh while you lay there fully-clothed. You have me at a disadvantage so I think you should remove your shirt." he said. She narrowed her eyes at him before smoothing her expression.

"Well, I guess fair's fair," she said, and slowly peeled her t-shirt over her head and then he forgot how to breathe. Her plump breasts spilled out from the tops of her lacy orange bra. The lace so delicate it was practically see-through, the sight of her brown nipples, hard and reaching for him had his mouth watering. Her waist was narrow, but her hips were round, she was perfect, and he was speechless.

She must have misunderstood his silence because her face fell, and she started trying to cover herself. He launched forward, straddling her body and grabbing her hands, pulling them down.

"Oh, no you don't. I wasn't done looking my fill," he murmured. He bent his head, trailing hot, open-mouthed kisses down her neck, along her clavicle, pulling her bra strap down to continue his journey. She ran her hands up his chest, his muscles tensing under her touch. She swirled her fingers through his chest hair before running down and over his six-pack. His skin began to heat, desperate to have her hands all over him, begging for her touch.

He reached around to the clasp on her bra but paused before he unsnapped it. She nodded her consent and he flicked it open, drawing it away from her body. He looked at her breasts, perfect handfuls he couldn't wait to get his mouth on.

"You're exquisite," he breathed, and she let out a sigh. He bent his head, drawing her nipple into his mouth, rolling his tongue over the sensitive bead. She gasped and her hands flew into his hair, tugging sharply at the strands. He licked and sucked at her, then moved to its twin and gave it the same attention until she was writhing and babbling incoherently. He pulled back, his breath rasping from him, and unsnapped her shorts. She lifted her hips and he pulled them down and dropped them on the floor.

She was wearing a pair of black cotton panties, so

simple but so sexy. She was unmanning him with every moment. His emotions were going crazy, this wasn't like him at all, but he was desperate for her. He needed to build his wall back up before she overwhelmed him and crumbled his defenses.

"I'm sorry it's not matching," she said quietly, and his eyes flew to hers, his thoughts quieting. Did she not know she was killing him? Destroying him with her sweetness and sexiness? He shushed her concerns and fed her a savage kiss full of teeth and tongue. He needed this to stop feeling so gentle and tender before she ruined him for other women. *Ha! What other women?*

He didn't think she'd like it so raw and harsh, but he was wrong. So wrong. She reveled in it. His fingers dabbled at the edge of her panties, waiting for her consent. She nodded eagerly and he ripped them off her and slowly slid two fingers deep inside her tight, wet heat. She soaked his hand and he had to bite his lip to keep from this all being over very quickly. She bucked wildly against him and shocked him by begging for more. He never thought she'd be like this, his cock ached, desperate to get to her.

He removed his fingers and fumbled at the zipper on his jeans, his hands struggling from shaking so much, he needed to get a hold of himself, needed them to slow down. He was meant to be making this memorable for her but he was rushing too much, too greedy to get inside her. She rolled her hips, moaning at the loss of him as he tried to unzip and shrug the denim down his legs to his knees.

The next thing he saw was her hand drifting down her stomach. His mouth ran dry, and he stopped breathing. His sexy little harlot was about to do something very dirty, and he didn't plan on stopping her. He watched as her fingers found her center and stroked slowly. She arched her back, and tilted her head back, moaning. He watched her hand stroke lower, and she pushed two fingers inside.

Fuck.

He couldn't tear his gaze away from what she was doing. He watched as she worked herself, taking her pleasure. It was the most erotic thing he'd seen in his life. He thought he would be showing her what to do this evening, but as usual, she took charge.

He sat back on his heels and continued watching as she rolled her hips into each thrust of her fingers, riding the waves. When she brought her other hand to her breast, pinching her hardened nipples, he pulled his cock from his underwear. He squeezed himself hard, then stroked slowly up and down, moaning as he watched her.

At his moan, she lifted her head, seeing him, her eyes widened as she took in his hand on himself. She met his hot stare, her honey eyes glazed with passion, then flicked them back down to his cock. She started rubbing her clit, faster and he could tell she was getting closer. He was so close already, he couldn't believe it, but he blamed her for being so damn sexy. None of the other women he'd been with would have dreamt of touching themselves in front of him. He changed his mind, he didn't want sweet and delicate, he wanted this. He wanted raw, carnal passion. He wanted *her*.

Moisture gathered at the tip of his shaft, and he slicked his thumb over the head, spreading it around.

"Blake," she sighed his name as she buried her fingers in her pussy again, thrusting in and out. The sound of her fingers sliding through her wetness filled the room and had him tightening his grip and pumping harder in long strokes. She removed her fingers and reached for him, but he grabbed her hand and set it right back where it had been.

"Aren't we gonna have sex?" she asked, her already husky voice deepening with her arousal. He had planned on it, but now he was here with her, there were so many things he wanted to do that one time with her wouldn't be enough, he needed to stretch out their arrangement.

"Not tonight, honey. We're gonna build up to that, we're going to explore all the things we can do together," he replied, panting as he felt his release coiling. "For now, I want to see you make yourself come." She bit her lip and his cock throbbed in his fist.

"God, do you have any idea what this does to me, to see you touching yourself like that?" he rasped. A slow, sexy smirk crossed her lips and she got right back to it. He saw her fingers glisten in the soft light and he vowed next time he would taste her. He bet she tasted sweet and sinful.

She moaned, her fingers working faster. She was panting, her gasps getting higher and higher, and he knew she was close. She seemed to enjoy watching him too, she didn't tear her eyes away from where he worked himself. God, he was going to burst any minute, but he wanted to watch her fall apart first.

"Pinch your nipples hard and rub your clit faster," he commanded, his voice thick with desire. Her eyes flashed at his words and her breath hitched. *Did she enjoy dirty talk? Jesus, they were in for a world of pleasure if she did.*

"Feels so good," she moaned.

"Looks real good, too," he huffed out. Damn, she was beautiful. A sheen of perspiration glittered along her mocha skin.

"Make yourself come, now," he demanded. She tipped her head back, getting ready.

"No, Justine," he said, and she lifted her head to meet his eyes. "You stay right here, I want to see your eyes as you come."

That was all she needed. She cried out and jerked against her fingers as she climaxed. That husky cry of hers, combined with the sight of her, tipped him over the edge. He tilted his hips forward as he came, hard, spilling over her thighs. When he was spent, he collapsed next to her, their ragged breaths filling the room.

*

"Oh my God, I knew it!" The piercing shriek pulled Justine from her vivid dream of her night with Blake.

Taylor? Justine bolted upright in bed, as did the half-naked man lying next to her. *Not just a vivid dream after all.* She saw Taylor standing in her bedroom, clapping happily as she took in the sight of Justine and Blake in bed together, then fist-pumped the air.

"I'm the best matchmaker *ever*! Fuck yes!" she yelled jubilantly. Justine glanced down and saw she was still in her underwear, as was Blake. He growled at the intrusion and pulled the duvet over Justine's body, shielding her from view. She tried to ignore the sweetness of his gesture, not wanting to think about the gooey feeling inside it gave her. She heard more footsteps pounding and then Christy was running into the room, shouting,

"What's going on, I heard screaming!" Christy stopped dead when she took in Justine and Blake in bed together and a grin split her face before she rolled her eyes and groaned. Justine watched as she reached into her jeans pocket, pulled out a $20 bill, and slapped it into Taylor's waiting hand.

"What are you doing here?" Justine grumbled, side-eyeing Blake as embarrassment tinged her cheeks.

"How did you get in?" Blake growled. *Note to self,*

Justine thought, *he's not a morning person.*

"It's wedding dress day," Christy pouted, at the same time Taylor said, "With this mystical contraption. I put it in the door, turned it and *alakazam*, it opened!" She held up her spare key triumphantly.

"Wiseass," Blake muttered.

Justine flopped back onto the bed, groaning, "Sorry babe, I forgot. Let me get dressed and we can get going." Both women stayed in the room, staring at them with goofy grins on their faces.

"I need you to leave so I can do that," Justine pointed towards the door.

"Of course!" and "Sorry!" they muttered and then she was alone again with Blake. He cleared his throat and ran his hand over his beard, rasping the strands. She wanted to look at him, to see what he was thinking, but she was scared she would see regret written all over his face.

She got up and grabbed some clean clothes from her dresser before facing him. He stood beside the bed, his arms folded across his massive chest. She let her eyes run over him, this warrior in front of her with his combat-honed, battle-scarred body displaying all kinds of strength. Her eyes dropped to the bulge in his boxers which she was disappointed she hadn't gotten her hands on last night.

Not that she was complaining at all, what they'd done had been amazing, but she wanted to do more. His thighs, broad with muscle, caught her attention. This man radiated strength, he was nothing like she had seen before. She shivered with desire. Damn how she wanted him. The force of it scared her, what did it mean? *He doesn't want a family or children and he's your client, he is definitely not Mr. Right, no matter how right he looks,* her mind argued.

When she looked to his eyes, she noticed he was doing

the same to her, running his stare over her body, leaving goosebumps behind. His nostrils flared briefly before he turned away and grabbed his clothes.

She went into the adjoining bathroom and quickly got dressed. She brushed her teeth and hair, trying not to focus on her friends downstairs who would have lots of questions that she didn't know how to answer. When she came back into her bedroom, he was dressed, honestly it was a crime to cover that body up. He had even made her bed perfectly.

She was discovering that he was very caring. First the incident with the fox, then looking out for her on her date, and covering her body just now with the duvet, then last night, once they were finished fooling around, he cleaned where he marked her. He wasn't nearly as cold and distant as he acted which tugged at her heart in a way she couldn't afford to look at too closely.

"Are you okay after…?" he trailed off, gesturing to her bed.

"Yes, thank you. Are you?" she said shyly.

"Uh-huh. I'm sorry, I didn't mean to fall asleep after," he said, looking uncomfortable.

"Don't apologize, I didn't mind at all."

Last night she had gone downstairs to get some more wine and when she came back, he was fast asleep. He looked so relaxed, so carefree, his perma-frown smoothed away by slumber. She hadn't dared wake him, especially knowing he suffered from insomnia. It warmed her inside to think that he'd been so comfortable and relaxed here that he let his guard down enough to drift off.

"I better get going then, you've got plans and I've got a basketball game to win," he said, and she smiled.

"I didn't realize you did that. Is that with Dean and Beau?" she asked.

He nodded. "I've played with them a couple of times now, but it's not a big deal." He shrugged it off. But it *was* a big deal. He was building relationships and making friends which was a huge step in his recovery process.

They headed downstairs and she was pleased to note her friends had made themselves scarce. She opened the front door and watched as he put his jacket on and grabbed his helmet. She felt awkward, not knowing how to behave, having never been in this situation before. Did he regret last night? Did he want to act like it never happened? Did he want it to happen again, to continue their agreement? *Whoa, slow down, do you want it to happen again? YES!*

"Have a nice game with the guys," she said. He stopped in front of her, and she stepped back to let him pass.

"I'll pick you up tomorrow for our stakeout," he said, and she thought she saw his lips twitch slightly. Then, he bent down and pulled her earlobe between his teeth, nibbling gently and her body sighed. God, she loved it when he did that.

"Thanks for dinner," he murmured, then pulled back and winked at her. "And *dessert*," he added, a playful gleam in those silver eyes and she nearly melted in a puddle of aroused, romantic mush.

She watched him get on his motorbike, swinging a powerful leg over the seat. There was something about the way he straddled it and revved the engine that really revved *her* engine. Then he was gone. With a sigh, she shut the door and went into her living room. Both women were standing there smirking at her.

"Did you cash in your V card?" Christy asked, crossing her fingers. Justine rolled her eyes and laughed.

"Not quite," she replied, but they both squealed

anyway.

"Come on, we're going to be late." She hustled them both out the front door. She could already see Taylor had rearranged her bookshelf so it wasn't alphabetized anymore, she was a dick like that.

They got in Taylor's car and as they drove, they peppered her with questions the entire journey.

No, they didn't have sex.

Yes, he did look like a Greek God.

No, she wasn't giving them all the dirty details.

"So, we know from the guys that you've been treating him. Is that why you kept saying he wasn't your type? Because you didn't want to step over that line?" Taylor asked.

"He isn't my type though. He's too serious, too cold, too brooding. He has more baggage than an airport carousel. He's not interested in settling down and having a family, and it's messy which I didn't want," she sighed.

"Then what are you doing, sweetie?" Christy asked, concern in her voice. Justine didn't know how to answer.

"I just can't get him out of my mind."

"I know that feeling," Christy laughed.

"We're not judging you babe, if he's the one then nothing else matters. We just don't want you to get hurt. We know you've been saving yourself for someone special, for your person. We just want to make sure you don't regret anything," Taylor said, reaching over and stroking Justine's hair.

"I appreciate it. I love you both for that, I do. But he's not the one and I'm tired of missing out on all these amazing experiences. What if I never find *the one*? And the next thing I know, I'm fucking eighty and shriveled and wishing I'd been a bit freer with my body?" She could tell neither of them knew what to say.

"If you know he's not the one, do you think you might still end up developing feelings for him? If you're going to be intimate with him for the first time it might be hard not to get attached," Christy said.

"If I do begin to develop feelings then I'll break it off," Justine replied, firmly.

"Do you already have any of those feelings?" Christy asked cautiously.

"You've seen that body, right?" Justine joked, changing the subject so she didn't have to examine her own emotions. Taylor let out a low whistle.

"Oh mama," Christy purred, and they all laughed.

"Honestly, I'm fine. But thank you both for being so caring," Justine replied, putting them at ease. But even as she said the words, something didn't sit right in her stomach. She pushed the feeling aside and focused on trying to help her bestie find her perfect wedding dress, no matter how much of a bridezilla Christy turned out to be.

Chapter 14

The following day, Blake pulled up outside Justine's house to pick her up for their stakeout. The stakeout wasn't actually necessary because he'd found the Trashcan Bandits last week, it was just raccoons digging through trash and knocking the cans over. He didn't know why he'd kept it quiet, it probably had something to do with the chocolate-haired, vanilla-scented vixen he was waiting for.

The image of her naked body had imprinted itself on his brain and he saw it every time he closed his eyes. She was his constant distraction. Yesterday he'd played like shit, too busy thinking about how she looked with her hand between her thighs. The guys had looked at him like they knew exactly who he was thinking about. Christy had probably blabbed to Dean as soon as she saw them in bed together, and he had definitely told Beau, the dude was such a little gossip queen.

Blake couldn't believe he fell asleep in her bed. Not only that, but he hadn't even heard Christy and Taylor enter the house the next day. He should have been on alert for any threats, especially while he and Justine had been vulnerable. Some trained assassin he was. His skills were getting rusty, as was his focus. He needed to be more careful, that could have been any maniac breaking into her house to hurt her. He couldn't let his guard down again.

He was distracted by Justine getting in the car, her scent wafting over him, reminding him that he still hadn't tasted her. *Soon,* he promised himself.

"Good evening," she said, looking at him briefly, her eyes shifting away nervously.

"Hey yourself," he replied, starting the engine, and driving off to the same spot they had parked the week before. She buckled herself in but remained pressed up against the passenger door, a rabbit-in-the-headlights expression on her face. He leaned forward to turn the radio down and she jumped when he accidentally on purpose brushed her knee. He sighed inwardly, was she going to act like this around him when they were alone? He couldn't have that. The way she kept shooting him sneaky glances had him wondering if she was actually worried that he had regrets about their time together, or did she have any herself? His only regret was that they'd not been able to continue in the morning.

He parked up on the road and quickly scanned the quiet residential street. When Justine darted another nervous glance at him, he pinched the bridge of his nose.

"Just in case you're wondering, I don't have any regrets about what we did," he said. Out of the corner of his eye he saw her shoulders drop as she relaxed. She unbuckled her seatbelt and crossed her legs.

"Do you?" he gritted out when she didn't respond. He turned to face her, his eyes capturing hers. She shook her head slowly, a coy smile flirting with her lips.

"Good," he grunted, and then lifted her onto his lap.

"What are you doing?" she breathed, already running her hands up his chest and gripping his shoulders tight.

"It occurred to me yesterday, that if you were saving yourself, you probably missed out on some traditional teenage experiences. Like making out for hours in a car somewhere," he said, brushing her hair back behind her ear.

"Yes," she said, somehow injecting a shitload of enthusiasm into just one word, *so sexy*.

"That's what we're going to do tonight. And that's *all* we're doing," *Even if it killed him.*

"That's it? Still no sex?" she asked, sounding disappointed.

He lifted an eyebrow at her. "You wanna have sex right now? Where little Timmy could be coming back from Scouts and get an eyeful, becoming scarred for life?"

She laughed. "Obviously not now, I meant later."

"We'll get there," he began, pulling her down to nip and suck at her delicate throat. "And we'll have plenty of fun doing it," he whispered, not wanting to admit he was drawing out their time together for as long as possible. Because once they had sex, that was it, their deal was done and he wasn't ready for it to end just yet. He trailed kisses up her neck, to the corner of her mouth where he dipped his tongue over the cute little beauty spot that rested at the crease.

They kissed for the longest time. He took the lead, playing with her, teasing her. He had to hold her still when she got restless and started arching into him and didn't that just churn his butter. He had been an idiot to think they could just kiss, and it wouldn't lead to anything else when he was dying to throw her in the backseat and whip out his handcuffs. He was harder than a steel pipe and definitely needed some alone time when he got home.

Then she took the lead, she taunted and teased him. Exploring his mouth, then moving away and kissing his cheeks, jaw and neck. He fought every instinct to pin her down and pound inside her until she was screaming his name. But he kept his word, and it was the hardest test of restraint he'd ever faced.

When he finally couldn't take anymore, he moved her back to the passenger seat and started the engine. He flicked on the air conditioning, needing it to clear the windows they had steamed up. While he waited, he looked at her. Her eyes were glazed, her lips swollen and pink, her cheeks flushed. She looked stunningly aroused and satisfaction flared through him.

A flash of movement caught his attention, he turned to look through the windshield. He watched as a man appeared on the sidewalk and got into a waiting car. There was nothing suspicious in the action itself, but he realized he had seen it last week too. It was the way the guy was walking, cautious like he was trying to keep quiet, moving quickly as though he didn't want anyone to see him. He cast furtive glances up and down the road and kept looking over his shoulder. As the car drove off, Blake put it out of his mind and tried to stop being so suspicious. It was probably just a couple of teenagers sneaking off together. This was a small town, nothing significant happened here. Hell, the biggest crime problem they had was raccoons.

He drove Justine home and chuckled as she stomped inside and slammed her door shut, obviously still annoyed he hadn't given her an orgasm. He went home and had a shower, jerked off while thinking about Justine, groaning her name as he climaxed. No other woman had ever invaded his thoughts like her.

He watched TV for a little while before finally heading to bed. He'd had the best sleep in years at Justine's house the other night. In her comfortable bed, with her scent surrounding him and feeling satisfied from their sexcapade, he'd drifted off, which was unheard of for him the last few months. Now tonight, as every night, she invaded his thoughts over and over until he was hard again.

"Jesus Christ, get a hold of yourself," he growled, shoving her out of his mind, annoyed that she plagued his thoughts so much.

At 4am he stopped trying to sleep and went to the spare bedroom that he turned into a gym. As he worked out, his thoughts drifted back to her and this time, he let them. He was already looking forward to seeing her again, but he was anxious about talking to her and opening up, then she would know exactly how fucked up he was.

On Wednesday, Blake turned up to Justine's office surprisingly eager for their session. He had a massive panic attack the day before at the station and he was tired. He just wanted this to be over with. He wanted to be back to normal, whatever that even meant anymore. He had to keep reminding himself that his journey was a marathon, not a sprint.

He chatted with Hilda briefly, she had a knack for drawing him into conversation, *damn small-town charm*. When it was time, he went into Justine's office and shut the door. She spun around in her chair, facing him. One long toned leg crossed over the other and damn, he tried not to get aroused but he was only human.

"Morning, Blake," she said in her bland, professional voice. God, that voice ticked him off. It just made him want to remind her that she'd been writhing in his lap, begging for him to make her come less than forty-eight hours ago. But he didn't; he was a gentleman like that.

"How are you?" she asked, sitting across from him when he took his seat on the couch. She folded her hands in her lap and smiled at him. He thought back to their session last week and how much things had changed between them in that time. He felt anxious about opening up but he realized he trusted her and he wanted her help. She had already done more than any other psychologist or therapist he had seen so if anyone could help him, it would be her. He ran his hand through his hair and his stomach churned as he prepared to open up and let her see the beast inside.

"Um, not great," he answered honestly. Her eyes widened and she sat up straighter in her chair, her brow pinched in concern.

"Really? Do you want to tell me about it?" she asked, hope lining her words. He met her honey eyes, beseeching him, begging him to open up and let her help. *A deal's a deal,* he reminded himself.

"I had another panic attack yesterday; it was pretty bad."

"Do you know what brought it on?"

He shrugged. "I was reading some case notes about a suicide and think it triggered memories of the incident in Anderson."

"How did you feel having another panic attack?"

He thought for a moment. "Frustrated, tired, fed up.

I'd felt like I was doing okay and then this comes along and reminds me that I'm not." He flushed at finally admitting that he wasn't okay. She came and sat next to him, facing him, her expression and eyes earnest. She was one of the most genuine people he had ever met.

"You shouldn't feel like this is a step back at all. Your progress won't be a straight trajectory showing immediate improvement. It'll be bumpy, you'll have setbacks and sometimes it might feel worse than ever but that's the journey and you can't let it discourage you," she said.

She was right. Of course he wouldn't be fixed at once. It had taken years of trauma to slowly break him down, he wouldn't be rebuilt in a few sessions. But he struggled to remember that at the time when the episodes hit.

"How do you feel when you're having a panic attack?" she asked. "Describe it to me."

He swiveled on the couch to face her better and their knees touched, but he didn't move away. He wanted to feel connected to her. He was enjoying talking to her and the emotional and mental connection they were creating. It felt like true companionship, something he couldn't remember having experienced before.

"My breathing starts getting out of control, that's what usually leads to me passing out."

"Okay, what else?"

"My uh…chest gets tight and burns, my vision starts to go, and my hands shake. I hear ringing in my ears and my entire body shakes. I also feel nauseated."

She smiled triumphantly and he felt himself smiling at her reaction before he wiped it from his face.

"Great, thank you. So, it sounds to me like it starts to attack some of your senses and your basic motor functions. There's a couple of things I can show you to help combat this while we're working through your thought process. They'll take practice, it'll be hard but you're a very focused and determined person, so I know you can do it," she said, and he felt his chest puff up with pride at her words. He *was* focused and determined, he had built his career around that. He'd just lost his way recently and needed to remember who he was. He would not be beaten by this and with her help, he would conquer it.

"The one I would like to work through today is the five to one technique. It's a grounding technique that's useful in situations of strong emotion, like panic. This will be most effective if you use it to try and pull yourself out of the panic attack by focusing on something else, to distract your mind, which is where this is all stemming from."

He nodded, trying to absorb what she was saying.

"It'll be difficult when you're in the throes of a panic attack, but this is why we practice, so you'll be able to recall it easier. It starts off with naming five things you can see," she added and then paused like she was waiting for him to start speaking.

"Oh, you wanna start now?" he asked. She nodded. "Okay, uh…" he looked around the room, feeling stupid because his mind completely blanked.

"Bookcase, desk, plant, pen and phone," he finished, and she smiled at him.

"Great! Now what are four things you can feel?"

"Like, emotions or physical sensations? Objects?" he asked, unsure.

"Anything, any of those. It's whatever you want to grab onto that will ground you, whether that's physically or mentally."

"Okay, uh, well I can feel the couch," he began, and he closed his eyes, feeling awkward again, but he wanted to concentrate.

"Denim," he said, touching his jeans. "Hungry and…" He cleared his throat. "Nervous." He opened his eyes to find her beaming at him, that damn smile that always made him feel like a superhero.

"You're doing great, you've got the hang of it! Now, what are three things you can hear?"

He closed his eyes again, needing to focus. He tried to shut out the world and used his instincts to home in on his hearing.

"I can hear…birds singing outside. Hilda talking on the phone, and my pulse pounding in my ears."

"What are two things you can smell?"

That was easy, it was her. He smelled her this whole time, her scent forever branded in him. He closed his eyes and inhaled deeply, getting the full hit. His jeans tightened over his crotch, and he inhaled again, reveling in the delectable scent of her.

"Vanilla and chocolate," he replied gruffly. There was a pause, and he opened his eyes to find her staring at him. Her cheeks slightly pink, she seemed to drift off somewhere, her eyes getting a faraway look before she came back to herself with a small jolt.

"What is one thing you can taste?" she asked, her voice slightly huskier. He blinked at the sound of it and tried to force himself to focus on the question and not on the sinful lips that had formed it. He couldn't taste anything except mint from his toothpaste. What he was dying to taste was her, but she didn't think she would appreciate that response.

"Mint," he answered eventually.

"And you're done!" she cheered and clapped her hands. His lips twitched at how adorable she was. "It's not very difficult but it requires focus and attention.

Having to think about everything to list will distract your brain from what it's trying to do, it disrupts the pattern of the attack," she explained. "It'll take some practice. It's hard to train your mind and we want you to get to a point where you'll be able to recall quickly, but don't be discouraged by setbacks."

He had reservations. He knew what he was like when he had an attack—nothing could break him out of it—hell, he'd been trying to do that for years. It sounded like a good technique, but he didn't know how successful he would be at implementing it and didn't want to disappoint her.

"So, let's go again and start from the top," she said.

They spent the rest of the session going over it again and again. She pushed him to come up with different answers each time and he got frustrated, growling, and snapping at her the more exhausted he became. But by the end, he felt a little…calmer? Like he'd been armed with a weapon for the next attack, that was how she put it. He found it sweet that she put it in a context that would speak to him and that he would understand.

When she walked him to the door to say goodbye, he was so desperate to kiss her that he had to clench his fists to stop himself from reaching for her. He knew she wanted to remain professional here and he could at least give her that after essentially blackmailing her.

He said goodbye and left her office feeling lighter than he had for a while, all thanks to her. The only problem was his old insecurities rearing their head. He'd let his guard down, he had been vulnerable and weak. He didn't want her seeing him like that and needed to work out how to reset the boundaries.

Chapter 15

Justine was late to the sleepover again. She got into her car and set off for Taylor's. As per tradition, she was already in her pajamas, this time she had gone for her favorite peach satin camisole nightdress. She looked around the streets as she drove, not expecting to see anybody else out this late at night. She hadn't expected to see anyone out so late last time either, damn that fox for running out in front of her and making Blake her late-night hero. She made a mental note to find out how the fox was doing.

Blake. She sighed at the thought of him. Their make-out session had thrilled her as much as it had frustrated her. She loved that he was thinking about how to make this as good as possible for her, and that he was taking his time and didn't just jump to sex straight away. Annoyingly though, seeing this sweet side of him was making her desperate. *Stupid, sexy, broody, broken man.*

Their session on Wednesday had blown her mind. She hadn't expected him to open up at all, she could see he struggled with it but eventually he'd given in. He had shown her a whole new side to him, the deep, emotionally vulnerable side that she didn't know existed and had been dying to find. He had opened up to her and she had been able to show him some of the techniques she'd been researching. His willingness to try them and his persistence pleased her.

The only problem was, he was ticking more and more of her Mr. Right boxes and that concerned her. She wanted to find her true love, it couldn't be Blake, and she was beginning to get attached to him which wasn't good.

Bright lights flashed in her rear-view mirror, distracting her, as a police cruiser pulled up behind her. The road ahead was deserted so they could only be signalling her. She pulled over, worrying. She had been so lost in her thoughts that she wasn't sure if she'd been speeding. She checked her mirror again and saw an officer stepping out of the cruiser, the headlights so blinding she couldn't see more than a pair of legs as they walked towards her.

"Just stay calm," she murmured, then smoothed her hands through her hair and down over her-

"Fuck!" she hissed when she remembered she was only in a nightie. Okay, that was it, she wouldn't *ever* turn up to the sleepover in her pjs again, she would always change once she got to Taylor's. She had definitely learned her lesson. She couldn't even cover herself with a blanket because it had gone to the vet with the fox the other week.

"Evening, officer," she cooed, hoping to flirt her way

out of the big, fat fine she was about to receive.

"License and registration, ma'am," came a familiar deep voice.

She looked up and saw Blake standing there, his arms folded across his massive chest. His expression deadly serious, more serious than he normally was. Her stomach fluttered, he looked so hard and aggressive, it sent a little thrill through her. She would definitely need to dissect *that* later.

"Blake?"

"I said license and registration, now," he demanded, flicking his gaze over her and then away.

"Oh, okay, just a moment," she rummaged in her purse. Thank God she had brought that with her at least. Would he go easy on her and just let her off with a warning? She found her license and held it out to him. He snatched it out of her hand. He seemed so tense, his jaw clenched as he studied her license, his shoulders drawn tight. Was she in serious trouble here?

Blake fixed her with a blank stare and then shook his head, letting out a disappointed sigh. He reached for the handle and popped the door open.

"Step out of the vehicle for me." His voice was firm, his jaw still clenched.

"Blake? Am I in some kind of trouble here? I'm sorry if I was speeding, I'll be more careful next time," she promised.

He stared down at her, his eyes cold and devoid of emotion in the moonlight, his look said *don't make me ask you again*. She reluctantly got out of the car and stood in front of him. His eyes took in her outfit and a muscle ticked under his eye. She suddenly felt very self-conscious despite him having already seen her naked. She tried to cover herself, but he grabbed hold of her arm and brought her to stand in front of her car.

"Place your hands on the hood of the vehicle. Now!"

She did as he said, gritting her teeth as she felt the evening breeze kiss the backs of her bare thighs. If she bent any further forward her panties would be on display. He started patting her down.

"Is this really necessary? Where exactly would I be hiding something?" she grumbled past the tidal wave of arousal that spread through her as his fingers stroked over her skin, gently, like he was caressing a lover, not a suspect.

"I pulled you over for disturbing the peace," he said, his voice low.

"What? That's ridiculous! When did I do that?" she demanded, her eyes rolling back in her head as he stroked over her ass. He bent forward and nuzzled the sensitive skin between her neck and shoulder, his beard rasping deliciously.

"Disturbing the peace in my pants," he murmured. His words took a moment to register then she burst out laughing, straightening and all her worry disappeared.

"Please tell me you didn't just say that?" she gasped through her giggles.

"I'm glad you found it so amusing," he grumbled, but she could hear the humor in his tone. She turned to face him. His eyes dancing in the moonlight and his pouty mouth had her laughing all over again. He crowded her against the car.

"Go ahead and get your laughs in now, honey. You won't be laughing in a minute, you'll be begging," he taunted, and cupped her breasts, stroking his thumbs over her nipples. Her eyelids fluttered closed, and her head dropped forward to rest on his broad chest.

"You're lucky I'm letting you touch me after a line like

that," she sighed in pleasure.

"That reminds me, I was looking for a concealed weapon," he said, grabbing her hips, he spun her back around. And slowly, so slowly, bent her forward at the waist, her round ass pressing into his pelvis, and she groaned as she came up against his hard arousal.

"I think I found it," she hissed.

"Shush, honey. You'd better let the professionals handle this."

She was only too happy to let him take control. He stroked down her spine, over her ass and pulled her nightie up and dabbled with the edge of her panties.

"I'm not even going to ask why you're driving around wearing only this, I'm just grateful," he groaned, pressing his pelvis into her harder. He palmed her cheeks, then stroked down the outside of her thighs before running his hands up the inside and cupping her sex.

"God, you're so wet already," he husked. She moaned as he stroked a finger over the material covering her, and her head dropped forward between her outstretched arms. He kicked her legs apart and she heard him moving then his head was between her legs. Her breath hitched in her throat in anticipation. Was he going to use his hands? His mouth? Were they going to have sex, finally? *Please God let us have sex!*

He placed gentle kisses to the cotton-covered globes of her ass, nibbling her cheeks through her panties before he buried his face between her legs. His tongue licking her through the material. She swayed on her feet from the pleasure and moaned loudly, the sound carrying through the quiet night, and she gripped the hood of her car tightly.

His tongue stroked her harder, the cotton grazing her sensitive bud in the most amazing way, sticking to her flesh. He ran his hands up the backs of her thigh and gripped her ass, pulling her into his mouth harder, she leaned into each stroke until she was nearly riding his face.

He worked a hand under the edge of her underwear and slid a finger inside her. She cried out, clenching around him. He pulled her panties to the side and stroked his tongue over the heart of her.

"Fuck, you taste so good," he growled, and ate at her again. She reached down between her legs and gripped the back of his head, rolling her hips into his mouth, desperate for release. She was so swept away by the sensations she forgot they were on the road in the middle of the night. He continued to lick and suck at her center, while his fingers slid in and out of her, causing little whimpers to leave her throat as her climax neared.

"Please, Blake," she moaned, and he grunted in approval. He sucked her clit hard and her orgasm slammed into her with fierce intensity, her cries echoed through the night. As she stood there, trembling from the force, he placed soft kisses to her thighs, before standing and turning her to face him, wrapping her in his strong arms. She reached to cup him, but he tilted his pelvis away from her.

"This wasn't about me," he said, and she stared at him. This was becoming a theme for him, giving her what her body needed but not taking anything for himself. It was too sweet, but she wasn't going to stand for it anymore. She rubbed herself against him, feeling him hot and hard in his jeans, the material abrading her bare skin.

"Why won't you let me please you?" she asked, rolling her hips against him again, gripping his shoulders to steady herself. She leaned up and fit her lips to his throat and sucked. He swayed forward slightly, his eyes fluttering closed and when she arched against him again, he met her halfway with a thrust of his own. His eyes shot open at the contact, molten silver entrancing her.

"Soon," he promised and then took her hand and drew her around to the driver's side door of her car. He bent down and placed a chaste kiss on her lips.

"You scared me," she said, changing the subject.

He smirked down at her. "I'm sorry about that. But, didn't you teach me that everything is heightened when our emotions are engaged? You're welcome."

Dammit, she had.

He patted her ass. "Go on, get to your sleepover."

She squinted at him. "How did you know that's where I was going?"

"Because Dean's a little gossip queen," he laughed. It took her a moment to tear herself away from him and that smug grin on his face.

"I'll escort you, make sure you get there safely," he said. She nodded and got in the car. It's just as well she didn't have far to go, her legs were like jelly after that orgasm. Diabolical man.

She drove off and true to his word, he followed closely behind her and when she pulled into the parking lot of the bar, he waited until she went inside Taylor's. Just before she walked in at the door, she turned back, and on a whim, blew him a kiss. He didn't respond but she could have sworn she saw a big, goofy grin on his face as he drove off.

*

Blake slammed shut the file he was reading and pounded his fist on the desk, hard. Pain shot through his hand. The previous sheriff had been a no-good dirty cop. A nasty piece of work and Blake was frankly pleased he was no longer around. He was resisting the urge to dig up his corpse just to kill and bury him all over again.

"You okay, boss?" Jim said, poking his head around the door, his kind face pinched with concern.

"Yes, thank you Jim," Blake tried to smile, not wanting to worry the old man. Jim fixed him with a look that said he didn't believe him but was good enough not to openly call Blake on his bullshit.

"You heading off?" Blake asked.

"Yeah, the book club should have disbanded by now," Jim sighed.

"Do they meet at your place?"

"Oh yes, every Saturday afternoon. Hil loves hosting and I don't mind, whatever makes her happy, but this book they're reading…" He clucked his tongue, a scandalized look crossing his face. "Fifty shades of something or other. It sounds like absolute filth, you should hear them tittering over it like teenagers!" he cried with indignation and Blake wiped a hand over his mouth, concealing his smile.

"I had to step out for a few hours," Jim's cheeks turned pink. "Anyway, Hil's been having cooking lessons with Justine, and I can't wait to see what exotic treat we're having tonight, it'll be *muy caliente*!" Jim winked and this time Blake couldn't stop his chuckle, mainly over Jim butchering Spanish.

Blake clearly wasn't a very good detective as it wasn't until Jim's words registered that he realized that Jim was married to Hilda, Justine's secretary. The knowledge that these two, kind-hearted, good-natured people had found each other and spent their life together warmed Blake's cold heart.

Blake stood. "Come on then, I'll walk you out," he said, clapping Jim on the back. "Tell Hilda I said hi," he added.

"Oh, you know my Hil, do you?" Jim asked, the note of pride in his voice was unmistakable and Blake's affection for the couple grew. Of course Hilda wouldn't reveal who Justine's clients were.

"Just being friendly," he lied.

They said goodnight and Blake went back to his desk, his thoughts once again returning to Sheriff Black. He flipped open the file and started reading again. It didn't take him long, the file was mostly redacted, but why would it need to be? Likely because it held something incriminating. Blake had been investigating Black since Jim had told him all about his predecessor. So far Blake had only uncovered a pile of cases that contained false statements, missing evidence and a lot of redacted documents.

He had reached out to a number of witnesses on some of these cases and had received the same story multiple times. Witnesses had been visited by two men, most likely the sheriff's cronies, because he couldn't be seen to do the dirty work himself, and coerced into changing their story. It looked like the sheriff had been a small-town mobster, someone you didn't want to owe a favor to.

Blake fumed at the idea of Sheriff Black ruling this close-knit, friendly community with fear. Blake wanted to make sure everyone here felt safe and valued and that they would be listened to. He was protecting this town now and dammit he would ensure he was protecting his people to the best of his ability.

The thing that bugged Blake the most was how Rebelle had gotten involved with him? She seemed like a kind, genuine woman. She ran an animal shelter, for Christ's sake. How could she be mixed up with such an evil, violent and abusive man? Blake remembered Jim said she had come in to make a complaint of harassment. He would have to take a look and see if a file had been created.

Maybe he would stop by and visit her, just to have a little chat and see if that unearthed anything. Blake would see if Jim knew anything more about her, he was pretty knowledgeable on all the town's history, maybe Blake could pop round for a beer one night and pick his brains. Jim was a good man with good values, the kind of man you could count on, and Blake was beginning to like him more and more.

He imagined himself and Jim talking over old cases at the kitchen table, over a couple of cold ones, while Justine taught Hilda to cook in the kitchen. Justine would drag Blake and Jim into helping them, offering samples to taste while Blake dabbled with her apron strings and murmured to her to keep the apron on when they got home. She would playfully slap his chest but then whisper in his ear that maybe he would be the one wearing it instead. They would all sit together and eat, and Justine would teach Jim Spanish while Hilda and Blake chatted about basketball, since he discovered she was a huge fan a few weeks back.

Blake shook himself out of the daydream. *Where the hell had that come from?* He was surprised at how right it felt, how peaceful it was, how perfect. He rubbed his chest trying to dull the ache that had appeared. Damn, this town was getting under his skin. *She* was getting under his skin. He had only seen her last night and yet he hadn't stopped thinking about her.

He couldn't explain how she affected him so much. Was it because she was working her way through his various problems? He'd opened up to her more than he had with anyone else, including Katie, and he was starting to like it. He liked that she knew him the most, that she wasn't judging him, that she was helping him yet still wanted to be intimate even though she knew his darkest thoughts, like she still found him worthy.

Last night had been incredible, his jeans tightening as he replayed it, focusing on her begging him. He loved that he brought out that side of her, a side no one else had ever experienced, it was all for him. She didn't put on a show of acting sexy, she didn't do things to be attractive, it was all natural.

After torturing himself with thoughts of Justine for another fifteen minutes he finally gave in and left the station. Maybe he would swing by her place on his way home and see if she was free. As he made his way to the cruiser, glancing down the street, he spotted the light on in her office. Ignoring the giddy feeling that tried to overtake him, he left his vehicle and headed in that direction. The closer he got to her office, the more his excitement mounted at the prospect of seeing her, it was embarrassing really. He gritted his teeth and tried to convince himself that it was just because he wanted to hurry up and get her naked again, but he couldn't fool himself, it was something more. Something he didn't entirely recognize.

He was about to enter her office when he nearly collided with someone. He had been so deep in his thoughts that he didn't notice anyone was around. He grunted in irritation at his lack of attention, he had neglected his training once again.

"Evening, Deputy Miller."

He looked down and saw Rebelle standing in front of him. Her eyes wide and darting between him and the door to Justine's office. She took a step backwards, then another and folded her arms across her chest, adopting a defensive stance.

"Rebelle, how are you?" he asked, pleased he had run into her.

"Fine, yourself?"

"Very well thank you," he replied, darting his eyes to Justine's office. If he'd been quicker, he would already be inside, and she would be in his arms. No one would have caught him but as it was, he didn't want to go in there and have a witness.

"How is she?" Rebelle asked, pinning him with her sharp stare.

"I'm not sure I follow?" Blake replied. *Shit, does Rebelle know about me and Justine?*

"Yes, you do. I followed up with the vet and they told me everything." Her doe-eyes lit with amusement. *Double shit, busted.*

"She's doing great, her leg has healed nicely," Blake said. His answer seemed to soften something inside this timid firecracker.

"I'm pleased. If you need any help at all just let me know, or swing by the shelter," she said.

"You too, Rebelle. And I mean that, I know you tried to make a complaint a little while ago. I guarantee you my full support if you ever wanted to come back and make another one."

She regarded him for a moment, she probably didn't trust him as far as she could throw him. But he needed her to know, he needed *the town* to know, he would protect them all, with his dying breath if that's what it came to. Unlike their previous sheriff.

"You've probably heard this before but, I'm different, I swear you can trust me." He reached into the back pocket of his jeans and pulled out his card, offering it to her. His outstretched arm hung between them until she reluctantly took it from him.

Awkward silence hung in the air. She glanced towards Justine's office and then away again quickly but stayed where she was. He couldn't go in and have Rebelle see him, but she didn't appear to be going anywhere. Why wasn't she leaving? He was impatient to get inside and wrap Justine in his arms, bury his face in her hair and inhale her mouth-watering scent. Jesus, who was he? His level of need to see Justine irritated him, he didn't want to become too attached. It was precisely the strength of his desire that made him leave. With a final, regretful glance towards the door, he said goodbye to Rebelle and left. He stormed back to his cruiser. Getting inside, he slammed the door with more force than was necessary. As he pulled away from the curb, he glanced around and noticed Rebelle was gone, she wasn't anywhere on the street. He drove home, not looking forward to a long night of cold showers and boredom. Hopefully, the boredom wouldn't be broken up by any panic attacks.

Chapter 16

Justine was packing up her stuff for the evening when she heard the door to the office open. She berated herself for not locking it like Blake told her to and for a moment wondered if it was him that had come to see her. Her stomach fluttered in anticipation at the thought. *Ugh!* She couldn't stop thinking about him, and how wonderfully skilled he was at particular *activities*. Heat pooled low in her belly at the memory of his mouth on her last night and a little moan nearly slipped out.

She pushed the thoughts out of her mind as her visitor came into the room, and she was surprised to see who it was.

"Hi Rebelle, how are you?"

Rebelle looked around quietly, her big eyes taking in all the details of the office, the action reminding Justine so much of Blake. Her heart clenched. *What ghosts haunted Rebelle to cause such an action?*

Rebelle swiped her tongue over her lip and shook her head. "It was stupid to come here," she muttered, squeezing her eyes shut. She spun on her heel and left the room.

"You'll regret leaving more than you'll regret whatever it was you came to say," Justine called after her, hoping her words reached Rebelle. She held her breath waiting for a response. Rebelle was a mystery to a lot of people in this town, Justine included. She usually stayed away from everyone and kept to herself.

The town talked. The majority of them believed that Rebelle murdered her husband, and they didn't trust her, she was a black widow, a bad penny, an outcast. No one wanted her around, believing she left a trail of disaster wherever she went, except Christy. Christy had become close with Rebelle when they were all at school together so if Christy liked and trusted her then Justine did too.

The silence stretched on until finally Rebelle peeked from around the doorframe and Justine was boosted by a flare of satisfaction.

"What can I help you with?" Justine asked softly.

Rebelle hung her head, her fingers picking at a hole in her denim shorts that Justine didn't think was there for fashionable reasons. She looked Rebelle over: her sandals were held together with some tape and the strap on her top looked like it had snapped and been tied back together to keep it up. She was too thin, her hair which had been so shiny as a child now looked dull and lifeless. Sympathy surged through Justine. *How much help did Rebelle need?*

"I was, uh, thinking that it might be nice to talk to someone," Rebelle mumbled, vulnerability pouring off her in waves. There was a pause and when she didn't say more, Justine spoke up.

"Well, thank you for choosing me to come and see, what did you want to talk about?" Justine sat in the armchair and gestured to the couch opposite for Rebelle to sit. Rebelle stepped into the room and walked over, perching on the arm like she was giving into the situation but not fully committing to it yet. She was a fighter though, Justine could see it.

She waited patiently for Rebelle to continue speaking, the situation reminding her of Blake's first few sessions where he refused to talk, just watching her with that hot, intense stare of his.

"Is there something in particular you wanted to talk about? Something you need help with?" Justine asked patiently.

Rebelle met her stare, tears pooling in those doe-eyes, magnifying them. "Yes," she breathed. "But, uh, money is a problem. I don't really have a lot spare. I was wondering if you had some kind of payment plan?" She nibbled her bottom lip nervously.

Justine only thought about it for a split second before she made her decision. She earned plenty from some of her other clients who paid top rate, money wasn't an issue, and she certainly wouldn't feel good about taking what little money Rebelle had to offer. She could feel herself being lured again by the challenge of being able to truly help someone. It was the easiest decision she'd made, but she could see the pride shining in Rebelle's eyes, she wouldn't take a handout from anyone.

"I do have payment plans but I don't think that's what we need," Justine began.

"Oh," Rebelle said softly, her shoulders dropping. Justine got up and went over to her desk and flicked through her calendar.

"What I think we should do is meet up every Thursday at 6pm for a coffee and a chat," Justine said.

Rebelle's head shot up; she fixed her with a questioning look.

"You can meet me here and we can catch up, like old friends do. I'll bring the coffee, and for that hour, we can talk about anything you like."

A ghost of a smile hit Rebelle's wide mouth.

"Anything." Justine repeated meaningfully. She came back to sit in front of Rebelle and held out her card. "If we're just having a friendly chat over a coffee then money doesn't need to come into it. Now you have my number too, so if anything comes up outside of our Thursday catch up, you can just call up your new friend—me—and we can chat."

Rebelle took the card and Justine noticed she had another piece of paper already crumpled in her fist.

"I don't know what to say. I don't think I can accept this," she whispered brokenly.

"Everyone needs a friend to talk to, that's all this is. I really can't wait for our first chat," Justine flashed her a bright smile and Rebelle let out a gentle chuckle.

"Thank you, that's very generous of you."

"Don't mention it. Now did you want a coffee now or to talk about anything? I have plenty of time?" Justine asked. Rebelle's expression shuttered, and she stiffened.

"No, thank you. I think I'll come back next week for our catch up if that's okay?" she replied.

"Absolutely fine, I'm looking forward to it already," Justine smiled again and Rebelle stood and headed for the door with Justine close behind her.

"I've been meaning to ask you actually, how's the fox doing, did you hear back from the vet?" Justine asked.

Rebelle regarded her quizzically. "What do you mean?"

"Was it able to be released back into the wild yet?"

"You've not spoken to Deputy Miller about the fox, have you?" Rebelle's mouth quirked up on one side.

"No, why?"

Rebelle filled her in, and Justine was stunned. She said goodbye to Rebelle and went back into her office to grab her things. That man was such an enigma, the more she learned about him, the more confused she became. All she knew was, she couldn't wait another night without seeing him. She left her office, hurrying to her car. She had to stop off at home first, there was something she needed to get.

*

She had stolen his address from his file. *Just another ethical violation to add to my growing list,* she thought as she knocked on Blake's front door. There was a pause before it swung open and then there he was.

"Well, well, well, what do we have here?" he smirked down at her, folding his arms over that powerful chest and leaning casually against the doorframe. He looked so smug, standing there in his hoodie and gray sweatpants that she took her time running her eyes over him, trying to unnerve him. Her slow, blatantly sexual perusal must have worked because the next thing she knew, she was being dragged inside.

"Get in here," he growled. She giggled and entered the hallway, the door closing behind her with an ominous *click*. Then they were alone, on his turf, surrounded by his scent. That seductive scent that turned her into a silly, silly woman who abandoned all her principles for a night in his arms, in his bed.

She tore her eyes away from him and glanced around his house, eager to see where he lived. The walls were exposed red brick with varnished wooden floors running throughout. Minimalist décor was definitely his style, very industrial loft-themed. The place screamed masculinity and she loved it. She turned to face him and arched a haughty brow.

"I know about your other woman," she said. He regarded her quizzically and began to open his mouth, but she interrupted.

"Don't bother making excuses, I know your little secret." His adorable secret that had sealed the deal for her. She followed the sound of the TV and headed into the living room. "Is she in here?"

He followed her and she watched as realization dawned on him and his cheeks darkened in the cutest way. Justine walked into the room, the exposed brick and wooden flooring continuing. There was a black leather couch and matching loveseat, a huge TV mounted to the wall was showing some kind of sport and an impressive-looking sound system took up the other wall. A black and glass coffee table held various remotes and a beer which was sitting on a coaster. If she hadn't already planned on sleeping with him tonight, the beer on a coaster would have sealed the deal.

She spotted a red fleece blanket piled in a mound on the couch. She looked back and forth between the blanket and Blake until he sighed and nodded. With excitement, she carefully pulled back the fold of the fleece to reveal the cutest little face she had ever seen.

"Hello angel," she cooed, and the fox's tail started pounding under the fleece. Justine reached out a hand slowly, not wanting to startle her. The fox sniffed her gently, then licked her hand and started squirming in the blanket, chittering away happily.

"She, uh, wants you to rub her belly," Blake said

gruffly, rubbing the back of his neck, his pink cheeks darkening another shade.

"Oh, does she?" Justine cooed again before delving into the warm, bristly fur. The fox squirmed even more and chittered again, getting excited, and Justine giggled when it nipped her playfully.

"She's adorable," she said, looking back at Blake who was watching her with a strange look on his face. The fox jumped up and grabbed a small rubber ball with her mouth before trotting over to Blake and dumping it at his feet expectantly. Her tail was so thick and glorious and there was only a slight limp when she walked. Justine's stomach twisted, even though it was an accident, the idea that she'd hurt the animal made her feel ill.

The fox shuffled impatiently on the spot and stared intensely at the ball. Blake pinched his nose, sighing and then kicked the ball out into the hallway. The fox charged after it, her claws scrabbling on the hardwood floors. Justine burst out laughing at the chagrined look on Blake's face.

"She fetches?" Justine asked as the fox trotted back in with the ball and dropped it at Blake's feet again. He kicked it away once more.

"It's been really great for strengthening Penelope's leg." He shrugged like it was nothing, but it was too obvious the work he had put into rehabilitating her.

"Penelope?" she asked, a smile forming on her lips.

"Yeah, Penny for short," he replied, picking invisible lint off his hoodie and avoiding eye contact. Justine sauntered over to Blake, not stopping until their torsos touched. She felt his pecs flex as they came up against each other and she peered up at him from under her lashes. His nostrils flared and his eyes heated, scorching her with their intensity.

"I see why you kept her a secret. You didn't want me to know that under that motorcycle-riding, leather-wearing, musclebound warrior façade, you had a marshmallow heart. Well, I've got news for you, tough guy," she paused, his closeness fogging her senses. His eyes dipped to her mouth, and he ran his tongue over his lips, slowly, like he could already taste her. "I already knew that," she murmured. Before she could blink, his arm snapped out and snaked around her hips, pulling her flush against him. She gasped as she came up against his erection. His dark chuckle consumed her.

"I think I'm going to hear that gasp a lot this evening," he said, his voice low and dangerous. He dipped his head, his lips a breath away and her eyelids fluttered closed in anticipation. His nose brushed against hers, her breathing deepened. He nuzzled across her cheek and down her neck, hovering there. She swallowed thickly as desire burned through her like wildfire, making her come alive. She had never felt like this with another, never *burned* for someone before. Would it be like this with any man or was it just her and Blake's chemistry? She had a feeling she knew the answer.

"You do something to me. I don't know if I like it," he murmured against her skin. He placed a soft kiss to the hollow of her throat, and she sighed, sinking deeper into him. He trailed his lips up her neck and teased the corner of her mouth, driving her wild. Just when she thought she couldn't take anymore, they were interrupted by a high-pitched bark.

Justine pulled back and looked down between their bodies and saw Penny sitting between Blake's feet. Her gorgeous tail curled around her neatly, patiently waiting for her ball to be kicked again. Blake muttered about the little diva cock-blocking him, and he scooped her into his arms like she was a child and disappeared out of the room. The action did funny things to Justine's insides.

He came back a few moments later. "I've given her some raw meat so that should keep her quiet for a little while."

Justine nodded, smiling at this tortured bad boy making sure his domesticated fox was happy.

"Shall we?" he asked, holding out his hand to her, his eyebrow raised in challenge, like he didn't expect her to go through with this. It was a challenge she was excited, and nervous, to accept. She placed her hand in his, watching his face closely as he tried to conceal his triumphant smile, and let him lead her upstairs.

When she made it to his bedroom, she let go of his warm palm and stepped into the center of the room, surveying everything. The room was decorated in warm tones, giving it a calm and soothing feel. Again, there was no clutter around, her OCD cheering once again. What drew her attention were the large canvases on the walls.

The first was of a forest filled with bright green trees and moss-covered rocks with sunlight peeking through the branches. The second canvas on the next wall showed a beautiful beach sunset, the contrast of sky against sand and water was breath-taking, the orange tones calling to her. The final canvas on the third wall was a waterfall in the middle of another forest, the sun's rays creating a rainbow through the water.

They were beautiful but not something she would expect to find in his bedroom. The images were serene and tranquil; it was then she realized their purpose. Blake was trying to create a soothing environment to help him relax, to ease his anxiety and let him sleep. Her heart ached for him. She felt his heat against her back, then his touch. He brushed her hair back over her shoulder and grazed his lips against her neck, her skin tingling.

"Are you sure this is what you want?" he murmured, his words vibrating through her. She closed her eyes and tilted her head back, resting her head on his shoulder, assessing her feelings. She couldn't think of anyone she would rather do this with, no one she desired more, no one she trusted more than him and her nerves evaporated.

"Positive," she replied, and he grunted in approval. He trailed more of those delicate kisses over her neck, his hands coming around and roving over her stomach before reaching up to cup her breasts. He squeezed them both, no sound in the room except his deep breaths in her ear.

She lifted her head from his shoulder, watching him work her. She marveled at such strong, hard hands being so gentle and loving. When he brushed his thumbs across her nipples she swayed on her feet, the pleasure so intense. He did it again, harder and a little moan slipped from her mouth. He spun her in his arms, her hands coming up against his solid chest and she met his heated gaze.

He cupped her cheek and slanted his mouth down over hers, she opened for him immediately, helpless to do anything but let him inside so she could taste him. Goosebumps covered her from head to toe when he stroked his tongue against hers and he swallowed her groan. She wrapped her arms around his neck, tangling her fingers in his soft hair. He pulled her roughly against him and palmed her ass, thrusting his hips against hers and she gasped when he hit her core perfectly.

"That's one," he grinned against her mouth, and she slapped him playfully before pulling him towards the bed. She pushed him down onto the mattress and stepped back, kicking off her shoes. Her hands slid down the zipper on her jeans and his eyes followed her every move. Finally he dragged his gaze to her face.

"It's okay if you don't want to do this, we don't need to do this or we can stop anytime you want," he rushed out.

"It's really wonderful that you're making sure I feel safe, in control and comfortable, it really is. But I need you to stop talking now, we're going to have sex and that's that." She arched a defiant brow at him, and the corner of his mouth kicked up in a grin that she felt all the way to her bones.

He reached behind him and pulled his hoodie over his head, her eyes drinking in his bare, sculpted chest, rope after rope of muscle defined from hard work distracting her. He tossed his hoodie aside and then leant back on his elbows, the taut muscles of his stomach popping.

"Then by all means, please continue," he said, his eyes roaming over her. She pulled her attention away from his six-pack and slid her jeans down her legs and pulled her shirt over her head and tossed it at him, hitting him squarely in the face. He laughed, the sound rusty as it pulled from him but soon died in his throat as he pulled her shirt away from his face and took her in, standing before him in her underwear. His eyes roamed her again, lingering, heating, setting her aflame. He swallowed and her eyes watched his throat bob. He continued to stare, not speaking and dread punched her in the gut. She'd gotten this all wrong, oh God what had she been thinking?

"You bought them," he said, his voice hoarse as he sat up.

"Well, yeah, I thought…" she trailed off, folding her arms across her body. She didn't want to think about what it meant that she'd bought the orange underwear from the magazine he pointed to that day in her office. That she actually bought it before even agreeing to their arrangement, she'd known deep down that it was inevitable. That *they* were inevitable. He reached out, gripping her arm and pulled her between his legs.

"It's a shame..." he sighed, shaking his head.

"Why?"

"You're a vision in this, but for what we're gonna do, what I'm *dying* to do with you, it needs to come off." As his words registered, her worries disappeared, desire left in their place. He unhooked her bra, drew the straps down her shoulders and it fell to the floor. His eyes moved to her breasts, something dark flickered in their depths, and she shivered in anticipation. He kept his eyes focused on her breasts as his hand moved to cup her sex. He stroked a finger over the heart of her.

"Christ, you're wet," he grunted, stroking her again. Her head tipped back as the sensations washed over her.

"Is that all for me?" he asked, his words dipped with his barely there control.

"Yes," she whispered, and he gripped the sides of her panties and pulled them down, she braced a hand on his shoulder, stepping out of them. He pulled her against him and laid back on the bed, her body covering his. The feel of their bare skin pressed together sent her pleasure skyrocketing, especially when his chest hair brushed her sensitive nipples.

He kissed her slowly, languidly, *adoringly*. He was ruining her for anyone else and she knew at that moment that she didn't regret their agreement. She didn't care about her questionable ethics. There was no man in the world she trusted more with her body, her pleasure, her first time than the man currently beneath her. She could never regret their pairing, or this moment, it was too perfect. How could anything this beautiful be bad?

He ran his fingertips over the bumps of her spine while his tongue dallied in her mouth, taking its sweet time. It was amazing, but she was impatient. She straddled him and rubbed herself against his hard length. He gripped her hips and eased her into a slow rocking rhythm that soon drove them both wild.

He flipped them, kicking off his sweatpants in the process and she looked down at him. A dark trail of hair led down to his long, hard cock. It was the first she had touched in real life, and she was…fascinated. She stroked over the flesh, hot and hard and the skin so smooth like satin. She squeezed the base and a breath stuttered out of him, she released him immediately.

"I'm sorry, did that hurt?" she asked, but he just chuckled.

"Honey, that didn't hurt at all," he replied, taking her hand, and curling it around him. "Do it again," he rasped. This time when she did, he thrust up into her grip, groaning. He dipped his head and sucked on her hard nipple. Her grip on him tightened as pleasure coursed through her and he sucked harder. She stroked her hand up and down, meeting his thrusts and then she felt his hand on her. He stroked a finger between her folds and pressed his thumb against her clit and she gasped.

"That's two," he whispered in her ear, sliding a finger deep inside her. She cut off the next gasp, determined not to give him anymore reasons to be cocky. He pumped his finger in and out, working a second one inside her, cursing when her muscles clamped down on him. The dark word on his lips spurred her on and she lifted her hips to meet his next thrust. Sensations flooded her and before long her orgasm was coiling, she clamped her lips together, refusing to make a sound.

"Do you know how good it sounds to hear you enjoying this?" he asked, panting slightly, a sheen of perspiration covering his brow. She shook her head, a small moan slipping out.

"It's very sexy," he added, closing his mouth over her nipple again and slid his thumb over her clit as he thrust his fingers into her. Her orgasm barreled through her, hard and intense, she writhed against him, moaning.

"Fuck," he swore again. When she came back to herself, she realized she was still stroking him and looked down. His cock looked even bigger than it had before, moisture gathered at the tip, and she wanted to know what he tasted like. She sat up and shimmied down, ready to taste him but he gripped her arms.

"No!" he shouted, and she jolted, surprised.

"Sorry, I would love nothing more than for you to do that, you really have no idea. But this will end far quicker than I want it to if you do," he said, laying her down and softly brushing her lips with his. He pulled back and opened the drawer of his nightstand, grabbing a condom. She watched, fascinated, as he rolled it on then settled himself in between her legs. She spread them wide to accommodate his bulk. She felt him against her core and arched up to meet him, already eager for more.

"Ready?" he asked. She nodded eagerly, and his mouth kicked up in amusement. How could she have ever thought that mouth cold and hard? It was hot, sensual. He held her hands and moved them above her head, dropping his head to lick her nipple and she felt him at her entrance. He gently thrust his hips, leaving her breast, and finding her mouth, rolling his tongue into her as he pressed himself inside.

She felt the burn as her body made way for his,

wincing and when he was finally seated inside her, he paused, letting her body get used to him. He continued to kiss her, in that wonderful way that made her feel like the only woman in the world, and then he began to thrust, slowly. The first few thrusts hurt but soon pleasure chased the sting away. He hit her deep and she clenched around him, moaning. He broke their kiss, hissing sharply.

"What, what happened?" she panicked. He thrust again, never slowing and her eyes nearly rolled in her head.

"Tight," he gritted out.

"Oh God, sorry!"

"No honey, it's a good thing." He withdrew, and then slammed into her again. "Oh, fuck, it's a *really* good thing," he choked out. He thrust into her again and another gasp slipped from her. The sound triggered something in him, and he pounded harder, she lifted her hips to meet him each time and gripped his thick biceps, hanging on.

Then he slowed the pace, rolling his hips into her like a wave and she began moaning as pleasure consumed her. He increased the tempo again and she clawed at his back. He fed her a hard kiss, teeth banging, tongues thrusting, and he moved a hand between them, sliding his finger over her bundle of nerves again and again until she couldn't hang on any longer.

With a cry, she flew over the edge, holding onto him tight and with a groan, he followed her. He rested his forehead against her breast, collapsing his weight onto her as they both tried to control their pounding hearts and gasping breaths.

"Are you okay?" he asked once his breathing had returned to normal. A slow smile spread across her face.

"*Mejor que bien*," she replied, and he laughed and shifted his weight, moving off her.

"Be right back." He kissed her temple and got up, heading into the adjoining bathroom. He came back a few moments later and climbed onto the bed. He laid down and rolled to his side, pulling her against him, her hot cheek resting against his damp chest. He stroked her hair, twining the strands around his fingers and she listened to the beating of his heart as it lulled her to sleep.

Chapter 17

Justine awoke a few hours later, the room dark and silent. She was alone. She was surrounded by Blake's scent, in his bed, but he wasn't with her. She touched the space where he'd lain. The sheets were cool: he had been gone for a while. Maybe he couldn't sleep and he'd gotten up, not wanting to wake her. She sat up, rubbing her eyes and decided to find him to make sure he was okay. She grabbed his hoodie from the floor, resisting the urge to bury her nose in the material, inhaling deeply, and instead slipped it over her head.

She stood up, her thighs and core aching. Her first time had been amazing, nothing at all like she'd thought it would be, all because of Blake. He had been so sweet and wonderful, making sure she was okay and sure of herself. Giving her pleasure and taking his own, hopefully he had enjoyed it as much as she had.

Would they do it again? Technically their agreement had been fulfilled: he had helped her lose her virginity, *expertly*, she might add. And he had opened up to her in their sessions now and was working on himself. Did they just end their personal relationship now? Did she even want to? The thought had a hollow feeling bloom in her chest. She couldn't imagine not being able to kiss him whenever she wanted or never getting to sleep with him again. That one time didn't feel like it was enough, she needed more.

She padded out of the room in search of Blake, crossing the landing but she only found the main bathroom and a spare room which had all his weights and workout gear. *No wonder he's so perfectly sculpted.* A dreamy sigh escaped her as she pictured him, gloriously naked. He was a work of art. She had *never* been interested in muscles before, but she was a changed woman now.

She went downstairs and peeked into the living room. Penny was snuggled up in her blanket nest, chewing on a bedraggled stuffed toy. When she spotted Justine, she let out a little bark and Justine laughed. She went over to Penny, the fox's tail bouncing happily the closer she got.

"Look how adorable you are, little lady," Justine murmured as she tickled Penny's cheeks. Penny chuffed at her in agreement and nibbled her hand gently, tickling her. Justine giggled and ruffled Penny's bristly fur and then Penny turned back to her toy, which now Justine realized was a cuddly fox. She smirked.

"Daddy's taken such good care of you, hasn't he? Soft bed, lots of toys and yummy food too," she cooed, trying to ignore the picture developing in her mind of Blake as a father. She needed to get rid of those thoughts immediately before her heart decided he could give her everything she wanted, he couldn't.

She left Penny and continued to search but didn't find Blake downstairs so went back to the bedroom. Maybe he'd been called into the station and decided not to wake her? She sat on the bed and crossed her legs. Should she call him to check? A noise from the adjoining bathroom drew her attention. She held her breath. Was she hearing things? Could someone have broken in and be hiding in there? Although the idea was ridiculous, a current of fear tickled the back of her neck. There was only one way to find out.

She tiptoed to the bathroom and paused outside to listen but heard nothing. She took a deep breath and swung the door open wide, patting the wall frantically for the light switch and flicking it on.

"Blake?"

He was sitting in the bathtub at one end, wearing only his sweatpants. His knees were pulled to his chest, his forehead resting on them, and his arms were wrapped around his legs. Her heart clenched at the sight of him.

"Blake, are you okay?" She took a step forward, but he didn't move. She nibbled her lip, he must've had a bad dream or attack and got in the bath. In her research she had read that it was very common. The bath was considered a place of comfort for some, the cold ceramic, walled in on each side, but still able to see everything around you, it was safe.

She lifted her leg over the side and settled in the bottom right in front of him. She hissed as the coolness of the bath came into contact with her ass and bare thighs. *Stupid, barely-there panties!* She reached out and settled a hand over his, his skin so cold. He surprised her by grabbing onto her hand and squeezing tight. After a while, he lifted his head slightly, his eyes were glassy and unfocused, his complexion pale.

"She screamed all the way down." The harsh rasp of his voice echoed around the room, jolting through the silence.

Her breath hitched—he was talking about the woman who committed suicide. This was a topic they hadn't discussed in their sessions yet. She waited, not wanting to push him. She wanted him to tell her in his own way, in his own time. So she just sat in the bath with him, warming his hand with hers and supporting him however he needed.

"I dreamed that I was there again. Taking the call, deciding to help because I was the closest and I could get there quicker."

More silence. Again she waited.

"But I couldn't, I couldn't help," he whispered brokenly. A lump rose in her throat at the pain in his voice. All her training evaporated out of her head; for once she found herself at a loss, she didn't know what to do to make him feel better.

"I hear her scream in my dreams, even when I'm awake." He lifted his hand and scraped it through his hair, shakily. She inched closer, trying to keep him calm and warm.

"She screamed all the way down and then silence. I don't know which was louder, that terrified scream or the resounding silence that followed. God, that silence…"

Suddenly he vaulted out of the tub and dashed to the toilet, throwing the lid back, he retched violently. She cried out and got up, standing behind him and she stroked his powerful back, uttering soothing words until he was finished. He flushed the toilet and pushed past her to brush his teeth, rinsing with mouthwash before facing her.

He ran his eyes over her body, a wicked gleam sparkling in their depths. His armor was back in place, gone was the vulnerable soul who needed help. Her body responded by readying itself. But her mind went on the defensive. She knew what he was doing, he'd felt weak and vulnerable in front of her and was trying to assert his masculinity to prove a point. Unfortunately, it was working.

"Let's go back to bed," his voice husky with promise.

"To sleep," she replied, firmly. The wicked gleam dimmed slightly but he reluctantly agreed. They got back into bed and cuddled together. This peace she felt when she was in his arms was becoming addictive. But she didn't sleep, and she didn't think he did either. She spent the rest of the night worrying over him and overthinking that worry. Was she worried as a psychologist over her patient or was it something more than that? Was she too invested in him? She pushed that thought away but more slammed into her. Was she even skilled enough to help him? And would they continue sleeping together? It annoyed her that the last thought bothered her as much as the one before.

In the morning they dressed in silence. He offered to make her breakfast, but she declined. She wanted to get home and study more techniques, desperate to help him. He walked her to the door, kissed her cheek and it was like they both knew their agreement was complete, there would be nothing more.

So why did she feel like crying?

*

Although it had only been a few days since he'd seen her, it felt like a thousand years had passed for Blake. When his session with Justine finally came around it went far too quickly. She had been completely unaffected by seeing him: the consummate professional and that just pissed him off. Especially as he suddenly felt like an awkward teenager harboring a huge crush whenever he was around her. He needed to see her, had come up with a hundred different excuses to stop by but had chickened out every time.

Their agreement was done, but he wasn't, not by a long shot. Their night together had been better than he could have imagined. It had felt so right having her around his place, it actually felt like a home for once. Blake, Justine and Penny made three. Having her around had relaxed him, for the most part, his mind drifting back to the little gasps of pleasure she made, the way she writhed against him and how good she felt in his arms. It had never been like that for him before.

Things with Katie had been good at the start, they were teenagers and had explored and grown together. But when he discovered her lie, their relationship had never recovered. Whenever they had sex, they had never connected in the way he and Justine did. Which was why he wasn't ready to accept their one-time-only deal. There were too many things he wanted to experience and to show her. And dammit, she still needed someone to look out for her, there were a lot of slimy men out there.

He couldn't deny it though, she twisted him up inside, it was agony and ecstasy at the same time and he wasn't sure if he liked it. Maybe it was because she pretty much knew most of his deepest, darkest secrets and still tried to help him, still treated him like a normal person. She had still trusted him with her body. God, he hoped she had enjoyed their first time. He was worried that he'd been too rough or aggressive but he couldn't help his reaction, another thing that had only happened with her.

Would she want to do it again? He wondered if she

would be up for extending their agreement. He had already put her in a difficult position the first time, blackmailing her like the asshole he was. She might be worried that if they continued, they would blur the lines and not be able to separate the roles of lover/psychologist/client. Whatever, he wouldn't get confused and he wasn't ready for it to end.

A knock on his office door distracted him, startling him out of his fantasy. He got up to open the door, berating himself once again for disappearing into a daydream and lowering his guard. When he opened the door, he was surprised to find Rebelle standing on the other side.

"Rebelle? Is everything okay?" He stepped aside to let her in. He shut the door and ushered her into one of the chairs opposite his desk and then sat facing her. She glanced around the room, her eyes wide, her gaze darting here and there, not settling on anything. Her hands gripped each other in her lap, her knuckles stark white. Clearly something was troubling her, and he'd be lying if he said he wasn't thrilled she had decided to put her trust in him.

"Rebelle?" he prompted, and she jolted at the sound of his voice. She nibbled her lower lip nervously, her brow furrowed as she faced him in silence. He didn't push her: she had something to say but was working up the courage, just like he'd done so many times before. He knew how it felt, to have to control your fear, to harness it and then overcome it by voicing your concerns.

Her expression smoothed, and her eyes shone brightly. "I'm scared," she whispered.

"What are you scared of, Rebelle?" He kept his voice gentle, but his anger rose by infinite levels, surprising him. He tried to reason that if it were any of his citizens sitting in front of him, he would feel the same. But he'd done some digging after looking into the previous sheriff, he knew exactly what kind of husband Black had been and could only imagine the secrets and scars that Rebelle hid. That was why he felt so strongly about protecting her.

She nibbled her lip again. "I know what you think, but I didn't kill him," she said fiercely.

"I never thought you did, not for one second."

"But there are people who think I did." She paused. "Dangerous people."

Blake stiffened. "Have you been threatened?"

She nodded almost imperceptibly.

"Who's threatening you?"

"I don't know," she whispered.

"You don't know?" he repeated, his brow furrowed with confusion.

She jumped up. "I knew you wouldn't believe me!" she hissed and headed for the door. "I shouldn't have come here."

He leapt up and went after her, being careful not to grab her in case she felt intimidated.

"I do believe you. Tell me everything, start from the beginning," he said earnestly, peering down into her delicate face and gesturing back to her seat. She reluctantly sat down, gripping the armrest tightly.

"It started after he died."

"The threats?"

She nodded. "They would turn up at the rescue center in the middle of the night, bang on the doors and walls, shouting abuse. It would last for a couple of hours, upsetting the animals and then they would get bored and leave." He noted that she said it upset the animals, though it clearly upset her too, even if she didn't want to admit it.

"Who is it?" he asked.

"I don't know, I've never seen them. It's so dark and I just try to stay hidden."

His anger rose again. No one should have to hide in their own home. He hardened his heart against her words, he had to remain clear-headed. "Do you recognize the voices?"

She shook her head.

"What do they do?"

"They call me a murderer, a whore, the 'black widow'. At first, they just used to taunt me and make noise. But now their words are filled with so much hate and anger, I don't think it's a game anymore."

He sat in silence, thinking, then, "Did he have a lot of friends outside the men at the station?" he asked, his mind whirring.

"Not really, maybe one or two, no one I can remember."

"Okay, have you got anyone you can stay with?" At his question she shot him a look that said *are you kidding me?* and he felt his mouth twitch at this hidden sassy side of her.

"I won't be driven out of the rescue center, the animals need me, I can't leave them, I won't." she said. He understood her loyalty, even admired her for it. He'd only had Penny a few weeks, but he would walk through fire for her. But staying there alone wouldn't keep Rebelle safe.

"Give me this evening to organize for someone to drive by each night. I'll get them to patrol the area late at night, maybe do some surveillance on the property for a few hours until early morning. I can't trust our officers if they were all loyal to Black. It could even be one of them doing this. I'll ask the sheriff in the next county if she can spare someone."

Rebelle nodded and relief flooded her features. God, she was so like Katie. But instead of feeling any romantic attachment, he just wanted to protect her. Like he should have protected Katie. Keeping Rebelle safe was his way of making up for not giving Katie the attention she needed, attention that could have kept her from taking her own life.

"Thank you, I appreciate that," she said.

"You have my number. If anything happens at all, call me. I'll let you know who will be coming by each night. And if someone else ever turns up, call me immediately."

Rebelle got up, heading towards the door and he picked up the phone to make the arrangements. She stopped and turned back to him.

"You were right, you are different," she said softly, and then left before he could respond. His throat tightened at her words; they were like a healing balm to his wounded pride. Ever since the suicide he'd questioned whether this should even be his job, but Rebelle made him remember this was why he loved his work. Because he cared. He should never have tried to shut the town out, too afraid to let them in. It was his connection to the town that made him so good at what he did.

He spent the next hour sorting out her security detail and wondering which of the officers that he trusted to guard his back was threatening one of their own.

Chapter 18

It had been nearly three weeks since Justine and Blake had slept together, or more accurately, two weeks, four days, ten hours and twenty-seven goddamn minutes. Not that Justine had been counting...like some lovesick fool. *No, not lovesick, just lust sick. Because you absolutely do not love him.* She was just obsessed with him, there, that was better, right? *Ugh, this was so not good.*

On the days in between their sessions, she felt like she was just existing. Nothing made her happy. She couldn't focus on anything and constantly thought about their night together, and all the ways she could end up back in his arms. She tried so hard to remain professional whenever she saw him. She kept her walls in place, not touching him, not looking at him too long and always making sure her smile was professional and not betraying all the thoughts flitting through her mind of things she wanted to do to his naked body.

Who knew what a filthy mind she had? She didn't even think about sex this much when she *hadn't* had it. Obviously she blamed Blake. He'd shown her how incredible it could be. But she'd spent so long fantasizing about him that she hadn't done anything about trying to find an *actual* boyfriend. She hadn't looked at her dating apps. She deleted any messages she got from previous dates who wanted to take her out again, and she hadn't gone back to Ladies' Night at the bar. She was behind on her plan, and she knew she needed to get back out there but for some reason, she just wasn't interested. And that reason was about to walk into her office.

For a smart person, she sure was stupid. She'd started to care for him more than she had anticipated. A feeling she couldn't name settled in the pit of her stomach and that was why she needed to push herself to go out and meet other men. She needed to take her mind off the client that she couldn't have. This thing wasn't serious, it was just an infatuation with her first lover which *any* woman would have.

She was distracted from her thoughts by Hilda's girlish giggle. Justine frowned. *What the fu*-she'd never heard Hilda make that sound before. Then Blake's large body filled the doorway and Justine couldn't breathe.

"You ought to watch that one, Justine. She may act all sweet and innocent, but I know a troublemaker when I see one," Blake teased.

Justine peered behind him to see Hilda tittering away and waving a hand to shush him. Justine glanced back at Blake and saw him smile, the joy in his expression nothing like the perma-frown that had been there when he first stepped into her office all those weeks ago. He seemed happier, lighter, and more engaged with people. Was the town working its way under his skin? She hoped so for, uh, the town's sake, yeah, the town, that was what mattered here.

Blake waved at Hilda and shut the door. Justine waited for him to get settled on the couch, noting that his eyes no longer darted around the room, looking for threats and planning escape routes. *Progress!* She sat down opposite, giving him her most professional smile. When he took in her smile, a muscle ticked under his eye, his lips pursing in annoyance.

"How have you been, Blake?" she asked, crossing her legs, the slit on her black dress spreading, baring slightly more thigh than was probably appropriate. She hoped he wouldn't notice but he saw everything. His eyes dropped and he clenched his jaw before swiftly averting his gaze. She tried to brush off the hurt that floated through her at his lack of interest, reminding herself she was meant to be behaving professionally.

"Good. I don't know, fine, I guess?" His words were a question, not an answer. He still had some work to do on opening up and talking about his feelings, but his progress so far was outstanding.

"Just fine?"

He nodded.

"Have you had any attacks this past week?" she asked.

He thought for a moment, then shook his head. A soft smile split her face at the news, a real smile this time, her professional one forgotten.

"Blake, that's wonderful!" she gushed.

His gaze snapped to hers and lingered on her mouth before his lips lifted in a smile that matched hers. *Two smiles in one session, dios mio, who is this stranger?*

"Any anxiety?"

His smile disappeared. "A little."

"Anything in particular that caused it?" she probed.

He looked away and out the window. When he didn't answer, she prompted him. He got up and started pacing behind the couch, tangling his hand roughly through his hair. Hair she longed to do the same to, knowing how soft it felt under her fingertips. She blinked and forced her attention back to the situation.

"I had another nightmare about the incident. I woke up sweating and shaking. I was sick again and it took a long time to snap out of it," he said, not meeting her eyes.

"A nightmare about the woman who committed suicide?" she asked, and he nodded sharply. Her eyes narrowed at him. He kept circling back to this incident, yes it would have been extremely traumatic but there was something else here and she was ready to start pushing his buttons to get the answers they both needed.

"Why does it bother you so much?" Justine asked.

"Excuse me?" His mouth gaped open in shock. "Did you seriously just ask me why someone committing suicide in front of me *bothers* me so much?" His words held a steely edge and a nervous twitch traveled up her spine at his anger. She had to work to hold the tension, *you're not his girlfriend, you're his psychologist. His mental wellbeing is what you need to work with, not worry about whether he's mad at you or not.*

"Yes," she replied simply.

He continued to stare at her in shock. "Because a woman *died*, Justine," he gritted out and began pacing again.

She sighed internally. *He's going to make this difficult on himself, isn't he?* "But *why* does it bother you so much?"

"Are you for real right now?" he shouted, his anger rising but she wouldn't back down from it.

She got up and went over to him, standing to the side to allow him to continue pacing. "Why does she bother you, Blake? What is it about *her*?" Justine pushed, her tone hardening. "You've seen plenty of people die. In battle, in the line of duty, what makes her stand out to you against all the rest?"

He continued pacing, stomping back and forth like a caged beast, his aggression coiled, ready to strike. "Because she *died*. Fuck!"

"Come on, Blake, why does she bother you?" Justine shouted back, ready to match him, to drive his anger higher until he burst and his mouth ran away with him. Until he told her what she wanted to hear.

"Because I *failed* her, that's why!"

Bingo! Now they were getting somewhere.

"You failed her." Justine repeated, her tone flat.

"Yes!" Blake growled at her, pain lurking in the depths of those silver eyes, lines of tension bracketing his mouth.

"You knew you weren't qualified to help her, you did the best you could. Better than most people could have, so why are you so fixated on her?"

"Because I failed her!"

"Like you failed your wife, Katie, who also committed suicide?"

"Yes, goddammit!" he barked.

And now we're at the crux of the problem. "You couldn't have helped either of them, Blake," she said.

He stared at her, his eyes wide, regret spilling from them. Regret he had no business feeling. He moved away from her and sat back on the couch, leaning forward and dropping his head in his hands. She came around and knelt in front of him.

"Blake?" she asked, worried she had pushed him too far. She placed a hand on his knee, trying to make a connection to ground him and make him feel safe. Thousands of thoughts and emotions must be tearing through him, but she was on his side. "You tried to help but at the end of the day, both women had *decided* to end their lives and nothing you could've said or done would have stopped either of them. They were in a place so dark that your light couldn't reach them, and that's not your fault," she said softly.

He raised his head and met her eyes, his watery with emotion.

"You need to let go of this guilt you've been carrying around for far too long. It's dragging you down."

"I can't," he whispered, voice cracking, and a single tear escaped, rolling down his cheek.

Her heart contracted in her chest and in that moment, she wanted to throw her arms around him. To kiss away his pain, to protect this fearsome warrior and keep him safe so nothing and no one would ever hurt him again. That wasn't how she should be feeling about a client, and it scared her.

She cleared her throat, trying to shove away her thoughts. "No one else is blaming you or finding you at fault, only you."

He nodded slowly.

"It won't happen quickly, but I want you to start right now. Each day I want you to *forgive yourself.* Take a moment, at some point in the day, and find a quiet place, find somewhere calm and forgive yourself. It will take time, but the more you do this, the more you believe it, you'll find the guilt slowly easing," she explained.

He nodded again, peering down at her, then cleared his throat and wiped at his eyes. "Sorry," he muttered.

"Don't apologize. There's nothing wrong with emotions, we all have them," she said gently.

He scoffed and then his eyes met hers. Their look lingered, his eyes heated, and his lips curled into a salacious grin that had her body betraying her once again. Her nipples hardened and arousal gripped her.

She longed to give in, but she knew exactly what he was doing, unfortunately her lady parts didn't care and just wanted him. He pulled her into his lap in a swift move that had her swooning. She straddled him, her dress pulling tight against her parted thighs, her body throbbing, desperate for his touch. He fit his lips to the hollow of her throat and goosebumps broke out over her skin.

No, this was wrong, all wrong. He was only trying to make himself feel better and prove a point. She knew him too well, knew exactly what he was doing, it had become a pattern. She pressed her hand to his chest and pushed him away. His eyes were glazed, his cheeks flushed and his lips plump, he was passion incarnate and if there was a more arousing sight, she'd never seen it.

"Blake, stop," she sighed.

His hands immediately relaxed their grip. "Is something wrong?"

She fixed him with a sharp, knowing stare. "You're not weak."

He looked at her quizzically. "What?"

"You're not weak because you've shown emotion. You're not any less masculine because you need help with your mental health. The ultimate test of strength for anyone is confronting your inner demons, no matter how scary, how hard, or how fierce they are, and you *win*. Strength of mind is what matters. You're not weak, you're not any less of a man for crying. You don't need to exert your masculinity through sexual aggression to remind me you're strong."

He gaped at her, he opened his mouth, but she held up her finger to stop him, she wasn't finished.

"I know you're a fighter, I know you're strong. I know you're a warrior and nothing will make me think otherwise. So, stop trying to dominate with your sexuality, it means nothing. It's all the work you're doing to combat your issues is what makes you strong, and because you fight to beat them every day, you could never be weak." She climbed off his lap. Her body screaming at her to get right back where she was, missing him already, but she needed to draw boundaries.

She couldn't meet his stare, afraid of what she would see. Instead, she went back to her seat opposite him, smoothing her shaking hands over her thighs.

"Now then, let's work on some more techniques to help you when you feel anxious. We'll start with a positive realization, let's find a place that calms you…"

*

The next day, Blake entered Justine's office, smiling in greeting at Hilda.

"Morning Blake, how are you?" she beamed at him.

"Very well thanks, and yourself?" he replied, genuinely interested in her answer. He was becoming such a chatterbox lately.

"I'm good. What are you doing here today? Jim's not causing any trouble, is he?" she asked, concern lining her face and Blake laughed.

"No, not at all. He's been raving all morning about the delicious paella you made last night," Blake said, and pink tinged Hilda's cheeks.

"That man's heart is in his belly: as long as you feed him, he'll stay happy," she said.

"Good to know," Blake chuckled again and then glanced towards Justine's office door. "Is she free?"

Hilda nodded and he winked at her before heading inside and shutting the door.

Justine looked up from her desk. He leaned against the door and stared at the woman who was twisting him up inside. Yesterday had been a revelation. She'd helped him break through a serious barrier and as a thank you, he had mauled her like some wild caveman beast in a pathetic attempt to redeem his masculinity in her eyes. But she had seen right through the attempt and called him on it, giving him a dressing down that had opened his eyes to his poor behavior. She had helped him yet again.

"Is everything okay?" she asked, getting up from her desk. He ran his eyes over her, taking in the leopard print dress that hugged her figure tightly, showing off every single curve that he was desperate to explore again. His eyes dipped to her orange high-heeled sandals. She really loved orange, didn't she? He would love to see her wearing those and nothing else.

He missed her. It had been so long since he had gotten to touch her, he was going out of his mind. Yesterday had just been an excuse to get his hands on her. He'd seen her expression, she wanted it too, which was why he had the confidence to come back here today.

"Everything is great," he replied, and he meant it. Their session yesterday had lifted something inside him, he felt like he could breathe easier. He tried to do his forgiveness mantra this morning, it felt a little silly and nothing had really changed but he knew he had to keep working on it. Like she said, it wouldn't happen right away.

"I just wanted to stop by to apologize for my behavior yesterday. I shouldn't have touched you in that way during one of our sessions, it was extremely inappropriate and I crossed a line," he said. He thought he saw a flash of disappointment cross her face. *Gotcha,* he thought smugly, and worked hard to keep the grin off his face. "Especially to try and prove a point, that was a shitty thing to do to you after everything you've done for me."

He meant it too, he did feel guilty over it. He had done it for the wrong reasons and that wasn't acceptable. This time it would be for the right reasons. He wanted to and so did she. He couldn't go another day, another minute without her skin against his.

"Thank you, I appreciate that," she said, narrowing her eyes as she perched on the edge of her desk.

"Great," he smiled, and took a step forward, closing the gap so there was only a breath between them. "Now take off your clothes." he commanded. Her eyes flashed fire at his order and her mouth parted.

"But you just said…" she floundered.

"I know, yesterday was wrong, it was during our session, emotions were running high, and I was doing it for the wrong reasons. Today I'm clear-headed, we don't have a session and I've been wanting you since we were last together. I know you want me too, so I'm done waiting. Take off your clothes."

Just when he thought he had her pegged, would have bet his house on her pulling that dress over her head without hesitation, she surprised him. She stood up, her breasts brushing against him. He fought a moan, his cock hardening in his jeans.

"You think you can come into *my* office and order me around, *cabrón*? Tell me what to do? No, no, no!"

His expression faltered slightly at her offended tone, and he was pretty sure *cabrón* didn't mean sexy hero. Shit, had he read this all wrong? Had his ego been lying to him?

"I'll accept your apology, maybe some groveling, either

way, get on your knees." The arch of her eyebrow, the rasp of her voice and that demanding tone, sent a jolt of arousal straight through him, warming his blood.

He tried not to smirk, he loved her like this. In control, independent, assertive, demanding what she wanted. It fired his blood. She wanted to play a game and he was ready and willing. He unleashed a wolfish smile and slowly dropped to his knees, staring up at her, admiring the curves of her body.

"I don't hear an apology," she sniffed primly.

He scrubbed a hand over his jaw, his palms rasping through his stubble. "I think I need an incentive."

She fixed him with a sharp look, but he could see amusement and arousal in those honey depths. Her hands gripped the material of her dress and slowly pulled it up, exposing more and more of those perfect thighs. She kept going, driving him wild with her slow, little striptease until she stopped before he could set his eyes on the prize. The room was quiet except for the sounds of their breathing.

She lifted one leg and settled her heel on his shoulder, the hard tip of her stiletto digging deep and he enjoyed the sting. Now he could see her panties, white lace. God, she was killing him. Using her heel, she drew him towards her, until his face was inches from her center. He could smell her scent and it ratcheted up his desire.

"Is this enough incentive?" She tried to keep her tone firm, but he could hear the underlying doubt in her words, doubt he didn't want her to be feeling. He buried his face, inhaling deeply before pulling her panties to the side and kissing her. She sucked in a breath when his tongue slid between her folds, she arched her back, pressing more firmly into his mouth.

The heel of those damn sexy shoes dug into his shoulder deeper, and he grunted in pleasure, he loved her reaction to him. She lay back on her desk and he grabbed her other leg, draping it over his shoulder, the other heel pressing into his back. He licked at her, then brought his hands into the mix, gripping her hip hard with one and pushing two fingers into her with the other.

She fisted her hands in his hair, arching her hips into his mouth and began moaning softly. She came hard, jerking against his mouth, her sex gripping his fingers tightly as she rode the waves. He pressed kisses to her inner thighs as her body quaked with aftershocks.

Never had he loved being with someone so intimately like he did with her, and he was determined to maximize her pleasure each time. She sat up, her cheeks flushed, her lips plump from being nibbled on.

"Your turn," she said, licking her lips and she stood, pushing her dress back down. Before he could say anything, she switched their positions, tugging him to his feet and pushing him against her desk. He was about to tell her she didn't need to do anything when his brain told him to shut the hell up. She had wanted to use her mouth on him the last time they were together, and he hadn't let her. He'd been plagued by fantasies of her plump lips wrapped around him ever since.

She rubbed her hand over his hard length, and he groaned, all thoughts evaporating from his brain. She continued rubbing up and down, pressing her body up against his, keeping them fully connected. She nipped at his neck and when her tongue stroked over his sensitive skin, the hair on the back of his neck lifted.

He didn't protest when she dropped to her knees and started undoing his jeans, he wanted this too much. Her hand reached inside and gripped him, squeezing tightly and his breath hissed through his teeth in pleasure. She pulled him out and stared at his cock with a mixture of arousal and curiosity on her face.

She cupped him, watching in fascination as she squeezed, stroked, and gently pulled at him. The actions had him fisting his hands at his sides to stop himself from doing something, anything but feeling the sensations coursing through him. She wrapped her plump lips around him and sucked. Her warm, wet tongue sliding around him, and he choked on the air leaving his lungs.

She swallowed and moaned, the sound vibrating along his cock, and she took him to the back of her throat. She reached up to cup his sac, gently squeezing and he pulsed in her mouth, ready to come. He grabbed her shoulders and pulled her to her feet, spinning her around and pushing her forward, bending her over the desk.

"Need to be inside you," he grunted. Lifting her dress, he tugged her panties down. "Shit, I don't have anything." *Fuck, why didn't I bring anything?*

"I'm on the pill and I'm healthy," she gasped out.

"Are you sure? I don't have anything, I'm all clear," he said. She nodded in agreement and he took a deep breath, then entered her from behind. She cried out in pleasure, clawing at the desk, her hips pushing back into him. He gripped her round ass and pounded into her.

"Fuck, you feel so good," he gritted out.

"So do you," she moaned back, looking at him over her shoulder.

He slowed his movements, pulling out of her then easing back in, the push-pull sensation driving them both wild. Her eyelids fluttered closed in pleasure and her head dropped forward. He slid a finger over her bundle of nerves, and she gasped, clenching around him. That sound did things to him. He sped up again, thrusting into her, stroking her until she was crying out again and clamping down on him. He followed her over the edge with his own cry, filling her up and then collapsed onto her back.

"That was..." she trailed off.

"I know," he rasped, trying to catch his breath. He placed delicate kisses to the back of her damp neck and slid out of her. He grabbed a tissue from her desk, cleaning up before tossing the tissue in the waste basket. She pulled her panties up and her dress down and he took her into his arms and kissed her. She gave in, immediately opening to allow him to explore her mouth before she broke away.

"Oh my God, Hilda's out there!" she gasped.

"Oh my God, she is!" he gasped back, matching her horrified tone, teasing her. She giggled and swatted at him playfully. "She'll probably tell everyone in town what you really do with your clients, and you'll develop a reputation for being a hussy," he teased again, and she laughed.

"I've never been considered a hussy before." She appeared far too eager at the prospect, and he laughed.

"I'd better get going," he said, and disappointment lined her beautiful face. "But I'll see you tonight? Penny misses you," he added, trying to save face in case she shot him down. *I miss you.* She just smiled again, a big beaming smile that seemed to brighten the whole room and nodded. He kissed her once, twice before reluctantly pulling away. He went to the door and winked at her before swinging it wide open.

"Thank you for the last-minute session, Dr. Rodríguez-Hamilton, you're a lifesaver," he called loudly, and watched as Justine smothered a grin. "Great to see you again, Hilda." The woman gave him a knowing smirk over her coffee mug.

He waved goodbye, whistling happily as he left the office.

Chapter 19

Justine couldn't stop staring at Blake. The way the firelight kissed his skin made him look even more delicious, edible even. She watched as he joked with Beau and Dean around the fire pit, a small smile forming on her lips. Dean let out a huge bark of laughter and Beau spat out his drink at whatever Blake had said and she wished she could hear them.

He was surprisingly funny, whenever he told a joke, *bam* her clothes were on the floor. He was dangerous. She'd seen a new side of him these last few weeks, he was more relaxed, unguarded, he teased her and was playful, she loved it. He was like a brand new person, one she was becoming increasingly attached to.

Taylor sighed deeply and rested her head on Justine's shoulder.

"Isn't Blake just the dreamiest?" she said in a breathy voice, mocking Justine. Justine shrugged her off, her cheeks flaming.

"That is so *not* what I was thinking," she replied defensively.

"Yeah, leave her alone, Tay," Christy admonished, and Justine shot her a grateful smile. "She can't help being so in *lurve*," Christy added, and then both women snickered at Justine's outraged expression.

"Shut the fuck up, he'll hear you!" Justine hissed, glancing at the men frantically. Both women fell about cackling. *I need new friends.*

"She didn't deny it," Christy sang.

"Interesting," Taylor added, stroking a hand over her fake beard like a TV detective.

"Seriously, shut up. And I don't," Justine added for clarity.

"I wouldn't worry, he looks at you like your vagina is the portal to unlimited whiskey and motorbikes," Taylor joked.

Justine rolled her eyes. "How charming."

"Seriously though, what's happening with you two? Has he explored your cave of wonders yet?" More snickering.

"Look at them, of course they're doing it!" Taylor said.

"Really, is that true?"

Justine stared back and forth between the harpies with their hopeful faces. She let the question hang in the air before checking the men weren't looking, then discreetly nodded. Being discreet was a waste of time as Taylor and Christy shrieked with joy so loudly that the men stopped talking and stared at them to see what all the fuss was about.

Christy glared at them and Beau and Dean turned back

to their conversation. But Blake was watching Justine, those silver eyes so hot and intense, she thought she would combust on the spot.

"We want details!" Taylor hissed. Blake must have guessed what they were talking about because a cute smirk crossed his face. He winked at her, turning her insides to mush before he turned back to the guys.

"Yeah, how was it?"

"When was it?"

"Just the one time?"

"Are you still doing it?"

"How big is it?"

"Enough!" Justine cried, then leveled a look at Taylor. "You know I'm not answering that last one, right?"

"I was just curious. It's not like I want an exact measurement, just a ballpark. I have my suspicions. Hey, how big are his feet?" Taylor began peering over the fire to try and get a look at Blake's feet.

"Stop it! You're unbelievable," Justine sighed, shaking her head.

Taylor placed a hand over her heart. "Thank you," she replied earnestly, and Christy snickered again.

"At least give us something, then we'll shut up, promise!" Christy said, and stretched out her pinkie, it was their thing. Justine linked their pinkies and then looked at Taylor.

"I'm not promising shit, just tell us."

Justine sighed. "Fine. It was about a month ago. Yes, we're still sleeping together. No, I don't know what it means and of course it's big, have you seen the size of the man!"

More cackling abounded which the men chose to ignore this time, too busy laughing at something else Blake said.

"Welcome to the club, my friend," Christy said, clinking her glass with Justine's.

"Gross, thanks for the reminder that you're doing it with my brother," Taylor muttered.

"Well close your ears darlin' because it's about to get real detailed. Dean really likes it when I take my hand and squeeze-"

"No! No, no, no!" Taylor shouted, jumping up and stomping inside the house, shaking her head. Justine laughed and turned back to Christy.

"Keep going…I want to know," she said. The men were talking quietly amongst themselves, except for Beau who was staring intently at Taylor through the glass door to the kitchen. *Interesting.* Christy leaned forward to whisper in Justine's ear. As she listened, her mouth ran dry, and her skin prickled with awareness. When Christy pulled back and saw the scandalized expression on Justine's face, she laughed.

"Is that even legal?" Justine choked out

Christy shrugged. "Darlin', I don't know, but it makes him see stars." She turned to stare at the man in question, a dreamy smile on her face. *Is that how I look at Blake? Does he look at me like that?* She turned to look for him but found him already watching her, the devilish expression on his face made her think that move might be something he would like after all.

When everyone said goodbye and started to leave Dean and Christy's, Blake came over to her and kissed her in front of everyone. Wolf whistles abounded and she was secretly thrilled he had made such a public claim on her. She'd never been the one in the group to have a boyfriend and she loved it. *Wait, boyfriend? Whoa, back up. He's not your Mr. Right and you know it.* But seeing the way he fit in with her friends, her second family, was almost too much, she wanted more. Blake's lips at her ear distracted her from her thoughts, his hot breath making her shiver despite the warm evening.

"I can't wait to get you into bed," he murmured. "The things I want to do to you..." trailing off, he growled low in his throat, and she sighed in response. The man was insatiable.

"Take me home then," she replied, leaning into his body. They said goodbye to everyone and left amid more whistles and jeers. He lifted her onto his motorcycle and sat in front. She wrapped her arms around him, resting her head on his strong back, right between his shoulder blades, like the space was made just for her.

They rode back to his place, he checked on Penny while she went upstairs, and she smiled as she heard him cooing at the fox. She loved his soft side. When he came upstairs, she was already naked, and he set to work. First, he made her beg in English, then in Spanish. Then she told him what she wanted to try, and it was his turn to beg.

*

"Journey? Are you serious?" Blake hooted, and Justine pouted, that gorgeous bottom lip of hers sticking out for miles and he had to restrain himself from nibbling on it. She wiggled in his lap, trying to get comfortable.

"How is that any different than Val Halen?" she countered, and he fixed her with his most serious stare.

"Oh, honey, it's very different."

She thought for a moment, and he used her distraction to openly stare at her, something he was doing more and more lately. Like he was unable to believe this stunning, intelligent, strong woman would be sitting on his lap, in his squad car, on a fake stakeout, debating the merits of eighties bands. He didn't want to jinx it, but life was pretty darn good right now, for the first time in...ever. He was lighter, carefree, and so calm, it was a strange feeling, but a blissfully liberating one.

"I know!" she shouted triumphantly, and he laughed, stroking his hand down her spine. "Heart! You've got to love Heart. *Alone*? Come on, you can't deny that song!" she said excitedly, then belted out the chorus, her voice causing little goosebumps to prickle across his skin. He couldn't deny it, especially when she sang it so beautifully that he felt it in his soul, but he wouldn't let her win that easily. He stroked a hand over his beard, thoughtfully.

"I'm not denying that song, but only that one," he added when she looked far too smug and pleased with herself. "They're no Mötley Crüe," he grumbled.

"Ugh, please! They're all hair and no substance," she sniffed demurely, folding her arms over her chest.

"Okay, name someone better," he challenged.

"I think the hard part would be only naming *one* band better, there are far too many."

At her words, he fixed her with a mock scowl. "Wiseass."

She hid her smirk. He dropped his hand to cup her ass and squeezed.

"Okay, person or band?" she relented.

"How about a duo?"

"Ooh, interesting but easy. Hall and Oates? Pet Shop Boys? Tears for Fears? The Eurythmics, wait, Wham!" She was so excited, but Blake faked a snore and she giggled.

"Did I tell you about the man who burst into the bar with a gun and demanded someone play eighties music?" he asked, seriously.

"No?"

"Luckily The Police turned up and sorted him out." he

joked, and she snorted, rolling her eyes but the gleam in them said she loved it when he was silly. She listed some more duos, but he vetoed each one.

"Fine, duos are a no go for you. What about…" she trailed off, thinking again and he took the opportunity to glance around outside, not seeing anything except a raccoon on the prowl. He really needed to tell her the Trashcan Bandits weren't real but he loved their stakeouts, this time she'd even brought binoculars, she was too cute. He turned back to Justine.

"Foreigner," she said quietly, her demeanor changing slightly. She ducked her head, her fingers twisting in her lap.

"Foreigner?" he asked. He'd heard of them but couldn't name any of their songs.

"They have this song, *Waiting for a Girl Like You,* it's a rock ballad and such an amazing love song," she sighed wistfully, lost in her thoughts and he studied her closely. "When I was a teenager, I dreamed I would be special enough for someone to sing it to me. In my opinion, serenading someone is the ultimate gesture of love."

She usually didn't reveal a lot about herself, it was normally him revealing all his deepest, darkest thoughts. He loved moments like this when he got a glimpse of her. He was always greedy for more so he could put the pieces of her together in his mind, creating the perfect picture.

"Did anyone sing it to you?" he asked, gently.

"Nope." She seemed so lost in the past and a hint of sadness tinged their conversation, he wanted to put that beautiful smile back on her face, the one he found so hard to resist.

"Yeah, I'm not surprised," he joked, her eyes flicked to his, shooting fire.

"Asshole!" she chided, slapping him playfully.

"What?" he asked, all innocence. "Singing in front of people is terrifying, it's the scariest thing you could ever do. So, I'm not surprised no teenager wanted to do that. I'm surprised you can do it now. I don't know how you manage it," he said.

She gaped at him, "Seriously? You realize you've faced *combat* before, right? Multiple armed terrorists? Bombings?" she said incredulously.

"Eh," he shrugged. "It was just a *couple* of terrorists. Anyway, it's crowds that get me: all those people, and performing in front of them? It would take nothing short of a miracle to get me to do that. What a nightmare," he shuddered, and drew her even closer. She laughed and threw her arms around his neck, kissing him, nice and slow. Exploring his mouth just how he liked, and every time he tried to stroke against her tongue she drew it away, teasing him. They came up for air half an hour later.

"Back to yours?" she rasped, her eyes clouded with desire, her husky voice trailing along his skin and setting him alight with anticipation.

"Yep!" he replied, and she climbed off his lap. He tolerated the loss of her only because soon she would be in his bed, underneath him, gasping in pleasure in that way that he loved. The thought had him belting up and reaching for the ignition in record time. As he did, he looked up through the windshield and something caught his attention. There was a man hurrying along the street, he looked around furtively before getting into a waiting car. It was the same man Blake had noticed before.

"Blake?" Justine asked when he didn't drive off. But he didn't reply, he just watched as the car pulled away from the curb, coming towards them. His intuition pricked him, telling him *something*, but he couldn't put his finger on it, it was like déjà vu. He knew what he was seeing was important, but he didn't know how.

It wasn't until the car drove past them and he saw inside that the prickle became something more. He recognized the driver as his fellow deputy, Austin, and the passenger was one of the officers from the station. And now Blake had a feeling he knew where they were going. Once they were retreating in his rear-view mirror, he started the car and pulled away, following them at a distance.

"Blake?" Justine penetrated his thoughts. He glanced at her. *Shit.* He didn't want to bring her with him, but her place was in the opposite direction.

"I've got a hunch that the men in that car are up to something. I can't turn around or I could be too late to stop them and I'm obviously not going to leave you in the middle of the street. So, you need to stay in the vehicle, and everything will be fine," he said.

He couldn't help but think he was overreacting, and he didn't want to scare her, but his instincts were rarely wrong. He'd relied on them to keep him safe in battle and on patrols with the sheriff's department. He trusted his instincts more than anything else in the world, so if they told him something wasn't right, then he was going to listen.

"What are you talking about? One moment we were kissing and planning to go back to yours and now we're following someone? Is it to do with the Trashcan Bandits?" Her tone was gleeful, and he bit his cheek. *Serves you right for lying about the stakeouts!*

"The Trashcan Bandits aren't real, honey. It's just a bunch of raccoons, I spotted them that first night we did a stakeout."

"What? But we've been doing stakeouts for weeks. Why wouldn't you say anything?"

"Because the more we got to know each other, the more we messed around and the more I looked forward to doing a fake stakeout with you," he sighed, feeling like shit for lying to her.

"They weren't fake to me," she huffed. He could just imagine that sulky bottom lip sticking out. The car ahead turned down a dark road and he followed.

"So, who are we following then?" she asked, a tremor of uncertainty escaping.

"I've seen this car leave at the same time on a few of the occasions we've been on our stakeouts. I think it has something to do with Rebelle. She said someone's been harassing her."

"Rebelle? Is she in danger?"

"I hope not. I hope they're just being idiots," he said, then filled her in on his visit from Rebelle the other week. They followed the car down the main road out of town; further along that road was the turn off for the rescue center. Blake prayed the car in front drove right past it, and that it wasn't what he thought.

But as they neared the turn off, the car spun sharply and headed down the dirt road to Rebelle's shelter. Blake cursed. He turned off his lights, not wanting the car in front to notice him pulling down the same road and draw their suspicion. A sense of dread hit Blake's stomach when he saw one of the men lean out the window and throw a beer bottle at the sign for the rescue center; glass showered down, glittering in the moonlight. His instincts were correct: they were about to make a big mistake.

Hot rage pulsed through him at the thought of these two officers whom he trusted to protect the town, harming and abusing one of their vulnerable citizens. Disappointment in himself came hot on the heels of the rage. How could he not have noticed what was going on with his own officers?

"*Pendejos!*" Justine spat, tutting over the falling glass. He nodded in agreement. He slowed the car and stayed back in the tree line, watching them drive closer to the barn. He killed the engine and glanced around. Where the fuck was the protection officer from the other precinct? He couldn't see anyone here. The rescue center was wide open to attack, leaving Rebelle vulnerable. He checked his phone and saw he had several missed calls. He dialed the number back and Sheriff Carlisle answered.

"Where the hell is your guy?" Blake demanded.

"I've been trying to reach you, where have you been? There was an incident at the county border, a large fire was set and we needed to pull our guy back to help out the fire department and investigate leads. I tried to let you know so you could get someone to cover but I'm sending someone else over now," she said. Blake tried to calm down, it wasn't her fault, and she was doing him a huge favor by having one of her officers help out every day.

"Okay, thanks. I'll check things out in the meantime," Blake replied and hung up. He opened the glove box and pulled out his firearm, checking it was loaded and the safety was off.

"Blake, what are you doing?" Justine's voice dipped slightly. *Fuck, what were you thinking bringing her here?* his mind shouted. He squeezed her knee and dropped a lingering kiss on her forehead.

"I'm just going to check that Rebelle is okay. I think they're just being assholes and trying to scare her, so I'll send them packing with a warning. Stay here and do not get out under any circumstances. Lock the doors when I leave."

"Blake, if you think they're just trying to scare her, why do you need your gun?" she asked, her brow pinched in worry.

"Honey, it's just a safety precaution, don't worry about me. Just stay here and think about all the things we're gonna do in bed when we get home later," he added, wanting to take her mind off things and fill her with the calm he wasn't feeling himself. She gave him a small smile and he kissed her lips briefly before getting out of the car. He shut his door quietly and waited for her to lock the doors before he shot her another smile through the windshield and left.

He crept up through the trees, his footsteps stealthy, not even crunching the dried leaves, his movements calculated, his breathing low. All his training had prepared him for moments like this, a covert attack. He kept his eyes focused in the darkness. The moon faded in and out of the clouds, lighting the way for a brief moment before plunging the world into eerie darkness again.

He approached the building, still scanning the area in the dark, and squatted down beside Rebelle's truck. He kept still, straining his ears for any sounds, his eyes picking up nothing.

"Get out here, you whore!" a voice shouted in the dark, menace and threat coating the words.

"Yeah, unless you want us to come in there and get you," a second voice jeered gleefully. They were clearly enjoying this, and Blake's blood boiled, his stomach turning at the realization that they wanted to seriously harm Rebelle. There was silence. It stretched on for an eternity. Blake inched around the side of the truck, moving closer.

The sound of smashing glass and laughter had his finger twitching on the trigger of his gun. He crept forward slowly, and a few feet away a figure shot past him and around the side of the building.

Blake needed to have sight of both men otherwise he was open to an attack himself. He didn't know what weapons they had and if he was incapacitated, he couldn't protect Rebelle. He leaned against the side of the building. He could hear murmurs, then a scuffle.

"I've got her!" one of the men shouted triumphantly. Blake's pulse kicked and tension set his shoulders as he peered around the side of the building.

"Fucking bitch bit me!" one of the men shouted then Blake heard a slap against flesh and promised himself both men would pay for any injuries Rebelle endured.

"Just fucking shoot her!" the other shouted. Blake rushed forward, only one man in his sights, but he needed to save Rebelle before they hurt her anymore. He ran to one figure, grabbing him from behind, trapping both his hands behind his back. The man used his trapped hands to his advantage and flipped Blake over his shoulder. Blake fell to the ground, the man jumping on him and raining his fists down. Blake blocked a punch to the face and raised his hand, cracking the butt of his gun over the man's temple. The guy grunted and slumped over. *One down, one to go.*

Just as he stood, Blake heard a scream, but it didn't sound like Rebelle.

"Justine?!" he shouted, fear pounding through his chest. She screamed again, the sound followed by a gunshot. The noise of the gunshot ricocheted all around him through the silent night.

Blake ran towards it, his heart in his mouth.

Chapter 20

Justine sat in the dark, peering out through the windshield into the trees and trying not to panic. *What if something happened to him?* She knew Blake could look after himself, Lord knows he was more than capable. But there were two men out there, potentially armed, who clearly had no concern over hurting someone if they were there to mess with Rebelle.

"Hasn't the poor woman suffered enough?" Justine muttered to herself. Rebelle hadn't come to see her yet, but she would, Justine knew she was probably working up to it. It took a lot of courage to face your issues and talk about them with a virtual stranger, just ask Blake.

She sat in the car, listening hard for any indications of trouble, chewing her nails nervously. So many times she reached for the door handle to go after him. She couldn't bear the thought of something happening to him although she wasn't prepared to acknowledge what her feelings *really* meant. That was a drama for another day.

Her eyes scanned the darkness. The pine trees swaying gently in the breeze had her seeing shadows everywhere she looked. A twig snapped close by. Her breath snagged in her throat, her blood pounding in her ears. Three meters away she spotted a man step out of the trees. Dressed head to toe in black, he blended with the night, but when the moon shone out from behind the clouds, he was illuminated. As was the gun he was holding, the moonlight bouncing off the metal. Justine gasped and ducked down in her seat.

She peeked out the bottom of the window, trying to stay hidden as she watched the man stealthily follow the same path Blake had taken. Justine's stomach twisted. Now it was three against one, and at least one of them had a weapon. Blake would have no idea. Justine sat up straight, she had to tell him, had to warn him that he would be ambushed. She grabbed for her phone, tapping the screen but it wouldn't come on; the battery must have died.

"*Mierda!*" she hissed, throwing her phone down in frustration. How could she warn him? Her hand reached out for the door handle even as her brain screamed *don't be that woman!* But she couldn't leave him out there vulnerable. It was Blake, he was *her man*, he had protected her before, and anyone would do the same, *he* would do the same.

She opened the door, stepping out quietly into the still night and easing the door closed. She didn't shut it properly, to avoid making any unnecessary noise. She took a deep, shuddering breath, then tiptoed forwards up the hill, towards the building. By the time she was there, she was terrified: there were too many noises she couldn't decipher, and it was too dark to see. But it was equally terrifying when the moon came out from the clouds and lit up the night, exposing her.

By the time she reached the building, the moon had disappeared again, and she could barely see a thing. She ignored her fear, she just needed to find him.

"Blake?" she whispered. Nothing. She inched around the corner of the building, she called him again but there was no response. The sound of shattering glass made her cry out in surprise, and she backed away, smacking right into someone. Strong arms wrapped around her middle, locking her in place and a hand clamped over her mouth, cutting off her scream before it could form. The stench of sweat, beer and gasoline invaded her nostrils and her stomach roiled.

"I've got her!" her captor shouted. He started dragging her away, but her fighting instinct kicked in. She managed to work her mouth free and clamped her teeth down on his fingers. He howled before loosening his grip.

"Fucking bitch bit me!" he shouted, rage fusing his words.

"Just fucking shoot her!" Another man shouted, and she realized the seriousness of her situation. She tried to run but he grabbed her arm and threw her against the building, her chin smacked against the brick, her teeth knocking together, and pain seared along her jaw.

He dragged her back and threw her to the ground. She bucked against him, working her leg between their bodies and kicking him away. She flipped herself over and tried to crawl away, gravel biting into her knees. She had to grit her teeth to keep from crying out. Her attacker grabbed her leg and dragged her backwards and she screamed as her bare leg scraped against the gravel, shredding her exposed skin.

"Justine!" Blake shouted but before she could respond, she was punched, hard. Her eye socket throbbed, and her vision blurred. A gunshot rang out, she caught a brief glance of her surroundings as the flash from the muzzle lit up the night. Rebelle stood behind Justine's assailant, gun in hand, a fierce expression on her face. The man fell forward, pinning Justine to the ground before rolling off her.

"Justine!" Blake shouted, his voice frantic.

"I'm here," she called out. She caught his scent as he bent down to her, he lifted her up and wrapped his arms around her, squeezing her tight. She winced in pain but didn't push him away, she was just glad he was there and was fine.

"Rebelle, is that you?" he called, pulling away from Justine and heading towards Rebelle. The moonlight shone down on them, and Justine watched as Blake pulled Rebelle into a bone-crushing hug. Jealousy rushed through her, and she tried unsuccessfully to put her feelings to one side. A scuffle to her left startled her, she shouted, "Blake!"

Blake turned at the same time, his gun raised as the man in black Justine had seen earlier approached.

"Whoa! Deputy Miller? It's Officer Davis, I was sent by Sheriff Carlisle?"

"Badge!" Blake barked, keeping his weapon trained on the man as he began to reach into his pocket, slowly. The officer withdrew his badge, tossing it to Blake along with a small flashlight. Blake inspected the badge before lowering his weapon, he tossed it back.

"Get these men in handcuffs. This one needs to go to hospital, the other one is around the side of the building, unconscious."

Officer Davis bobbed at him before setting to work quickly. Blake flicked his eyes to Justine before turning back to Rebelle, murmuring softly to her, and gently taking the gun from her hand. He then called an ambulance and only when it turned up, did he have time to deal with Justine. He glared at her injuries before sending her off in the ambulance, saying he'd meet her at the hospital.

Justine felt like crying. She knew he was just doing his job, but he didn't need to be so cold with her, she had been through a traumatic ordeal. Maybe Blake didn't care for her at all?

*

Blake paced back and forth like a caged animal. What the hell had she been thinking coming after him like that? His heart had finally started to slow its rhythmic pounding, but his fear still burned hot and bright. Why hadn't she listened to him and stayed in the car? Did she know how much worse the situation could've been? He squeezed his eyes shut at the thought, *don't go down that road*. Why the hell had he even brought her in the first place? It was his fault for being stupid, he knew he should've dropped her at home first. But then God knows what would've happened to Rebelle if he had taken that detour and not made it back in time.

"Fuck!" he shouted, kicking the chair in the hospital waiting room in frustration. He couldn't have won either way. He sat down, slumping forward, dropping his head in his hands. The sound of her scream, the fear on her face. He had been ready to tear the world apart to protect her. But he'd failed. *Again.* Seeing her bloodied, bruised and in pain made him feel ill. He could barely look at her without rage consuming him.

Both offenders were in custody and would be

prosecuted to the fullest extent of the law. On checking Austin's car, Blake found rope, zip ties, gasoline and matches. He shuddered at the idea of what they had planned for Rebelle. They admitted to setting the fire at the county border to draw the police away from the rescue center but wouldn't talk anymore. It seemed like they had wanted to exact revenge for the 'murder' of Sheriff Black. Blake was ashamed they had been part of the same unit as him. He was now conducting a full investigation into their backgrounds and the backgrounds of any officers they were affiliated with. He would ensure nothing like this would ever happen in his town again.

He was distracted from his spiralling thoughts by Justine coming towards him. He took in her injuries: the black eye, bruised chin. Her thigh was bandaged, causing her to limp slightly. His stomach clenched sharply as he saw her wounds, and his simmering rage returned full force, choking him.

"I'll take you home," he said gruffly, not waiting for a response, he needed to get out of there. He left the hospital to pull his car around the front, feeling calmer by the time he pulled up outside the exit. He helped ease Justine into the passenger seat and they drove to her place in silence. He didn't trust himself to speak yet.

The drive was mercifully short and when they pulled up outside her house, he got out and helped her out of the car, gripping her so tightly, he never wanted to let her go. He helped her inside and into her kitchen, dropping her keys on the table and scrubbing a hand over his mouth.

"You can leave, if you need to go and check on Rebelle," she muttered. *Was that jealousy in her voice?*

"I'm not leaving until we've had this out," he said firmly, stopping in front of her.

"Had what out?"

"What the hell were you thinking?" he roared. She jolted, her eyes blinking rapidly in shock. She opened her mouth to reply but he wasn't done.

"You only had to do one thing, Justine! Stay in the goddamn car, and you wouldn't even do that!" She tried to talk again but he held up his finger. "I'm not finished," he stated, and she raised her eyebrows at him, a sassy look crossing her face. He knew he was overstepping the line, but he had never dealt with his emotions well and he needed to get this out.

"Do you even know what could have happened to you? What it looked like they were planning to do? You just got caught in the crossfire and look what *happened* to you!" He jabbed a finger towards her injuries. His breathing became ragged as he took in her face again and he fought back all the scenarios of her getting hurt that tried to bombard him.

"Are you done?" she asked.

"No," he said gruffly, tugging her to him, cupping her cheeks gently before pressing his lips to hers. He was trying to be mindful of her wounds, but his kiss was urgent. His lips pressed firmly against hers like he was trying to seal them together, to keep her in his arms. As long as she was in his arms, he could keep her safe. His kiss was his apology for letting something bad happen to her, for not protecting her better, for failing her. His kiss was a promise that nothing bad would ever happen to her again. His kiss was everything he could offer her, and she took it.

She met his urgency with her own, nibbling at the seam of his mouth to get him to open up and let her in. Their tongues stroked together, and his breath huffed out of him. When they drew apart, chests heaving with their breaths, he brushed her hair behind her ear and stared down at her. He watched as her eyes filled with tears and his chest ached as they spilled over.

"Don't cry, honey, I'm sorry," he murmured, swiping at her cheeks, catching the droplets.

"I was fine until you yelled at me!" she cried. God, he could be a dick sometimes, he needed to learn to control his emotions better. That was one of the reasons he had to see a psychologist in the first place. He tried to reach for her again, but she stepped back, bumping into the kitchen table.

"No! Now it's my turn, don't you *dare* come into my house and shout at me!"

He didn't have the guts to point out that she was shouting at him for shouting at her.

She wasn't done. "I came after you because you were in danger and I wanted to warn you. How could I leave you out there with someone who had a gun? I didn't want you to die, jeez what a terrible person I must be! *Pinche estúpido!*" she yelled, sarcasm dripping from her words.

"Okay, I get it, I'm sorry," he said, reaching for her again. She reluctantly let him take her hand. "It's just, when you screamed, and the gun went off, I thought I'd failed again…" he trailed off, looking away. The sound of her scream replaying in his ears, so similar to another scream that haunted him, both echoing in his mind. His throat constricted and his chest started to tighten. *Oh no, not now, please!* He gripped at his chest, his breathing becoming more labored. He knew what was coming.

"Blake?" Justine stared at him with concern. He turned away from her, trying to overcome the attack. He tried to walk but his legs turned to jelly, his vision began to cloud. He felt hot, his palms dampening as his breath sawed in and out of his chest. His stomach churned as the panic took over. He tried to fight it, but his mind turned to mush.

He stumbled out of the kitchen and into the hallway, not wanting Justine to witness his meltdown. He needed to break in private. *No, remember your techniques!* His brain shouted through the fog. He tried to think. There was the five to one technique but that was no use, he was too far gone, he couldn't breathe, and his sight was shot to shit from his panic attack.

"Come on Blake, you know what to do." Her calm voice penetrated the fog. He tried to recall a positive realization but couldn't think of anything. He tried 'then and now' but he couldn't focus.

"Come on!" he growled in frustration.

"Come back to me, I know you can do it, you've done it before, remember?" she said. She was right, what was it last time? He'd focused on listing objects, picking a color. *Okay, you can do this,* he chanted. His stomach lurched, and his chest burned from the struggle to breathe properly. He opened his mind to pick a color and the color orange slammed into his brain again. *Orange...basketball, Justine in that orange slinky dress, she looked so beautiful in that. Those silly orange earrings she wore that dangled delicately, teasing her neck, making me want to kiss it, she does have a very kissable neck.*

Images filled his mind, and his stomach began to settle. *Justine's orange heels digging into my shoulders while I made her fall apart after our first disagreement, the sexy orange pajamas she wore when I pulled her over that night, she looked stunning in the moonlight...*his vision began to clear and the tightness in his chest eased up slightly. *The orange bra and panty set she wore when we had sex for the first time, God, that night was amazing, she was amazing. The orange candle that flickered on the table that same night when we ate our first dinner together, her eyes shining at me across the table as she called me courageous, and* *thanked me for my service.*

As he came back to himself, he was aware he was crouching down in her hallway. She crouched beside him, stroking her palm across his back in soothing circles. He turned to face her, his embarrassment at suffering another panic attack in her presence written all over his face.

"There you are," she whispered, a soft smile playing on her lips. He nearly broke, then and there. This woman was incredible. She was open, honest and fearless. What had he done to deserve her help? Her kindness and care were unparalleled. And he'd shouted at her like a *cabrón* and then had a meltdown. *Fantastic.* He stood up, shaking out his legs.

"Sorry about that," he mumbled.

"Don't apologize, don't you see the progress that you made? You pulled yourself out of it!" she gushed and tugged his arm, pulling him back into the kitchen. "How did you do it? Which technique was it you used?" she asked excitedly.

"Uh, it was positive realization," he lied. He couldn't tell her he thought about her, she would probably think it was crossing another boundary and her ethics would put another mark against her name.

"That's amazing, you're amazing. This calls for a celebration!" She hurried over to the refrigerator and grabbed a bottle of champagne, their argument forgotten. Opening the cabinet and snatching up two glasses, she came back to him.

"It really doesn't," he said, feeling embarrassed again but also enjoying her happiness.

"Every win counts and needs to be celebrated accordingly," she said, popping the cork. She poured a glass and held it out to him, waggling her eyebrows. He chuckled and accepted the drink, she held hers out.

"To you, for fighting, and winning." She glared at him until he repeated the words back to her. She pushed him, no matter how much he fought and how ungrateful he seemed, but words couldn't describe the gratitude he had for what she was doing. They clinked their glasses and then she put one arm around his neck.

"You didn't fail me, Blake. Your intuition told you something bad was happening and you raced up there with no hesitation. You saved Rebelle. You saved me. This is what you were made for." She whispered the last part and he soaked up her words as they began to patch up the broken space inside him. He realized that these negative feelings wouldn't last forever. Finally he had hope, something he hadn't had in a long time. *What would I do without her?*

She gripped his jaw and pulled him down for a kiss, a kiss he quickly deepened, slanting his mouth over hers. He slowed the pace down, just the way she liked, and he smiled against her mouth when her breath hitched. God, he lov—*liked* that sound. She sighed into him, the sound teasing him, pushing the boundaries of his self-control.

He pulled her firmly against him, his palm splaying across her back, and she gasped as she came up against his hardness. He swallowed the sound, tangling his fingers in her hair, tilting her head for better access and slid his tongue into her mouth as she ground her hips against him. He spun them around and laid her down on the dining table, not breaking contact once.

They kissed until she started whimpering and he pulled back to look down at her. Her hair tangled around her, lips swollen, cheeks tinged red from his beard. If there was a more beautiful woman, he hadn't met her, because she didn't exist.

He pushed her top up, exposing more of her

delectable brown skin, then her bra, revealing her breasts. Her nipples were hard, begging for his mouth. He dropped his head to suck on one, then the other. Her legs scissored against his thighs and her nails clawed at his scalp. He loved her passion, bathed in it and it fired his own. She didn't play games, she showed him exactly what she wanted, she was perfect.

*

Justine thought she should probably stop him, they had both had a rough night, but as his mouth worked its magic, all rational thought fled. She needed him as much as he needed her, she was too emotionally on edge from this evening's incident, she needed his comfort.

This time it didn't seem like he was doing it to make a point, like he had previously. It was borne from want and need. His movements were clumsy, his desire too great for calculated, purposeful touches designed to drive her wild. She met his urgency with her own. She was tumbling down a rabbit hole, falling endlessly, drowning in him and she never wanted it to end.

He tugged at her clothes, his hands fumbling with the zipper on her jean shorts until she helped him. He hooked his thumb in the waistband and tugged them down, leaving her in those orange panties that he liked so much. He stared down at them, his eyes fixed, then shook his head and tugged them off, baring her. His gaze fixed on her again, staring between her legs before he dragged his eyes to meet hers. Her stomach clenched at the raw desire she saw banked in the molten silver depths.

He held her stare as he pushed a finger inside her. He withdrew it, slowly, and when he thrust again, he added another and curled them in that way that made her see stars. He continued to work her in that same lazy, unhurried way, the intensity of his stare ratcheting up her need until she surrendered, shouting his name.

He withdrew his fingers and thrust inside her while she was still riding the waves of her climax. He pounded into her, rattling the table, scraping it across the floor with his movements and she loved it. She loved him. The knowledge filled her as her second orgasm barreled into her and she had to bite back the words as they tried to escape her throat.

He still watched her, his expression unreadable as she orgasmed, unable to hide away from what he made her feel. She was raw, vulnerable, and exposed. His jaw clenched and she felt him pulse inside her. He grunted and closed his eyes, his head tilting back in pleasure.

What did she do now? How did she act? Did he already know she loved him? He looped his arm under her knees and wrapped the other around her waist, lifting her, and he carried her upstairs. He gently lay her on the bed and tucked her in before he joined her, curling his big body around hers. His unique, mouth-watering scent enveloped her and, without a word he fell asleep, holding her tight.

She turned in his arms, trying not to wake him, and watched him as he slept. She stroked her thumb over the furrow between his brows, smoothing it away, and in his sleep, he relaxed. His panic attack had nearly caused one of her own. Watching him go through that had been harrowing. It had been harder to witness this time over all the others. For the first time, *she* had panicked and forgotten how to help him. All her training had disappeared out of her mind, all her studies and research gone, and she'd been helpless. Because she loved him.

Justine didn't know when it had happened, probably weeks ago, but it only solidified in that moment. When her heart had torn apart watching him struggle, and after that she just wanted to wrap her arms around him and tell him everything was okay, that she had him and would never let him go. She had failed him. She had forgotten until the last minute to even say anything. Her love for this wonderful man who was so brave and fearless had turned her into a failure.

The knowledge settled like lead in her stomach as she realized this is how it would be now, and she couldn't help him like that. She couldn't continue to treat him now that she had developed such a deep, emotional attachment to him. She could no longer be objective. A sob caught in her throat at the thought of not treating him and working with him. She buried her face in his chest, his arms tightening around her in his sleep.

She would have to refer him to someone else, she wouldn't be able to see him anymore, it wasn't right. It hadn't been right in the first place, but it had been easier to justify when it was just sex. If she had known what this would turn into, would she still have done it? *Yes, in a heartbeat.*

She laughed bitterly as she realized she had fallen in love with the one person she was convinced she never would. Goddammit, she had no one but herself to blame. He didn't love her, he didn't love anyone, and he definitely didn't want a family or children.

She couldn't stay like this. She was tempted, so damn tempted, but she couldn't do that to herself, couldn't condemn herself to living a life of continual heartbreak, loving someone who couldn't love her back or give her what she'd always dreamed of.

He mumbled something in his sleep and gripped her tighter. She had tonight. She would spend her last night in his arms, memorizing his face, breathing in his scent and she would remember this moment always.

Lila Dawes

She didn't sleep, and when the sun came up, she slipped away quietly, leaving him in her bed as she went into her office early. Once there, she dug through her contacts, and, her heart breaking, she made the call.

Chapter 21

Blake's instincts were all out of whack. When he'd woken up yesterday morning alone in Justine's bed, something hadn't felt right, and not just because she wasn't there with him. The brief message he received from her hadn't felt right and the two times he popped into her office to see her, she hadn't been available. These were all completely innocent things individually, but when combined with his gut feeling, they made him suspicious.

Something had changed the other night, when he had kissed her, stripped her. When he had seen her orange panties something had stirred inside him, he didn't know what it was, but it hovered there even now, just out of reach. Things between them had shifted, this wasn't just a casual friends-with-benefits scenario anymore, that was for sure, but he didn't know what it was.

The L-word circled his brain, but he dismissed it

immediately. He didn't love her, he didn't love anyone. But he did care about her deeply, she was his closest friend. The way she was helping him made him truly believe for the first time that he could get better. He knew he'd never be cured, this would never go away completely, there was too much scar tissue for that. But he could manage it, because of her and her amazing skills. She had become so special to him and for the first time, he didn't panic about what the rest of his life looked like, he was enjoying what it currently was far too much.

Until that niggling feeling came back. He tried calling her, but she didn't answer. He messaged her but she hadn't seen it yet. He was worried and that feeling just wouldn't go away. He needed to practice some of the techniques she taught him, his anxiety was getting the better of him.

He would see Justine this morning for his session and make sure she was okay, and when he saw she was, he would kiss her, then when she tried to take it further, he would resist her. He would resist her until he couldn't anymore and then he would give in and let her have her way with him until she had satisfied her carnal lust. Just the thought had him grinning like an idiot.

He got dressed and went downstairs, passing his home gym. He hadn't been working out as much lately. He usually did that to help ease his stress and anxiety, but recently he hadn't felt the need. He gave Penny a quick cuddle goodbye, she grumbled at him, berating him for leaving her again and then he got in his cruiser. As he buckled up, his phone rang and he huffed, annoyed that something was coming between him and getting to Justine quicker. He pulled out his phone but didn't recognize the number.

"Deputy Miller," he answered.

"Hi Blake, this is Dr. Patrick Hall. Just thought I would call to introduce myself and see if we can get our first session arranged?"

"What for?" Blake asked. He didn't recognize the name, he wasn't expecting a call from anyone.

"For your treatment? Dr. Rodríguez-Hamilton said you've made some significant improvements in the last few months which is fantastic to hear."

"Justine said *what?*"

"It's difficult accepting when you've done all you can for a client, but it just goes to her credit that she's aware she lacks the experience to continue and chose to seek help. I can't wait to start working together," Dr. Hall said. Suddenly that niggly feeling made sense; a roaring sound filled Blake's ears.

"What do you mean, first session?" Blake gritted out, a pit in his stomach forming.

"Oh, jeez. Have I put my foot in it? Has she not told you yet?"

"Told me what?"

"Dr. Rodríguez-Hamilton, Justine, has put in a transfer for you to my office so you'll no longer be working with her. I'm your new psychologist."

*

She heard him before she saw him. He banged into the building, stomped into her office coming face to face with her, fury pulsing off him in thick waves. Hilda ran in behind him but Justine signaled everything was fine, so she closed the door.

"Who the fuck is Dr. Hall?" Blake spat. Last time she'd seen him, his eyes had been warm with affection and desire, melting for her. Now they were cold, hard and terrifying.

She swallowed nervously and smoothed her hands over

her blouse. She had been dreading this moment, she'd known exactly how he would react, but she still hadn't been prepared to see him. She wasn't prepared for how good he looked and the effect he had on her. She wasn't prepared for the way she wanted to throw herself into his strong arms, bury her face in his neck and beg him to love her. The image tore her insides apart and she steeled herself.

"Deputy Miller, please take a seat," she said, fixing her professional smile on her face. He sneered when he saw it. She knew he hated it, but it was necessary.

"I'll stand. Explain. Now." Each word punctuated with his rage.

"Dr. Hall is much more qualified than myself to treat you. I'm afraid I've done as much as I can with you."

"Bullshit."

"Deputy Miller, stop cursing in my office." Her firm tone momentarily seemed to take some of the wind out of his sails, but he rallied.

"How could you do this? After everything?" He shook his head.

"Dr. Hall is a renowned specialist. If I continued to treat you when I knew someone was better qualified that would be detrimental to your progress, so I reached out to him." Her heart was pounding in her ears as she took in his stony expression.

"You didn't even tell me, Justine!" he shouted, and she jumped at the sudden lift in volume.

"I was going to," she lied, her voice quiet because deep inside she knew she'd been too much of a coward to tell him.

"When? Before our next session? Which starts in two minutes?"

"I'm sorry, Blake."

When she said nothing further, his eyes narrowed, his piercing stare making her heart pound and her palms sweat. She shifted uncomfortably on the spot.

"What's going on?" he asked, reaching for her hand. His gentle tone, full of concern, cracked something inside her and she spun away, choking back the words that lodged in her throat.

"Nothing's going on," she said, and he came around to face her.

"Don't lie to me. I know you well enough by now."

She marched back to her desk and began shuffling papers. "I'd like you to leave now, Deputy."

"Justine, honey, what's going on?" The endearment, the concern, *damn this man.*

Tears sprang to her eyes. "Nothing's going on."

He gripped her shoulders, tingles branching from his touch.

"Justine, tell me, what's-"

"Please leave, Blake!" She couldn't hold it back any longer.

"Honey, whatever's going on, we can handle it together, you know I'll help you any-"

"I love you!" she shouted at him. Not exactly coming out how she had dreamed, but it had been bubbling inside her. He reared back like she'd slapped him. Her words hung in the air between them, and she wished she could snatch them back and tell him she was kidding, tell him he'd misheard but it was too late, the words were out there. His mouth floundered open and closed, his eyes darting around.

"No, you don't," he said softly, shaking his head.

"Don't tell me what I feel," she replied, fiercely. She crossed her arms over her chest, then she saw it, the moment his expression softened to one of pity, and it broke her heart even more.

He didn't love her.

"I can't treat you anymore, it's not right. I can't separate myself from you enough to be able to help you objectively."

"Then don't. Why do we have to stop what we're doing? Things are going just fine, they've never been better!"

"Do you love me?" The words left her mouth before she could stop them, and he blanched but didn't respond. It was all the answer she needed. "The lines are blurring," she said.

"Why can't we just continue on as we are, being together?" he tried again.

She wanted to, oh, how she wanted to, but she wouldn't do that to herself. She needed to walk away while she could still put herself back together. She shook her head. He gripped her shoulders again, his fingers digging into her flesh and she looked up at him. His brows were knitted together, his eyes wide in desperation.

"I'm offering you more than I've ever offered anyone else," he said.

"That's not true," she whispered, and he spun away from her.

"You know I didn't want to marry her. She tricked me, and I had no choice!" he shouted.

"Yes, you did. You made one, didn't you?" she countered.

"I was just a kid. I didn't want to stay with her, but I didn't know any better."

"Exactly, you were just a kid and yet your guilt over Katie is stopping you from moving on in life, from finding love again." Even in the midst of her emotional breakdown she was helping him, putting him first.

Because even if it wasn't with her, she wanted him to find love, he deserved it.

"Don't turn this back on me, you're abandoning me when I need you most! Look how far I've come. You're willing to just throw it away? How could you betray me like this?" His voice rose again with his anger, an undercurrent of hurt in his words. She didn't respond, there was nothing to say. She was done.

"So that's it?" he asked, spreading his arms wide.

"Dr. Hall is wonderful. He's going to do great work wi-"

"Don't," he interrupted. He scrubbed a hand over his face and looked away. He shook his head and when he turned back to her, his expression blank, his eyes emotionless. "To hell with this, and to hell with you." He walked out, slamming the door behind him as he went.

She sank down onto the couch and buried her face in her hands and cried the tears she had been too stubborn to shed for days. Hours later, when she picked herself up, she realized that she'd missed at least two appointments. There was a soft knock on the door before Hilda poked her head in.

"I've canceled all your sessions for today," she said.

"You didn't need to do that," Justine replied, trying to sound like she hadn't been crying for two hours.

"Yes, I did." The kindness in Hilda's face brought about a fresh wave of tears.

"I've been so stupid," she said, her voice cracking as a fresh sob broke through.

"Nonsense." The word came out so matter of fact that Justine nearly smiled. "You've been *living*, dear. I can't tell you how wonderful it's been to see you so happy these last few months. I had been so worried about you before." Hilda said.

"But I've done something terrible!" Justine cried. "I slept with a client."

Hilda just shrugged. "Eh! What're you gonna do? Come on, let's go to my place. You might be teaching me traditional Mexican cuisine, but I've been working on my cocktails. I've got Palomas!" Hilda winked at her.

"Hilda, it's eleven o'clock in the morning."

"Well, it's five somewhere. Come on, let's go."

Justine smiled. She didn't think she could face Christy and Taylor just yet. She knew they would be sympathetic and supportive, but she felt so stupid. She had ignored their advice and done the opposite of what they told her. She wiped her tears and grabbed her belongings as Hilda got ready to lock up.

That day she drank a shitload of Palomas while she poured her heart out to Hilda who was a fantastic listener. By the time Justine stumbled home that evening, she was convinced that in the morning she would feel fine. She would be fine without Blake, in fact, she was pretty sure she was already over him.

However as soon as she got into her bed, and smelled his lingering scent on her sheets, she promptly burst into tears and realized alcohol was a dirty liar. She wasn't over him at all and she decided to go and cry herself to sleep on the couch instead.

*

Blake had a face like thunder for the rest of the week, although there were positives to this: it meant everyone left him the fuck alone. His mood was getting darker by the day and no amount of cuddles with Penny or workouts were calming him down. And he knew exactly who was to blame. He couldn't even think her name without nearing a rage blackout. Now he was mad again, goddammit!

How could she do this to him? They had been doing so well. He'd trusted her, he had opened up to her and let her inside the battlefield of his mind. And she'd abandoned him, right when he was making progress.

Blake stomped around his office, pacing back and forth. He had barely slept since his encounter with Justine and counted three panic attacks in four days. He overcame them all but only by using the techniques she taught him, fixating on the color orange again and of course all that did was bring about images of her. He couldn't get her out of his mind, she had worked her way inside, hollowed him out and then left him to pick up the pieces. He hated to admit that at the core of his anger was hurt.

There was a knock at his door.

"What?" he barked.

The door opened, Jim poked his head around and Blake instantly felt guilty at his display of temper.

"I've got that report you wanted, on the Monday night incident," Jim held the file out and Blake sighed, ushering him in. Jim placed the report on Blake's desk and hung back. "Everything okay, Deputy?" he asked. Blake sighed again, a regular noise he was making this week.

"Yes, thank you, Jim. Just a few things on my mind. How are you?"

The older man looked surprised to be asked. "I'm fine, son," Jim replied, he kept talking but Blake didn't hear anything else. For some reason, definitely *nothing* to do with the fact that Jim called him *son*, he got a lump in his throat.

"...so what do you think?" Jim's thick, southern drawl brought him back.

"About what?"

"Fishing tomorrow? My buddy Len can't make it and I

need someone to take his place."

Blake had never been fishing in his life, hadn't really had any interest in it before, but suddenly he wanted to go more than anything.

"Sounds great," he replied, and clapped Jim on the back, the older man smiling like a loon.

"Come on, it's getting late, and I bet the book club will have left now. I got some steaks we can throw on the grill. You like Palomas? Hil's been making tons of the stuff."

Blake held up his hands. "That's nice of you, Jim but you really don't need to do that for me."

"I know I don't need to, I want to," Jim replied. Blake hesitated. "I ain't getting any younger, son." Jim added, giving Blake a push towards the door.

Blake smiled and let Jim push him again before giving in. They rode back to Jim and Hilda's house in separate cars and when he walked in the front door the place immediately felt like home. Hilda took his coat and began fussing over him like she was his mom, and he would be lying if he said he didn't enjoy it a little.

Jim grilled the steaks while Hilda grilled him. He was seriously impressed with her interrogation techniques. Blake didn't know how it happened, but he ended up telling them everything that happened between him and Justine and apologizing to Jim for his foul mood these past few days.

"Well shoot son, any old fool could see it was lady troubles," Jim said with a tsk.

Blake snorted. He got the feeling that Hilda knew more than she let on. Not surprising considering how close she and Justine were. This time when he thought of Justine the flash of hot rage that seemed to accompany him the last few days was down to a light simmer. Then he proceeded to tell them about his mental health struggles. He didn't flinch once while explaining what had happened to him over the years, the first time that had ever happened.

"Are your panic attacks worse right now?" Jim asked, distracting him and he nodded. "Well, I hate to say it, son, but I think you need to see this new doctor of yours before you take any more steps back. You don't want to undo all the hard work you and Justine have done just because of your little ol' pride." Blake opened his mouth to protest but Jim held up his hand.

"I know you want to work with Justine but that's not possible right now. You need some space from each other to sort out your feelings."

"Feelings?" Blake asked, confusion clouding his features. He saw Jim shoot Hilda a look that he didn't appreciate, because it seemed to say, *this kid is an idiot.*

"Jim's right, dear. I know you don't want to hear it, but you need to put your health first," Hilda added. Damn, they were right. He would be stupid to hold off meeting with Dr. Hall just because his pride didn't want to end what he and Justine had.

"Anyway, we need to get you fighting fit if you're planning on making that bid for sheriff sometime soon," Jim said, a twinkle in his eye.

"You think I could do it?" Blake asked hesitantly. He had been thinking about it more and more recently. The town and its residents had become such a part of him that he couldn't imagine ever leaving. This was the step he had planned on taking way down the line when he was well again. But, who knows, maybe he could do it sooner than he thought?

"You'll make a damn fine sheriff, son," Jim said, and Hilda nodded in agreement. After talking until late, he finally left, both Jim and Hilda hugging him goodbye, even though he would be back in the morning to fish.

When he got home, he sat on his couch, playing with Penny, watching sports, and thinking. His mind made up, he took out his phone. He knew it was late, but he still rang Dr. Hall and left a message asking to arrange an appointment for his first session.

Chapter 22

Before Justine knew it, weeks had gone by. She floated through the days aimlessly, not paying attention to anything in particular. She couldn't even say how many clients she had seen which she should probably feel bad about, but she didn't. She didn't feel anything, except the aching chasm in her chest where her heart had been.

She made it through the days and when she finally went to bed, she sank into the sweet relief of sleep. But even then she couldn't escape the pain: he was always there. And when she awoke in the morning, with tears on her face, she started the whole cycle again.

She was torn between feeling grateful that she had finally known love, and regret that she now knew how painful it could be. Why did it have to be him? She had never suspected in a million years it would be him; he was the opposite of everything she wanted. But now, she couldn't picture life without him. So far it was bleak.

She wondered how he was doing. How were his sessions going with Dr. Hall? Had he made any more progress? Was he sleeping? How was Penny? And the final one that rattled through her brain, did he miss her? She'd spotted him earlier in the day laughing with Bob, the shared owner of The Rusty Bucket Inn. Seeing him was like taking an ice pick to the heart and burning alive all at the same time. She had tried so hard to move on but seeing him that morning had put her back to square one. She felt like she was missing a limb, the ache unbearable. He looked gorgeous, carefree, and easy-going. He didn't look like he was missing anyone or heartbroken at all. He was thriving, while she was barely hanging on.

That afternoon, she was sitting in her office, a silent tear trickled down her cheek while she tried to rally herself.

"Knock-knock."

She looked up and saw Taylor and Christy standing in the doorway.

"Hey buddy," Christy crooned, and they both walked slowly towards her like they were approaching a bear in the wild. Guilt instantly ate at Justine. She had shut them out, not wanting to admit how stupid she had been with Blake.

"Hey beautiful, how are you?" Taylor asked.

Justine swiped at her damp cheeks, brushing away her tears. "What are you guys doing here?" she rasped. They came over to stand beside her, each dropping down to hug her.

"Hilda called us, she's worried about you," Taylor said, sympathy pouring from her.

"Want to tell us what's wrong?" Christy stroked Justine's hair and she leaned into the touch, seeking comfort from her oldest friends. They waited for her to speak. She opened her mouth but didn't know what to say.

"We're definitely not going to judge, especially her, she's got no room to judge anyone," Christy hiked her thumb at Taylor as she spoke. Taylor frowned at her, the action causing a small snicker to work its way free from Justine.

"Thank you both, but I don't think I want to talk about it just yet. I thought I was doing okay but then today I realized I'm not, and I'll just cry if I talk about it," Justine said.

"That's fine, we're here when you do feel ready to talk," Christy said.

"How about singing? You haven't done that for a while and my regulars miss you. I miss you. And it's a great way for you to express how you're feeling without having to talk to anyone," Taylor added.

Justine thought for a moment. Taylor was right. She hadn't sung for a while, and it was how she usually dealt with anything that was bothering her. She needed to pull herself out of this funk and it made sense to use this as her outlet. The idea was bolstered by the fact that Blake didn't go to the bar when it was busy, so there was no danger of him turning up and her going to pieces.

"Why don't you come to the bar tonight? We can have a drink, you can sing your heart out, then we can drink, we can play pool and then maybe drink?"

"Basically, we're gonna drink. I've got a bottle of Patrón with your name on it," Taylor teased, and Justine smiled for the first time in weeks.

"Sounds great. Thank you both, really, you're amazing," Justine said, and hugged them tightly. She walked them out of the building with promises of seeing them later. Instead of heading back into her office she stopped by Hilda's desk.

"I know I probably overstepped but-" Hilda began but Justine didn't let her finish. She wrapped her arms around Hilda and squeezed her tight.

"Thank you," she whispered. Hilda hugged her and rubbed her hand over Justine's back soothingly.

"Any time, dear."

Later that night, Justine sat on stage at The Rusty Bucket Inn, the crowd gathered in tight around her. Her stomach dipped in apprehension, she looked into Christy and Taylor's excited faces. She could do this. She could do this *without* crying. And maybe when she did do this, she would feel better. She took a deep breath, strummed the opening notes on her guitar, opened her mouth and let her pain pour out.

*

Blake went along to his first session with Dr. Hall, dread bubbling his stomach. The man's office was busy and cluttered, nothing like Justine's clean, mess-free office. The receptionist was a young bombshell who tried to flirt with him, but he missed seeing Hilda. Although he actually saw her plenty at the moment, given how much time he was spending with Jim. He found her presence comforting, and right now, he really needed comforting.

Blake had to sit and wait in the reception instead of going straight in. The longer he sat there, the moodier he became. When the receptionist finally said he could go in, he got up and with a sigh entered the office. The office was full of deep mahogany bookcases and wood-paneled walls, it was very dark and imposing. Once again, he thought of Justine's bright, open office where he felt at home.

"Ah, Blake! Lovely to see you, please take a seat." Dr.

Hall came towards him and pumped his hand enthusiastically. Dr. Hall's hairline had long gone but he had kind eyes set in a round face. He was dressed entirely in tweed which just made Blake think of Justine in all her sexy dresses. At least with Dr. Hall being all tweed-clad and male, Blake was unlikely to spend most of his sessions hiding an unwanted erection, like he had with Justine. *Hello, silver lining, my name is Blake.* Unless he kept *thinking* about her. He pushed her image out of his mind and took a seat on the dark brown leather chair, the doctor sitting opposite him.

"How are you doing?" Dr. Hall asked.

Blake shrugged. "Fine, and you?" The doctor laughed but Blake didn't think he'd said anything particularly funny.

"I'm great, thank you for asking, I don't get that often! Now then, I've read through all the notes Justine made on your progress and it sounds like you did some fantastic work together, which I'd like to continue. Today I think it would be good to just get to know each other, what do you say?" Dr. Hall's wide smile stared at him, and Blake had to admit the man was hard to dislike.

They spent the session trading information about each other which Blake knew was so Dr. Hall could establish trust, it was exactly what Justine had done. He actually revealed more than he thought he would. It seemed that working with Justine had made him more comfortable about opening up.

He missed her sassy, inappropriate questions though. He missed her intense stare as she tried to work him out. He missed her scent, her raspy voice teasing his ears, her curvy body. Hell, he just missed *her*. His anger at her had faded, now he was just hurt that she had given up on him, that she had abandoned him when he wanted, *needed* her most. He'd seen her around town and every time his heart jerked in his chest and his throat dried. She was without a doubt the most stunning woman he had ever seen, and he was lucky that for a short while, she had been with him. Goddammit he missed her.

Dr. Hall was outlining the structure of their sessions going forward and explaining where he would like Blake to work on specific areas, starting with his anxiety around crowded spaces. By the time their session was over he actually felt hopeful for what they would achieve together.

*

A few weeks later, Blake was on his couch, drowning his sorrows with Penny, when his phone rang. He pulled it out and sat up straight when he saw the name on his screen.

"Taylor? What's wrong?" he demanded, worried her ex-boyfriend, Dale, had come back into the picture.

"Nothing is wrong with me," Taylor began, her voice crackling through the line. Where was she? "I just need you to hear something," she added, and he heard a door opening, then glasses clinking and people cheering, then silence.

"What?" he asked, and then he heard it. Justine singing, her husky voice caressing him through the phone, and goosebumps broke out all over his body. Her voice cracked on each line, the pain in her words searing him. She was singing John Waite's *Missing You*. It was one of his favorite songs, but he would never forget the way she sang it. Her voice cracked again on the last line and a sob came down the line and an answering lump caught in his throat.

She was in pain, and he couldn't bear it, he needed to see her. Now. To tell her everything was all right, that they would be okay, that he missed her, that he needed her. The sound of her voice faded, and he wanted to roar at Taylor to take the phone back to Justine's singing.

"I don't know what you did." Taylor's voice came back down the line, devoid of emotion. "But you need to fix it. Now." Then she hung up. He stared at his phone for a moment before leaping up and grabbing his helmet and leather jacket. Penny followed him to the door, chittering away before he turned to her.

"I'll be back. Daddy needs to go and get Mommy." The words struck in his chest; he had never wanted a family before but now he couldn't imagine not having one, not having a wife, more pets, *children*. The image of a little girl with dark wavy hair and light honey eyes, the spitting image of her mother wove its way into his mind uninvited.

He'd created a family for himself here in the town. Jim and Hilda were like the parents he'd always wanted. Beau, Dean, Christy and Taylor were the friends he was so lucky to have and strangely Rebelle felt like a little sister he needed to look out for. How could he ever have thought that he didn't need any of them? And especially Justine? He left the house and jumped on his bike, gunning the engine, roaring out of the drive and off to the bar.

When he arrived, he could hear how many people were inside and his pulse started pounding at the thought of going in there when it was so packed. It sounded like half the town was inside, definitely more people than he'd anticipated. Even though he and Dr. Hall had done some great work, he was emotionally charged and if he went in there, surrounded by so many people, he could trigger an attack. He weighed up his options and decided to wait it out. Sure enough, Taylor was soon kicking everyone out.

Then he saw her. She came out, her arms around Beau and Dean as they held her up.

"Taylor was right, that bottle of Patrón did have my name on it," she slurred, and then giggled.

"Some of us would have liked a shot or two," Beau grumbled, wincing as she stumbled and stamped on his foot.

"Justine?" he called, not knowing what else to say. Her eyes swung to him and widened, her smile falling from her face.

"Hey Blake, long time no see," Dean said, his features were tight but there was a hint of hurt in his voice that gave him away. Blake had been avoiding Beau and Dean since his fallout with Justine, not wanting anyone to have to pick a side.

"I'm sorry about that, man."

"I guess now we know why the radio silence." Beau tilted his head to Justine. Blake nodded.

"I get it," Dean said, his hard features giving way to understanding.

"Justine, can we talk?" Blake asked.

Justine nodded and then shrugged Beau and Dean off her, they took a step back. Blake held out his hand to her, but she ignored it, pushing past him, the action hurt more than he thought it would. He turned to face her.

"I miss you." He hadn't been planning on saying that, but it slipped out and he couldn't deny it.

She blanched. "No Blakey, you miss your therapist. You're just suffering from transference."

"That's bullshit." he spat, and she shook her head again. She blinked, first one eye and then the other. She was really wasted and probably not up for this conversation, but they were having it out whether she liked it or not.

"It comes from reliving a painful or traumatic experience with someone. We went over plenty of those so it's really not a surprise," she muttered. He started to speak but she interrupted him. "You were vulnerable, you're getting your feelings mixed up because you were attached to me. It happens all the time, you weren't the first and you won't be the last," she said quietly, her mouth twitched, and her eyes turned sad. "I mean, it's not like you love me or anything, r-right?"

The hesitancy in her voice made his chest constrict. He couldn't say the words and he couldn't lie to her. Maybe she was right, maybe he did use her to help him when he had attacks. It was thinking of her that brought him back. But was that because he had fallen victim to transference? Shit, was she right? He was so confused. He didn't know what it was, he just wanted her. But he couldn't give her what she wanted, love. He cared about her, respected her and he had to be honest with her. He shook his head and her face twisted. All of a sudden, she bent forward at the waist and vomited all over his shoes.

"Okay, time to take you home," Beau said, coming around and looping an arm around her shoulders, steering her away. Blake just stood there like a moron, trying to sort out the maze of thoughts.

"We're here for you too buddy, don't shut us out." Dean clapped him on the back.

"Thanks, man." Blake said, then Dean went to help Beau get Justine into a car. Blake took himself home, more unsettled and confused than ever. He couldn't be suffering from transference, he truly cared about her. It couldn't be that, could it? When he walked in the door, Penny was waiting for him, she peered behind him expectantly and he sighed deeply, sadness smothering him.

"Sorry Penny, I shouldn't have gotten your hopes up."

He stroked her before she trotted off in disappointment. *What else am I gonna fuck up tonight?* He went to bed but lay awake for hours replaying the scene with Justine over and over again in his mind. He had a session with Dr. Hall the following day, he would ask him about transference then.

He didn't get a chance. Dr. Hall wanted to go straight into understanding his triggers and his techniques for coping with his attacks.

"What techniques do you find most effective?" he asked, making notes on his pad. Justine never made notes, she gave him her full attention. What he wouldn't give for her full attention right now. *Guess you never know what you have until it's gone.*

"I've tried all the ones that Dr. Rodríguez-Hamilton taught me, but I find some hard to recall in the moment. Well, except for one…" Blake trailed off.

"Which one?" Dr. Hall prompted.

"It's an association technique. I needed to find a focus point in the middle of my attack, to distract myself from what was happening," Blake explained.

"And what did you pick?"

For some reason, Blake didn't want to share it with him. It felt too private, they were his memories.

"A color," Blake said, reluctantly. "Orange."

Dr. Hall was quiet for a moment, just watching Blake pensively before he spoke again. "Why orange?"

"I'm sorry?"

"Why do you use orange to ground yourself? What does it mean to you?"

Blake thought about it for a moment, then all at once, the images rushed through him. Justine in her orange dress the first time she helped him, when he began to start trusting her. The orange underwear she wore when she gave herself to him, trusting him in return with her body, her first time. The little orange carrots on her pjs the night they rescued Penny and he saw her caring, nurturing side and her fierce independence. The heels of her orange shoes digging into his back as he made her scream during their first make up session, the orange candle flickering in her eyes over their dinner together when he learned more about her.

All stand-out moments in the relationship that had become so vital to him. His mind was never alone, it was full of her. The color represented so much, it was safety, security, comfort, trust, calmness and… His chest ached at the final realization.

"It's love. It means love," he choked out, emotion burning his throat. It was Justine he saw in those moments, not because of transference. Because he needed her to ground him, yes, but because she was his *world*. He couldn't believe it, all this time he loved her, no wonder he was so damn miserable without her.

Shit, he needed to tell her, she was hurting right now because he'd said he didn't love her back. How could he not love her back? She was the best damn thing that had ever happened to him, how could he be so fucking blind? The knowledge settled in him with a quiet acceptance. Of course, he didn't recognize this feeling for so long: he had never felt anything like it before. Love. Selflessly given.

He needed to tell her. Would she even believe him now? She had accused him of missing her because of transference, which wasn't true at all now he knew how he felt. Hell, he had a new psychologist who was helping him a great deal and he was pretty sure he wasn't in love with him. Dr. Hall smiled at him quizzically. Scratch that, he *definitely* wasn't in love with him.

How could he prove to her that he needed her, not to help him with his mental health, but because he couldn't imagine his life without her? Couldn't imagine his life without fake stakeouts, barbecues, and debates about eighties music with the woman who twisted him inside out.

His session with Dr. Hall finished, the minutes dragging by. It nearly killed him but instead of going to find Justine to tell her how he felt, he went back to the station. He needed a plan, he couldn't just come out with it. She would never believe him, especially after their conversation last night. Over the following days, he caught glimpses of her, and fought the urge to rush over to her and drag her into his arms and reveal his newest secret.

He finally figured it out on Saturday while reading reports and shooting the breeze with Jim. He ran out of the station and down the main street to Iris Motors and found Dean fixing a car while Taylor was hiding his tools. When she spotted him, Taylor fixed him with a glare so deadly he was shocked he didn't collapse on the spot, but he ignored her.

"I'm so glad you're both here. I know how to fix it, but I need your help."

He had his plan, now he just hoped he was strong enough to carry it out.

Chapter 23

The last thing Justine felt like doing was going to The Rusty Bucket Inn on a Saturday night.

She just wanted to stay at home, re-alphabetize her DVDs since Taylor had at some point messed up her system again, eat ice cream and wallow in self-pity.
Fun times.

But Taylor had called her and begged her to come in, she had accidentally booked Justine to sing again and now there was a huge crowd expecting to see her. Justine didn't understand how it had happened, but it wasn't like she had anything better to do, other than the wallowing thing, that is. Her only solace was that there would be no chance of running into Blake if it was as crowded as Taylor said it was.

She showered, for the first time in days, she was still too depressed to stay clean. She wasn't bothered if she repelled men, she only wanted one. The one she couldn't have. The ache hadn't dulled, if anything it had grown over time, especially after seeing him the other night. She braided her wet hair, swiped some make-up across her face and stepped into her favorite burnt orange jumpsuit. She added some jewelry, grabbed her guitar and drove to the bar. The parking lot was rammed. *What the hell's going on?*

She pushed the door open and immediately the noise level assaulted her. The place was packed. The whole town must have turned out for tonight, including some people from the next town over. She weaved her way through the sweaty crowds to find Taylor at the bar.

"What the hell happened, Taylor?" she shouted over the hubbub. Taylor's eyes gleamed at her across the bar, her energy off the charts.

"I know, it's crazy right?" she shouted back and only then did Justine notice that not only were Taylor and Kayleigh serving customers, but so were Beau and Dean, while Christy acted as bouncer, shouting at customers who were too amped up. She may be tiny, but she was fierce; no one messed with her.

Justine stared around and spluttered. "Are all these people here to listen to me sing?"

"Not exactly," Taylor hedged.

"What?"

"Don't hate me, okay?" Taylor shouted back and her eyes flicked over Justine's shoulder. Justine felt heat at her back and then she caught that sinful scent that turned her inside out.

"They're here to listen to me sing."

His voice rasped right in her ear. She gasped and spun around and found herself staring into those beautiful eyes. His mouth quirked at her.

"I do love it when you make that sound." His eyes roving over her had heat flaring throughout her body, pooling between her legs at the blatant arousal etched on his face. Someone bumped into her, and she was crushed against his solid chest, her palms pushed back, his muscles flexing under her touch. Awareness sizzled between them.

"Blake, what are you doing around all these people, we need to get you out of here!" She started panicking, she didn't want him to have an attack from being in a crowd this size. Her eyes darted around the bar, trying to find the nearest exit.

"Why would I leave when everyone came to see me?" He cocked his head, smiling down at her and again her stomach clenched at the sight. *Damn he's beautiful.* But how was he managing to be around this many people?

"I don't understand?"

"You will soon," he replied, and brushed a kiss across her cheek.

She wanted to pull back, but she had missed him too damn much, so instead she leaned into his touch. He cupped her cheek, brushing his thumb across her jaw and the world melted away as they looked at each other, his eyes shining down at her with…no, she knew he didn't love her.

"Blake, showtime!" Taylor shouted.

The spell was broken, the crowd roared back into focus and Blake was no longer in front of her, he was lost in the throng. Panic consumed her as she worried about him.

"Good evening, ladies and gentlemen and welcome to another epic night at The Rusty Bucket Inn!" Taylor's voice boomed out around the room. "We've got a very special guest this evening which I know is why you're all here and eager to watch the show."

Justine forced Blake out of her mind, she needed to get up to the stage quickly. She tried to push through the crowd, but it was so thick that she barely made her way to the front of the stage before Taylor was announcing her.

"Now, give it up for our very own Citrus Pines Deputy Sheriff, Blaaake Miller!"

The cheers were deafening. *What the hell is going on?* Justine looked around the bar, so confused. Music filled the bar and then that deep voice echoed around the room. Her eyes flew to the stage and there he was.

"I'd like to dedicate this song, and all the eighties love songs, to my very own love, Justine."

His *love*? Her? Was this some kind of joke? The tender note in his voice suggested it wasn't. The look in his eye as he stared down at her, had her heart filling with hope. He couldn't love her because he *didn't* love her, he didn't love *anyone,* did he? The song built in the background, and he began to sing, his voice soulful, deep and surprisingly pleasant. When he sang the first line of the song, she realized what it was.

"Oh!" she cried, her hand flying to cover her mouth as her eyes filled with tears. It was the song she had told him about on their stakeout, *Waiting For A Girl Like You.* The one she had always wanted someone to sing to her, wishing she was special enough. Was she *finally* special enough? He smiled down at her and winked, then continued to sing about how he had been waiting for a girl like her to come into his life.

He worked the crowd, giving them what they wanted. She'd never seen him exude so much confidence, and the effect was breathtaking. Pride filled her up. She laughed through her tears as someone threw their underwear on stage, probably Taylor.

As the song built, everyone else melted away and it was just the two of them. Tears spilled over her cheeks as he serenaded her, but she didn't care. When the song ended, the crowd applauded and raucous cheers abounded, but she just stood there, too shocked to move. What did this all mean? She didn't want to jump to any conclusions. He stepped down from the stage and came to her.

"What did you think?" he asked, ducking his head sheepishly. His cheeks turned pink. He was so freaking adorable.

"I don't understand, Blake. Help me understand?"

He pulled her into his arms and her palms naturally settled over his chest. "That was my love gesture to you. I love you, Justine. And it's not transference, I swear to you. I'm not in love with my new psychologist. I'm just in love with you."

She shook her head, still confused. "But..." she trailed off.

"I needed to show you what you mean to me. That I would be in the middle of a crowded room for you, that I would get on a stage for you, that I would sing a song I seriously dislike, for you. I would face my biggest fear for you, I would do anything for you. You saved me, you're my love, my *everything* and I was an idiot not to see it."

"But..." she started but he wasn't finished.

"You broke me apart, opened me up and got me talking about my issues, you made me whole. You were my new beginning. I don't know where I would be without you. The stars feel closer, the moon is within my reach, and I feel like I can do anything, all because of you. But more than that, you made me the man I am now, the man I wanted to be *for you*. You're my family and I can't wait to have a life with you and Penny, to have kids with you. I love you honey, not just your psychology brain, I love your independence, your authenticity, your caring nature. I just want you, in my arms, in my life, in my *soul*, forever."

His words set her alight, happiness flooded her. More tears spilled down her cheeks. Was she really getting everything she dreamed of?

"Kids? You're sure?" she asked, taking a shuddering breath, terrified she hadn't heard him right.

"Lots of them, mini versions of us, and more foxes," he nodded. She laughed, her hands covering her mouth in shock.

"I love you too, Blake. So much. I'm so proud of you for everything. You amaze me, and I can't believe this is happening!" she sniffled.

He bent his head and whispered in her ear, "Am I Mr. Right?" She detected a hint of doubt in his words.

"God yes, *mi amor,*" she gushed, and he dipped his head, his lips slanted over hers to feed her one of those slow, lazy kisses she loved. She opened up and let him in and as he stroked her tongue against his, his moan vibrated through her. Cheers and whistles erupted around them, and they broke apart.

"I need to get you back in my bed," he growled and nipped at her earlobe. She laughed and threw her arms around him. He hugged her tight, like he was afraid to let her go, and her heart sighed with happiness. She pulled back sharply, remembering something.

"Wait a minute, you *still* don't like that song?" she accused.

He shrugged. "It's growing on me."

She burst out laughing again and he gripped her tighter. Then they were surrounded by their friends, the women hugged Justine while the men did a lot of back-slapping and throat-clearing, with talks of allergies and dust in their eyes before they all faced each other in a circle.

"Thank you, Taylor and Dean, for helping me pull this together and getting everyone here," Blake said, and Justine shot them both a grateful smile.

"Are you kidding, look how many people are here? I'm gonna make a fortune!" Taylor cried, rubbing her hands together gleefully.

"Congrats, I'm so happy for you both," Beau said, smiling at them.

"Thanks, man," Blake replied.

"Although, I hope it's okay, you know, that I kissed her first?" Beau had a wicked gleam in his eye. Justine watched as a deadly calm settled over Blake before he arched a brow at Dean.

"He pulled this shit with me too. I got your back, bro," Dean said, cracking his knuckles and then both men charged at Beau.

"Men," Christy tutted. Taylor shook her head, but Justine just watched as Blake caught up to Beau and threatened to hurt him in all the ways the government had taught him. She laughed at Beau's horrified expression and Blake met her stare and quirked a grin at her.

Oh yes, life would be very interesting indeed, now that she had finally found her Mr. Right.

Four months later

"How's Rebelle doing?" Blake asked, taking Justine's hand, and leading her around the car, carrying her guitar case in his free hand and heading towards the door to the bar.

"Blakey," she began, using the nickname she called him when she was drunk that time. He liked it, but only from her mouth. When Dean and Beau called him that, he beat their asses. "You know I can't talk about that," she sighed.

He tugged her hand gently and she stopped walking and turned to him. He took in that beautiful face that brought him to his knees. A frown puckered his forehead as he spotted the dark circles under her eyes. Guilt flared in him as he thought of the full nights' sleep he'd gotten last night, he needed to be more considerate of her restlessness at the moment. Other than those circles, she glowed brightly in the moonlight.

"I thought she just met you for a chat?" he asked.

"It's a professional chat," she said. "Would you want me telling everyone what you say in our little chats?" she asked, dropping her voice seductively. He smiled down at her, and she beamed at him in return. She always did that, met his smile with hers and it made him smile that much harder.

"The chats you're referring to take place in the privacy of our bedroom. Now lucky for you, I'm a gentleman and don't share the filthy things you say to me. But maybe Dean and Beau would like to know what a minx you are?" he teased, and her eyes widened.

"You wouldn't?" At her horrified gasp, he barked out a laugh. He loved making her gasp, preferably in the bedroom but anywhere worked for him.

"I guess you'll just have to convince me to keep quiet," his voice lowered, and he drew her against him.

"Hmm, how on earth would I do that?" she replied. He pretended to ponder her question, stroking his hand up and down her back.

"Well, I have a few thoughts of my own but I'm happy

to let you use your imagination," he dipped his head down to kiss her. Just before their lips met, she pulled back, clapping her hand over her mouth. Her skin suddenly had a slight green tint to it.

"Sorry," she said after a moment.

He sighed. "Honey, if you don't feel up to it, then don't sing tonight."

"But I want to," she pouted, and he laughed again, dropping a kiss to her forehead and her eyelids fluttered closed, she liked it when he did that.

"Okay then, but I warn you, I'm not standing in the front row, it could be a splash zone," he joked, and she snorted at him.

They pulled apart and walked into the crowded bar. The noise immediately hit his ears and he waited for the spark of fear to follow but it didn't. Who would have thought when he first came to town and entered this bar, nearly a year ago, that this is where he would end up? *Definitely not me*, he thought as a wave of gratitude washed through him. Damn, he was lucky. Sometimes he lay awake at night, not from insomnia, he didn't struggle with that anymore, but just counting his blessings.

Thank God he'd met Justine, she was everything to him. She had kickstarted his life again, setting him on the hard road to recovery, teaching him how to control his attacks, to value himself, build himself up not tear himself down, she gave him back his self-respect. Then when she had done all that, she handed over the reins to someone she trusted.

He'd been doing great work with Dr. Hall. It was hard, and sometimes it felt like he was taking a step back, but his attacks were almost gone. He would never be cured of them, he still had anxiety, but they weren't setbacks anymore. He could manage them now and each one reminded him just how far he had come. His mental health was strong enough now that his previous sheriff was ready to support and help Blake begin his campaign to become sheriff of Citrus Pines. It would be a long road, but he was ready to show his commitment and support to the town where he'd found his home.

Justine had also given him a new lease of life. He had love, close friends, the town, and she had also given him the chance at a dream he never thought existed for him: *Fatherhood*. He looked down at her, glowing with their secret, and he was so happy he could burst, so happy he could make this dream of hers come true too.

He couldn't wait to watch her grow and to experience this journey together, she would be an amazing mom. Even now, she cradled her stomach protectively, it was wonderful to see but she wasn't too far along and wanted to wait a bit before telling everyone. He coughed discreetly and when she met his eye he nodded to her hand. She snatched it away, shooting him a grateful smile, luckily none of their friends were paying attention.

Christy hugged Blake tightly, then drew Justine away for a chat. Taylor high-fived him over the bar, because apparently she was still a teenager, and Dean slung an arm around his shoulders.

"You ready to get your ass handed to you on the court in the morning?" Dean asked, a competitive twinkle in his eye.

"Why, is someone else playing for you?" Blake deadpanned and Dean shoved him away, muttering something that sounded suspiciously like *cocky asshole* under his breath. Blake laughed.

"Anyway, it'll be two against two tomorrow, one of Beau's L.A buddies will be joining us. His name's Will. You'll like him, he's cool," Dean added.

"Awesome, someone new to beat. Where is Beau?"

"The dude bailed on us," Dean said, hiking a thumb over his shoulder and Blake turned to see Beau and a petite brunette seated at one of the tables by the stage.

"Got you a whiskey," Dean said.

"Thanks man, let me just set this up and I'll be back," Blake said, pointing to Justine's guitar case. He walked away, pausing to kiss Justine's cheek and murmur in her ear. He watched as her cheeks flushed prettily and he smiled to himself as he walked away. Goddamn he was lucky.

He walked past Beau's table then paused again.

"Excuse me, ma'am," he said to Beau's date, flashing his badge. "Just let me know if this idiot bothers you and I'll have him out of here in two seconds flat," he said, shooting her a winning smile. His eyes met Beau's over her head and the fire in them promised Blake he would pay for that on the court tomorrow. Blake walked on, clapping Beau on the back as he immediately began explaining to his date that Blake was just kidding. Served Beau right for ditching them tonight.

Blake hopped up onto the little stage and set up Justine's guitar and positioned her microphone for her. He stepped down again and made his way back to the bar, patting Justine's ass as he went. She shot him a look that promised all sorts of delights when they got home later. He joined Dean, taking a sip of his whiskey as Taylor came back over.

"How's things, Tay?" he asked.

"Fine, although I have been meaning to talk to you," she said. He noticed she wasn't her usual bubbly self tonight.

"Oh yeah?" he asked.

"Dale's back," Dean muttered, putting his beer bottle

down on the bar with more force than was necessary.

Shit. "Want me to pay him a not so friendly visit?" Blake asked Taylor.

"Not yet, he didn't do anything really. He just showed up with a buddy, had a drink and left." She shrugged nonchalantly, but the tightness in her jaw suggested she was more worried than she was letting on.

"Call me next time he turns up and I'll swing by, just to let him know I'm around and keeping an eye on you, I'll make my presence known."

"Thanks, B," she said and squeezed his hand before turning away and grabbing the microphone.

"There's something bugging her, she won't let me in," Dean said quietly, his brows drawn in concern.

"She's just a private person and probably wouldn't want you to worry. We'll keep her safe, try not to worry about it, man." Blake clapped Dean's back and Dean nodded.

Taylor announced Justine's performance and a roar of cheers, applause and whistles went around the room, with Blake cheering the loudest. He watched his love take the stage and settle on her stool.

Christy and Dean tried to drag him towards the front of the stage, along with the rest of the crowd, but he stayed back at the bar with Taylor. Just because he was better with crowds didn't mean he wanted to tempt fate. Besides he was a little on edge tonight, his stomach fluttering with nervous anticipation. His mind anxiously running through the speech he would deliver later, when he and Justine were alone, that ended with the question he'd been dying to ask for months. *God, I hope she says yes.*

Justine started her set with classic Wet Wet Wet and as soon as she opened her mouth and sang, goosebumps covered him. God, she was extraordinary. During the song, her eyes searched for him, a jolt moved through him as they connected, and heat soared across the bar between them, so thick he could almost reach out and grab it. She winked cheekily and he smiled.

Taylor moved beside him. Should he be concerned about her too? He felt they were close enough that she would be honest with him if anything more was bothering her. As he watched her, he noticed she wasn't watching Justine, her eyes were fixed just slightly to the left of the stage, on Beau and his date.

"I'm so happy for you, B," she said quietly, turning her attention back to him. "Everyone is finding their love."

"It'll be your turn soon," he said. She laughed, the sound harsh.

"You're funny. I didn't know you were funny," she deadpanned, and he snorted at her sarcasm. He watched her eyes flick back to Beau before moving away again too quickly. He wondered if that was the reason her light shined a little less brightly tonight. He opened his mouth to ask what the deal was with her and Beau, but then thought better of it. Judging by the way he had seen Beau watching Taylor these last few months, he would find out soon enough.

"This next song is for *mi amor*," Justine said, and his eyes found hers again over the crowd. Everyone in the bar turned to stare at him but he didn't care, he only had eyes for her. She began to play and after a few bars he recognized a Mötley Crüe song and laughed, shaking his head before mouthing *te amo*. She smiled and nodded back at him, and contentment settled in him, greeting him like an old friend.

What a life he had; a wonderful woman, his mental health healing, an amazing job and friends, a gorgeous fur baby and an actual baby on the way.

Lila Dawes

Had he mentioned how lucky he was?

The End.

Fancy a sneak peek at book 3 in the series, Sweet Surrender? Turn the page…

Chapter 1

"Oh Beau, your breath smells like garbage..."

"I'm not usually a fan of receding hairlines but it really works for you!"

"Is that as big as it gets?"

Taylor snickered to herself, mimicking Beau's date as she watched the woman gushing over him. They sat across the table from each other, his date talking while Beau stared at her with open-mouthed amazement.

Ugh.

Taylor looked away before she was sick. She wrenched open the dishwasher. A cloud of steam attacked her face and she breathed in the heat, reveling in it. Pulling out a tray, she began drying off glasses, stacking them along the back bar of her pride and joy, The Rusty Bucket Inn.

Her break from the loved-up couple didn't last long as

her eyes were inexplicably drawn back to them. *God, I hate him,* she thought, staring at his stupid smug face beaming down at his stunning date whose breasts were making an enthusiastic escape attempt from her skin-tight dress.

You're just jealous your breasts don't look like that. She glanced down at her less than impressive chest and sighed before her eyes lifted to the *happy* couple again.

Unfortunately, Beau didn't have any of the things Taylor just mentioned. His hairline was damn near perfect, his thick hair a deep chocolate brown that Taylor guessed was attractive, if you liked that kind of thing. His breath was always minty fresh, like he ate mints all day long. And his dick? Well, she didn't know about that but she sure as shit didn't think it was small. The guy was a giant and he radiated big dick energy. *Ugh, stop thinking about his dick!*

Taylor hated the way women fawned over him, just because he was hella tall, tanned and absolutely *stacked* with muscle? Pssh. Okay yes, he had nice hair that was just begging to be stroked and she could admit his mouth was pretty great, his full, wide lips always smiling. And fine, she would concede that a girl could get lost in those thickly-lashed dark eyes that curved suggestively at the edges.

BUT.

None of that meant a thing when the guy's personality was a big, fat bag o'dicks and *that* she damn well knew for a fact. She just made it her mission to ensure that everyone else knew it too, like a public service. *You're welcome, America,* she snorted to herself as she hip-checked the dishwasher shut and grabbed a cloth, wiping down her bar lovingly. She sighed over every chip the cloth snagged on the handcrafted oak top, her stomach dipping each time like she was touching an open wound.

The bar itself had been what she'd fallen in love with when she first looked around the place and she'd built the idea for the Inn around it. She had put her blood, sweat and tears into this place, renovating the bar as well as the rundown cabins. She'd created a place for folks to come and let their hair down with rooms they could book into if they needed to get away. She'd been running the place for ten years now. It was her life, her passion, the thing that got her out of bed each day. There had been tough times, but she worked her ass off to bring in the customers and it was finally paying off.

On her periphery she saw Beau saunter past the bar, not even glancing in her direction, as he headed down the hall to the restrooms. Looking around, Taylor spotted only a couple of people left in the bar, the hardcore regulars who stayed until closing most nights.

Taylor rang the bell that signaled closing time and was met with the now customary boos from her clientele which she just laughed off. She began going round the tables collecting the empty glasses, stopping by Porter, one of her regulars, who was slumped over on his stool.

"Come on Porter, quit faking it or I'll call Dina to come pick your ass up. Then you'll be sorry," she said, shaking the older man.

"You wouldn't do that, would you? Not after last time," the old man replied, slurring slightly. His horrified expression had Taylor chuckling. His wife was a scary lady; no one fucked with Dina.

"Then you'd better git!" Taylor flicked him with her cloth, her Southern accent deepening with her sass. Porter grumbled at her again but slid off his barstool and patted her hand affectionately. Taylor watched as he wandered out the bar, beginning his long walk home since she had confiscated his car keys. She always took the keys of the regulars; she wouldn't have anyone driving drunk on her watch.

The last few stragglers left, and Taylor collected their empty glasses before stopping at the table next to Beau's date. She eyed the woman critically. The blonde curls bounced with every movement, as did her impressive rack, inflating with every breath.

Don't do it! Taylor's brain screamed. But she was feeling particularly vicious this evening. *Jealousy's a bitch but so am I.*

"I just want to say, well done. You're a better woman than most," Taylor gushed. The blonde looked at her, confusion tried to pinch her forehead but her vast quantities of Botox made it near impossible.

"Excuse me?"

Taylor plastered a smile on her face. "It's *so* great that you're giving him a chance. Rehabilitated criminals need love too, am I right? I mean, sure, he *killed* that guy with his bare hands, but I bet he feels real bad about it."

The blonde's face dropped. "What?"

"Oh shoot, did he not get to that part yet in his 'about me' section? Well, don't I feel like I put my foot in it. Forget I said anything." Taylor waved her hand dismissively and then headed back to the bar, trying to smother her evil grin. She stacked the remaining glasses into the dishwasher. A moment later the clack of stilettos echoed through the bar as Beau's date skipped to the door.

"Come back soon!" Taylor called after her with a little wave then laughed as the door slammed shut behind her, bathing in her triumph. Seconds later, Beau came back from the bathroom and stopped in his tracks as he took in the empty bar. His steely gaze found Taylor's and narrowed dangerously before he headed her way. His long, muscled legs ate up the distance between them. He stopped in front of her and folded his arms across his chest, covering his blue t-shirt with the Superman 'S' on the front. She gulped as she took in his expression.

Shit.

Acknowledgements

Thank you so much for choosing to read this book, I hope you loved Blake & Justine's story as much as I did. Please consider leaving a review, these are hella important for indie authors and mean the world to us!

An enormous thank you to my awesome critique partners, Andrea, Anna P, Anna L, Mimi and Michelle for all your support and feedback. I don't know where I would be without you. All the messages, video calls, voice notes, rants and late-night chats are so much fun and the best part of this process – other than the actual writing, ha!

Thank you to all my amazing ARC readers and reviewers, your feedback means the world and I'm so grateful for you all. And of course a massive thank you to my fabulous editor for all her hard work getting this ship shape.

I also want to thank all the service men and women for everything they have given up to keep us safe. What they do is incredible and without them we wouldn't have the freedom we do. Unfortunately they don't all come home or they come home with mental scars as well as physical. There are some amazing projects and charities out there so have a read on how you can help.

Lila Dawes

https://combatstress.org.uk/

https://www.ptsduk.org/

https://www.wwfs.org/

https://cst.dav.org/

About the Author

Lila is a thirtysomething writer living in Derbyshire, England with her *cough* parents *cough*. She loves romance, sharks, cats and has an ~~un~~healthy obsession with Henry Cavill.

Color of Love is her second novel in the Citrus Pines series, head to Amazon to check out book one, It's Only Love if you haven't already read it. Lila is a huge fan of the romance reading and writing community so why not say hello, she can be found on Instagram, Facebook, Pinterest, Tiktok and Goodreads.

Printed in Dunstable, United Kingdom